STRAVAGANZA
City of Masks

STRAVAGANZA
City of Masks

Mary Hoffman

Acknowledgements

Many thanks to my three consultants, Dottoressa Silvia Gasparini of the University of Padua, Abele Longo, my Italian teacher, and Edgardo Zaghini of the Young Book Trust. Thanks also to Stevie and Jessica for being such a good audience. And to Scottish Widows, whose windfall took me back to Venice for a quick reality check.

First published in Great Britain in 2002 by Bloomsbury Publishing Plc
38 Soho Square, London, W1D 3HB

A CIP catalogue record of this book is available from the British Library
ISBN 0 7475 6093 5

Printed in Great Britain by Clays Ltd, St Ives plc

10 9 8 7 6 5 4 3 2 1

For Rhiannon, a true citizen of Bellezza

'Every time I describe a city, I am saying
something about Venice.'
Italo Calvino, *Invisible Cities*

'... everye man conceived in his minde a high
contentation every time we came into the
Dutchesse sight ... Neither was there any that
thought it not the greatest pleasure he could
have in the world, to please her, and the greatest
griefe to offend her ...'
Castiglione, *The Book of the Courtier*, 1561

Contents

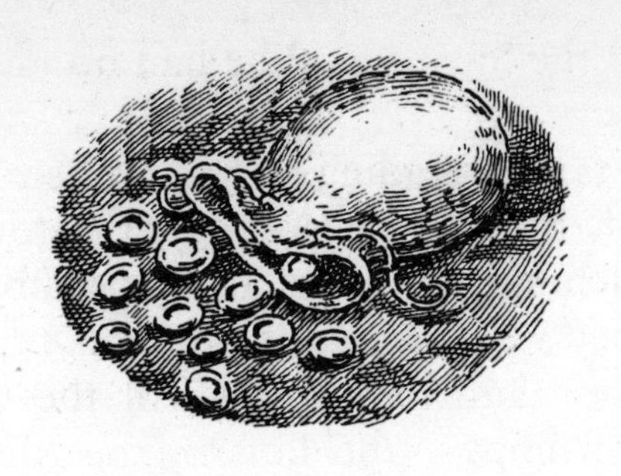

Prologue: *Reading the Future*

In a room at the top of a tall house overlooking a canal, a man sat dealing cards out on to a desk covered in black silk. He made a circle of twelve cards, face up, methodically moving widdershins, placed a thirteenth in the middle of the circle, then leaned back and contemplated the pattern.

'Strange,' he murmured.

The card in the middle – the most important one – was the Sword, signifying danger. Rodolfo was used to that symbol setting the tone of his readings. It was no surprise either to see the Queen of Fishes as the seventh card, to the right of the Sword. Danger often appeared close to the most important woman in Bellezza and the water queen was obviously the Duchessa. But the Princess of Fishes was the first card, to the left of the Sword, and he had no idea what she could signify.

It was the oddest reading he had ever seen. The only number cards to appear were fours, all four of them, one from each suit – Fishes, Birds, Salamanders and Serpents. They were ranged like guards on either side of the Princess and the Queen. All the other cards were major trumps – the Lovers, the Magician, the Goddess, the Tower, the Spring Maiden and, most disturbingly, Death.

Rodolfo looked at the array for a long time before sweeping the cards up, shuffling them thoroughly and setting them out again. Princess of Fishes, Four of Serpents, the Lovers, the Magician ... By the time he set the Sword down in the middle, Rodolfo's hands were shaking. He had dealt exactly the same pattern.

Hastily, he swept the cards up again and wrapped them in their black silk. He stowed them in a drawer of the carved desk and removed from another a velvet bag containing glass stones. Closing his eyes, he put a hand in the bag and drew out a handful of the stones, which he cast lightly on the desk top, where they glittered in the candlelight.

Each nugget of shining glass had a silver emblem embedded in the middle. Wonderingly, Rodolfo identified a crown, a leaf, a mask, the number 16, a lock of hair, a book— He started when he saw the book.

Then he stood up. 'Silvia again,' he murmured, holding the piece of smooth purple glass containing the silver crown. He walked to the window and looked out over his roof-garden. Lanterns swung gently between the trees, illuminating the flowers and leaves, bleached of their vivid daytime colours. In the distance a peacock screamed.

He walked back to the desk and took a pair of twelve-sided dice from a drawer. Six and ten he threw, eight and eight, seven and nine – wherever he looked tonight the number sixteen kept coming up. That and the symbols of a young girl and danger. Whatever it meant, it was linked with the Duchessa and he would have to tell her about it. Knowing Silvia, she would not tell him whatever significance his divinations had for her, but at least she could prepare herself for whatever new danger was approaching.

Sighing, Rodolfo put away his means of divination and prepared to visit the Duchessa.

Chapter 1

The Marriage with the Sea

Light streamed on to the Duchessa's satin bedcovers as her serving-woman flung open the shutters.

'It's a beautiful day, Your Grace,' said the young woman, adjusting her mask of green sequins.

'It's always a beautiful day on the lagoon,' said the Duchessa, sitting up and letting the maid put a wrapper round her shoulders and hand her a cup of hot chocolate. She was wearing her night-mask of black silk. She looked closely at the young woman. 'You're new, aren't you?'

'Yes, your Grace,' she curtsied. 'And if I may say so, what an honour it is to be serving you on such a great day!'

She'll be clapping her hands next, thought the Duchessa, sipping the dark chocolate.

The maid clasped her hands ecstatically. 'Oh your Grace, you must so be looking forward to the Marriage!'

'Oh, yes,' said the Duchessa wearily. 'I look forward to it just the same every year.'

*

The boat rocked precariously as Arianna stepped in, clutching her large canvas bag.

'Careful!' grumbled Tommaso, who was handing his sister into the boat. 'You'll capsize us. Why do you need so much stuff?'

'Girls need a lot of things,' Arianna answered firmly, knowing that Tommaso thought everything female a great mystery.

'Even for one day?' asked Angelo, her other brother.

'Today's going to be a long one,' Arianna said even more firmly and that was the end of it.

She settled in one end of the boat gripping her bag on her knees, while her brothers started rowing with the slow sure strokes of fishermen who spent their lives on the water. They had come from their own island, Merlino, to collect her from Torrone and take her to the biggest lagoon festival of the year. Arianna had been awake since dawn.

Like all lagooners, she had been going to the Marriage with the Sea since she was a small child, but this year she had a special reason for being excited. She had a plan. And the things she had in her heavy bag were part of it.

'I'm so sorry about your hair,' said Lucien's mother,

biting her lip as she restrained herself from her usual comfort gesture of running her hand across his curly head. The curls weren't there any more and she didn't know how to comfort him, or herself.

'It's all right, Mum,' said Lucien. 'I'll be in fashion. Lots of boys at school even shave theirs off.'

They didn't mention that he wasn't well enough to go to school. But it was true that he didn't mind too much about the hair. What really bothered him was the tiredness. It wasn't like anything he had ever felt before. It wasn't like being knackered after a good game of football or swimming fifty lengths. It had been a long time since he'd been able to do either of those.

It was like having custard in your veins instead of blood, getting exhausted just trying to sit up in bed. Like drinking half a cup of tea and finding it as difficult as climbing Everest.

'It doesn't affect everyone so badly,' the nurse had said. 'Lucien's one of the unlucky ones. But it has no relation to how well the treatment is working.'

That was the trouble. Feeling as drained and exhausted as he did, Lucien couldn't tell whether it was the treatment or the disease itself that was making him feel so terrible. And he could tell that his parents didn't know either. That was one of the scariest things, seeing them so frightened. It seemed as if his mother's eyes filled with tears every time she looked at him.

And as for Dad – Lucien's father had never talked to him properly before he became ill, but they had got on pretty well. They used to *do* things together – swimming, going to the match, watching TV. It was when they couldn't do anything together any more that Dad started really *talking* to him.

He even brought library books into the bedroom and read to him, because Lucien didn't have the strength to hold a book in his hands. Lucien liked that. Books that he knew already, like *The Hobbit* and *Tom's Midnight Garden*, were followed by ones that Dad remembered from his boyhood and youth, like *Moonfleet* and the James Bond novels.

Lucien lapped them all up. Dad found a new skill in inventing different voices for all the characters. Sometimes Lucien thought it had been almost worth being ill, to find this new, different Dad, who talked to him and told him stories. He wondered if he would turn back into the old Dad if the treatment worked and the illness went away. But such thoughts made Lucien's head ache.

After his most recent chemotherapy, Lucien was too tired to talk. And his throat hurt. That evening Dad brought him in a notebook with thin pages and a beautiful marbled cover, in which dark reds and purples swirled together in a way that made Lucien need to close his eyes.

'I couldn't find anything nice enough in WH Smith,' Dad was saying. 'But this was a bit of luck. We were clearing out an old house in Waverley Road, next to your school, and the niece said to dump all the papers in the skip. So I saw this and rescued it. It's never been written in and I thought if I left it here on your bedside table, with a pencil, you could write down what you want to say to us when your throat hurts.'

Dad's voice droned on in a comforting background sort of way; he wasn't expecting Lucien to reply. He was saying something about the city where the beautiful notebook had been made but Lucien must have missed a bit, because it didn't quite make sense.

'...floating on the water. You must see it one day, Lucien. When you come across the lagoon and see all those domes and spires hovering over the water, well, it's like going to heaven. All that gold...'

Dad's voice tailed off. Lucien wondered if he'd thought he'd been tactless mentioning heaven. But he liked Dad's description of the mysterious city – Venice, was it? As his eyelids got heavier and his mind fogged over with the approach of one of his deep sleeps, he felt Dad slip the little notebook into his hand.

And he began to dream of a city floating on the water, laced with canals, and full of domes and spires...

Arianna watched the whole procession from her brothers' boat. They had the day off work, like everyone else on the lagoon islands, except the cooks. No one worked on the day of the Sposalizio who didn't have to, but so many revellers had to be fed.

'There it is!' shouted Tommaso suddenly. 'There's the Barcone!'

Arianna stood up in the boat, causing it to rock again, and strained her eyes towards the mouth of the Great Canal. In the far distance she could just see the scarlet and silver of the Barcone. Other people had seen the ceremonial barge too and soon the cheers and whistles spread across the water as the Duchessa made her stately way to her Marriage with the Sea.

The barge was rowed by a crew of the city's best

mandoliers, those handsome young men who sculled the mandolas round the canals that took the place of streets in most of Bellezza. They were what Arianna particularly wanted to see.

As the Duchessa's barge drew level with Tommaso and Angelo's boat, Arianna gazed at the muscles of the black-haired, bright-eyed mandoliers and sighed. But not from love.

'Viva la Duchessa!' cried her brothers, waving their hats in the air, and Arianna dragged her eyes from the rowers to the figure standing immobile on the deck. The Duchessa was an impressive sight. She was tall, with long dark hair, coiled up on the top of her head in a complicated style, which was entwined with white flowers and precious gems. Her dress was of thin dark blue taffeta, shot with green and silver, so that she glittered in the sunlight like a mermaid.

Of her face there was little to be seen. As usual she wore a mask. Today's was made of peacock feathers, as shimmering and iridescent as her dress. Behind her stood her waiting-women, all masked, though more simply dressed, holding cloaks and towels.

'It is a miracle,' said Angelo. 'She never looks a day older. Twenty-five years now she has ruled over us and ensured our happiness and yet she still has the figure of a girl.'

Arianna snorted. 'You don't know what she looked like twenty-five years ago,' she said. 'You haven't been coming to the Marriage that long.'

'Nearly,' said Tommaso. 'Our parents first brought me when I was five and that was twenty years ago. And she did look just the same then, little sister. It is miraculous.' And he made the sign that lagooners use for luck – touching the thumb of the right hand to the little finger and placing the middle fingers first on brow and then on breast.

'And I came two years later,' added Angelo, frowning at Arianna. He had noticed a rebellious tendency in her where the Duchessa was concerned.

Arianna sighed again. She had first seen the Marriage when she was five, too. Ten years of watching and waiting. But this year was different. She was going to get what she wanted tomorrow or die in the attempt – and that was not just a figure of speech.

The barge had reached the shore of the island of Sant'Andrea, where the church's High Priest was waiting to hand the Duchessa out on to the red carpet that had been thrown over the shingle. She stepped down as lightly as a girl, followed by her entourage of women. From where they were on the water, Arianna and her brothers had a good view of the slim blue-green figure with the stars in her hair.

The mandoliers rested on their oars, sweating, as the music of the band on the shore floated over the water. At the climax of silver trumpets, two young priests reverently lowered the Duchessa into the sea from a special platform. Her beautiful dress floated around her in the water as she sank gently; the priests' shoulder-muscles bulged with the strain of keeping the ceremony slow and dignified.

As soon as the water lapped the top of the Duchessa's thighs, a loud cry of 'Sposati' went up from all the watchers. Drums and trumpets were sounded and everyone waved and cheered, as the Duchessa was lifted out of the water again and surrounded by her women. For a split second everyone saw her youthful form as the thin wet dress clung to her. The dress would never be worn again.

'What a waste,' thought Arianna.

*

Inside the State Cabin of the barge another woman echoed her thought. The real Duchessa, already dressed in the rich red velvet dress and silver mask that was required for the Marriage feast, stretched and yawned.

'What fools these Bellezzans are!' she said to her two attendants. 'They all think I have the figure of a girl – and I do. What's her name this time?'

'Giuliana, Your Grace,' said one of them. 'Here she comes!'

A bedraggled and sneezing girl, not now looking much like a duchess, was half carried down the stairway to the cabin by the waiting-women.

'Get her out of those wet things,' ordered the Duchessa. 'That's better. Rub her hard with the towel. And you, take the diamonds out of her hair.' The Duchessa patted her own elaborate coiffure, which was the exact duplicate of the wet girl's.

Giuliana's face, though pleasant enough, was very ordinary. The Duchessa smiled behind her mask to think that the people had been so easily deceived.

'Well done, Giuliana,' she said to the shivering girl, who was trying to curtsey. 'A fine impersonation.' She glanced at the amulet on a chain round the girl's neck. A hand, with the three middle fingers extended and the thumb and little finger joined. It was the islanders' good luck token, the *manus fortunae* – hand of

Fortune – signifying the unity of the circle and the figures of the goddess, her consort and son, the sacred trinity of the lagoon. But it was doubtful that this child knew that. The Duchessa wrinkled her nose, not at the symbolism but at the tawdriness of the cheap gold version of it.

Giuliana was soon warm and dry, wrapped in a warm woollen robe and given a silver goblet of ruby red wine. She had taken off the peacock mask, which would be preserved, along with the salt-stained dress, along with twenty-four others in the Palazzo.

'Thank you, Your Grace,' said the girl, glad to feel the iciness of the lagoon's embrace receding from her legs.

'A barbarous custom,' said the Duchessa, 'but the people must be indulged. Now, you have heard and understood the conditions?'

'Yes, Your Grace.'

'Repeat them.'

'I must never tell anyone how I went into the water instead of Your Grace.'

'And if you do?'

'If I do – which I wouldn't, milady – I will be banished from Bellezza.'

'You and your family. Banished for ever. Not that anyone would believe you; there would be no proof.' The Duchessa glanced, steely-eyed, at her waiting-women, who were all utterly dependent on her for their living.

'And in return for your silence, and the loan of your fresh young body, I give you your dowry. Over the ages many young girls have been so rewarded for lending their bodies to their betters. You are more fortunate than most. Your virtue is intact – except for a slight incursion of sea water.'

The women dutifully laughed, as they did every year. Giuliana blushed. She had the suspicion that the Duchessa was talking dirty, but that didn't seem right for someone so important. She was longing to get home to her family and show them the money. And to tell her fiancé they could now afford to be married. One of the waiting-women had finished undoing her hair and was now briskly braiding it into a coil around her head.

*

Tommaso and Angelo rowed behind the Barcone as it travelled slowly back across the lagoon to Bellezza, the biggest island. On deck the Duchessa stood in a red velvet dress with a black cloak thrown over it, which blurred the lines of her figure. The setting sun glinted off her silver mask. She now matched the colours of the Barcone, was one with her vessel and the sea. The prosperity of the city was assured for another year.

And now it was time for feasting. The Piazza Maddalena, in front of the great cathedral, was filled with stalls selling food. The savoury smells made Arianna's mouth water. Every imaginable shape of pasta was on sale, with sauces piquant with peppers and sweet with onions. Roasted meats and grilled vegetables, olives, cheeses, bright red radishes, dark green bitter salad. Shining fish doused with oil and lemon, pink prawns and crabs and mounds of saffron rice and juicy wild mushrooms. Soups and stews simmered in huge cauldrons and terracotta bowls were filled with potatoes roasted in olive oil and sprinkled with sea salt and spikes of rosemary.

'Rosmarino – rose of the sea!' sighed Angelo, licking his lips. 'Come, let's eat.' He tied up the boat where they would easily find it after the feasting and the young people went to join the throng in the square. But no one would eat just yet. All eyes were fixed on the balcony at the top of the cathedral. There stood four brazen rams and in a moment a scarlet figure would come out and stand between the two pairs.

'There she is!' the cry went up. And the bells of Santa Maddalena's campanile began to ring. The Duchessa waved to her people from the balcony, unable to hear their wild cheers because her ears were firmly stopped up with wax. She had failed to take this precaution on her first appearance at the Marriage feast – but never since.

Down in the square the feasting began. Arianna sat under one of the arches, with her legs tucked under her, a large heaped plate on her lap. Her eyes darted everywhere. Tommaso and Angelo steadily ate their way through mounds of food and kept their eyes on their plates. Arianna was content to stay with them for the time being; the moment to slip away would be when the fireworks started.

*

Inside the Palazzo, a rather more refined feast was in progress. The Duchessa was disinclined to eat much while wearing her silver mask; she would have a substantial meal sent up to her room later. But she could drink easily enough and now that the day's farce was over, she was happy to do that. On her right sat the Reman Ambassador and it took a lot of the rich red Bellezzan wine to put up with his conversation. But it was her single most important task for the evening to keep him sweet, for reasons of her own.

At last the Ambassador turned to his other neighbour and the Duchessa was free to look to her left. Rodolfo, elegant in black velvet, smiled at her. And the Duchessa smiled back behind her mask. After all these years, his bony hawklike face still pleased her. And this year she had a particular reason to be glad of that.

Rodolfo, aware as so often of what she was thinking, raised his glass to her.

'Another year, another Marriage,' he said. 'I could get quite jealous of the sea, you know.'

'Don't worry,' said the Duchessa. 'It can't beat you for variety and slipperiness.'

'Perhaps it's your young oarsmen I should envy, then,' said Rodolfo.

'The only young oarsman who ever meant anything to me was you, Rodolfo.'

He laughed. 'So much you wouldn't let me become one as I recall.'

'Mandoliering wasn't good enough for you. You were much better off at the university.'

'It was good enough for my brothers, Silvia,' said Rodolfo and he wasn't laughing any more.

It was a delicate subject and the Duchessa was surprised he had brought it up, especially tonight. She hadn't even known of Rodolfo's existence when his brothers Egidio and Fiorentino had applied to the Scuola Mandoliera. As was her right, she had selected them for training and, as was her practice with the best-looking ones, she had taken them as her lovers.

It was only when the youngest brother turned up at the School that her heart had been touched. She had sent Rodolfo to university in Padavia and, when he had returned, equipped the finest laboratory in Talia for him to do his experiments in. And then they had become lovers.

The Duchessa reached out and briefly brushed the back of Rodolfo's hand with her silver-tipped fingers. He took her hand and kissed it.

'I must go, Your Grace,' he said in a louder voice. 'It is time for the fireworks.'

The Duchessa watched as his tall thin figure walked the length of the banqueting-hall. If she had been an ordinary woman, she would have wanted a confidante at this moment. But she was Duchessa of Bellezza, so she rose from her seat and everyone stood with her. She made her way alone to the window-seat, which overlooked part of the square and the sea. The sky was a dark navy blue and the stars were about to be rivalled in brightness.

In a minute, she must gesture to the Reman Ambassador, Rinaldo di Chimici, to take his place beside her. But for a moment, with her back to the throng of Senators and Councillors, she removed her mask and rubbed her hand over her tired eyes. Then she caught sight of her reflection in the long window. She regarded it with satisfaction. Her hair and brows might have been helped to stay dark and glossy, but her violet eyes owed nothing to artifice and her pale skin was only lightly etched with lines. She still looked younger than Rodolfo, with his silver hair and slight stoop, though she was five years older than him.

*

The crowd in the square was getting merry with wine and the sheer pleasure of a three-day holiday. The Bellezzans and islanders knew how to enjoy themselves. Now they were dancing in ragged circles, arms linked, singing the bawdy songs that traditionally accompanied the Marriage with the Sea.

The climax of the evening was coming. Rodolfo's mandola had been spotted making for the wooden raft floating in the mouth of the Great Canal, which was loaded with crates and boxes. Everyone was expecting something special for the Duchessa's twenty-fifth Sposalizio – her Silver Wedding.

They were not disappointed. The display began with the usual showers of shooting stars, rockets, Reman candles and Catherine wheels. The faces of the Bellezzans in the square turned green and red and gold with the reflected light from the display in the sky over the water. All eyes were now turned away from the Palazzo and from the silver-masked figure watching at the window.

Arianna and her brothers were in the square too, jostled and crowded by their fellow-islanders.

'Stay close to us, Arianna,' warned Tommaso, 'We don't want you going missing in this crush. Hold Angelo's hand.'

Arianna nodded, but she had every intention of going missing. She took the hand that Angelo held out to her, brown with the sun and calloused from fishing, and squeezed it affectionately. They were going to get into such trouble when they went back to Torrone without her.

After a pause, the dark blue sky began to brighten with the fire-pictures of Rodolfo's set pieces. First a giant brazen bull pawing the sky, then a blue and green wave of the sea, out of which grew a glittering serpent. Then a winged horse flying above them and seeming to sweep down into the water of the canal, where it disappeared. Finally, a silver ram seemed to emerge from the sea and grew massively large above the watchers before it dissolved into a thousand stars.

Angelo let go of his sister's hand to join in the applause.

'Signor Rodolfo has excelled himself this year, hasn't he?' he said to Tommaso, who was also clapping. 'What do you think, Arianna?' But when he turned to look at her, she had gone.

Arianna had laid her plans well. She had to stay on Bellezza overnight. The day after the Sposalizio was the city's great holiday and no one but a native-born Bellezzan was allowed to stay on the main island. Even the other lagooners, from Torrone, Merlino and Burlesca, had to return to their islands at midnight. The penalty for breaking this rule and remaining in Bellezza on the Giornata Vietata – the forbidden day – was death, but no one in living memory had taken the risk.

Arianna was not taking any chances; she knew exactly where she was going to hide. At midnight, the bells of Santa Maddalena would ring out once more and at the end of their peal every non-Bellezzan, whether islander or tourist, must be away in their boats across the water. Tommaso and Angelo would have to go without her. But by then Arianna would be safely hidden.

She slipped into the cavernous cathedral while everyone outside was still gasping 'Ooh!' as the fireworks were let off and 'Aah!' as they fizzled out. Santa Maddalena was still ablaze with candles but it was empty. No one to notice a slight girl running up the worn, steep steps to the museum.

It was Arianna's favourite place in all Bellezza. She could always get into it, even when the cathedral was so thronged with tourists that they had to queue all round the square and be let in in batches, like sheep going through a dip. They didn't seem to care much for the museum, with its dusty books and music manuscripts in glass cases. Arianna hurried through the room with the four original brazen rams and out on to the balcony where the Duchessa had stood an hour or two earlier, between the two pairs of copies.

Arianna looked down into the square, milling with people. So many, it would be easy to mislay one. She couldn't pick out her brothers from the many swaying revellers but her heart went out to them. 'Don't be soft,' she told herself sternly. 'This is the only way.' She settled down beside one brazen leg, clinging on to it for comfort, as she got the best grandstand view of the end of Signor Rodolfo's display. It was going to be a long, uncomfortable night.

*

Lucien woke to feel the sun on his face. His first thought was that his mother had been in and opened the window, but when he came to more fully, he saw that he was out of doors.

'I must still be dreaming,' he thought, but he didn't mind. It was a lovely dream. He was in the floating city, he knew that. It was very warm and yet still early in the morning. The beautiful notebook was still in his hand. He put it in his pyjama pocket.

He stood up; it was easy in the dream. He was in a colonnade of cool marble, but between the columns, where the bright sun splashed in, were warm pools of light, as comforting as a hot bath. Lucien felt different; he reached up to his head and felt his old curls. This was definitely a dream.

He stepped out into the square. There seemed to have been some huge party going on; the few people who were about were sweeping up and putting rubbish into bags – not plastic bin-bags, he noticed, but more like sacks made of rough cloth. Lucien gazed at the huge cathedral opposite him. It was vaguely familiar, but something about it was not quite right.

He turned the other way and looked out over the water; this was the most beautiful place he had ever been in. But more beautiful still was being able to walk about in it. Lucien had almost forgotten what it was like to do that.

But a moment later, the dream changed completely. Someone came up on him from behind and grabbed his arm, dragging him back into the cool shadows of the colonnade. A fierce boy, about his own age, whispered in his ear, 'Are you mad? You'll be killed!'

Lucien looked at him in astonishment. His arm really hurt, where the boy was pinching it. In his real life Lucien couldn't have borne such a touch; it would have made him cry out in pain. But the point was, he could feel it. This wasn't a dream at all.

Chapter 2

The Scuola Mandoliera

The night had been just as uncomfortable as Arianna expected. Up on the rams' gallery it was freezing cold, in spite of the warm cloak she had brought with her. She had changed into her boy's clothes as soon as she had slipped out on to the loggia, taking cover in the dark and the knowledge that everyone's eyes were turned towards the fireworks still exploding out over the lagoon.

At midnight, the bells rang the hour from the campanile, nearly deafening Arianna, but she pulled her woollen fisherman's hat further down over her ears and shrank back against the bulk of the cathedral. When they stopped, she stepped forward and leaned over the marble balustrade, watching the crowd streaming towards the water and the waiting boats. Somewhere among them, tagging reluctantly at the end, would be her two brothers, going home without her.

Arianna pulled further into the shadows when she heard the old monk who looked after the museum going on his rounds. Her main fear now was that he would lock her out with the bronze rams until late the next morning. She had slipped a piece of wood in the jamb of the door out on to the loggia, just in case, but she needn't have worried. The old man lifted a blazing torch just high enough to see the balcony was empty, pushed the door to and shuffled on his way.

Arianna breathed out loudly and settled down to the long night between the two pairs of rams. They felt like some sort of protection, standing on either side of her, the left pair with their left forelegs raised, the right pair mirroring them, even though they were not exactly company.

'Good night, rams,' said Arianna, making the sign of the hand of fortune and covering herself with her cloak.

*

She was woken early, by the shouts of the people who had come to clear up the Piazza after yesterday's revels. She stretched her cold, cramped limbs and rubbed the sleep out of her eyes. She walked stiffly to the balustrade and looked down over the square to the colonnade behind the bell-tower. And froze.

There was a stranger there, a boy about her own age, risking death. He was obviously not Bellezzan, not even Talian by his clothing. Arianna had never seen anything so outlandish as what he was wearing.

He was as out of place as a dog in the Council chamber. And yet he seemed totally oblivious of danger, warming himself in the sunshine and wearing an idiotic expression like a sleepwalker. Perhaps he was touched in the head?

Arianna didn't hesitate. She picked up her bag and slipped off the loggia, past the sickening drop to the floor of the great cathedral, and flew down the museum steps and across the Piazza.

*

'What do you mean, killed?' said the boy, stupidly. 'Who are you? And where is this?' He gestured helplessly at the glittering sea, the silver domes of the cathedral and the bustling square.

'You *are* mad,' said Arianna with satisfaction. 'How can you be in Bellezza on the Giornata Vietata, the one day of the year forbidden to all except natives, and not know where you are? You haven't been kidnapped, have you?'

The boy shook his black curls but said nothing. Arianna saw at a glance what she was going to have to do, though she hated him for it. She dragged him back into the shadow of the bell-tower and started yanking off her boy's clothes, unaware of the effect she was creating.

The boy watched in astonishment as her brown hair tumbled out of the fisherman's hat and she stood in her feminine if rather old-fashioned underwear, pulling a skirt out of her bag.

'Quick, stop gaping like a fish and put on my boy's clothes, over those weird ones of yours. You've only got minutes before someone spots you and hauls you up before the Bellezzan Council.'

The boy, moving as if in a dream, obediently pulled the rough woollen trousers and jerkin on, still warm from the body of the extraordinary girl, while she dressed herself in more clothes from the bag, talking all the time. She seemed absolutely furious with him.

'Almost a year it's taken me,' she fumed, 'to get this disguise together and now you've ruined everything. I'll have to wait another year. And all to save the life of some half-crazed stranger – what's your name, by the way?'

'Lucien,' he said, grasping the one remark he understood.

'Luciano,' said the girl, making his name as different in her mouth as his whole life seemed to be in this place, this 'Bellezza' as she called it.

Lucien was sure that wasn't the real name of this city, just as he knew his real name wasn't Luciano, but he decided to accept the girl's version. Nothing made sense here anyway.

'What's yours?' he asked, clinging on to the little ritual of meeting that was common to ordinary life and this place.

'Arianna,' said the girl, tying her loose hair back with a lacy scarf. She looked at him critically. 'At least you won't attract so much attention now. Good job we're the same size. But you're done for the minute someone questions you. You'll have to stay with me.'

'Why were you pretending to be a boy anyway?' Lucien asked.

Arianna heaved a big sigh. 'It's a long story. Come on. We'd better get away from the Piazza and I'll tell you. Then you can tell me how you got here on this day of all days. I'd have sworn I was the only non-Bellezzan in the city.'

She led him through a passage under a big clock and then along a maze of narrow streets, up and down little bridges, across narrow waterways and through small deserted squares. It seemed as if most of the city were still asleep. Lucien followed her, silently enjoying walking without feeling breathless, being able to keep up with this incomprehensible energetic girl, aware of the sun warming his shoulders through the coarse jerkin and being happier than he could remember for a long time.

They came to a square with a small closed-up theatre in it, where sleepy-eyed stallholders were setting out vegetables and a man was opening up a café. Arianna checked her purposeful stride and eyed the man for a long time before diving into the café. Lucien went in after her.

Inside there were delicious smells, sweet and acrid mixed together. Workmen stood at the bar drinking small cups of black coffee. Arianna gestured Lucien to sit at a table, then brought over two mugs of chocolate and some crumbly pastries.

'So,' said Arianna. 'What's your story?'

'Tell me yours first,' said Lucien. 'Why are you so angry?'

'I suppose it's not your fault,' said Arianna, relaxing a bit for the first time since he'd met her. 'You didn't mean to mess everything up for me. It's just that I've been planning today for a long time. If you really don't know anything about Bellezza,' here she lowered her voice to a whisper, 'then you don't know that today is the one day in the year when all visitors are banned, on pain of death. It's the Giornata Vietata – the day after the Marriage with the Sea.'

Then, as Lucien showed no sign of recognition, 'You *do* know about the Marriage with the Sea, don't you?'

'Just assume I know nothing about anything,' said Lucien. 'It will be easier that way.' He wanted time to see what made things tick here, or at least what made Arianna tick.

'On that day,' she explained, 'every May, the Duchessa has a wedding ceremony with the sea. She's lowered into the water and when the water has reached her middle, the marriage counts as having taken place and the city's prosperity is guaranteed for another year. I know, it's crazy, but that's what lagooners believe. The next day, in accordance with tradition, anyone who wants to train as a mandolier can put himself forward to the Scuola.'

'Hang on,' said Lucien. 'What's a mandolier?'

'Someone in charge of a mandola, of course,' said the girl impatiently. 'The Duchessa chooses the best-looking ones and then their fortune is made. And everyone knows what she does with the very handsomest.'

She was looking at him expectantly. Lucien felt, as he had ever since he met her, that he had no idea what she wanted him to say.

'How does that involve you?' he asked cautiously.

'Put *him*self forward,' she stressed. 'All mandoliers are male. Don't you think that's wrong? I am just as tall and strong as a boy my age, stronger if they're like you (with a contemptuous glance at Lucien's build), and good to look at, if that's what matters.'

She paused again and this time he was not at a loss. 'You are good to look at,' he said.

Arianna hurtled on, not acknowledging the compliment she had asked for; it was just a fact she had wanted to establish. 'I mean, this city is ruled by a woman.'

'The Duchessa,' said Lucien, glad to have understood something.

'Of course la Duchessa,' said Arianna impatiently. 'The trouble is, she makes all the rules, so if she wants handsome male mandoliers she'll have them.'

'But what would happen to you if they found out?' asked Lucien.

'You mean what *would* have happened,' said Arianna bitterly, mangling her pastry to crumbs. 'I can't put myself forward now, dressed as a girl, can I? I'll be lucky not to be caught and executed. And so will you. We just have to hope no one here knows we're not Bellezzans,' she added in a whisper.

Lucien concentrated on eating his cake, which was something he could understand. He closed his eyes and let the almonds and sugar melt on his tongue. Nothing had tasted so delicious for a long time.

'Have mine too, if you're so hungry,' said Arianna, pushing her plate over.

'Thanks. Look, I'm sorry for messing up your plan. As you said, I didn't know. And thanks for saving me, if that's what you've done.'

'There's no "if" about it. Now tell me what you're doing here, so I can see if it was worth it.'

It was a long time before Lucien answered. He had no explanation to offer. Everything around him was strange – the people, the language they were speaking, which he was pretty sure was Italian and yet he understood it. The fierce, beautiful girl sitting opposite him, who also seemed to be Italian, and yet could understand him. The women coming into the café, who were wearing masks. It was bizarre.

Yet nothing equalled the strangeness of how he felt inside. He was well, strong, in spite of what Arianna thought of him. He felt he could run up mountainsides, swim across the lagoon, and yet – he couldn't explain why he was here in this beautiful, odd city and not lying in his bed in London.

If he were in a dream, it wouldn't matter what he said. But no dream had ever been like this. In the end he just told her the truth.

'I can't explain how I got here but I'm from somewhere else. From London. In England. When I'm there, I'm very ill. In fact, I think I'm probably dying. I have cancer and I'm having chemotherapy. My hair has all dropped out. I'm tired all the time. I fell asleep thinking about a city floating on the water and when I woke up, I was where you found me and my hair was back.'

Arianna reached out and tugged his curls. Feeling the resistance she gave a little gasp and made a sign with her right hand, holding her thumb against her little finger and touching her forehead and chest.

'*Dia*,' she whispered. 'It is true. I don't understand all those words you told me but I believe you. You come from a great city a long way from here, where you are very ill and now you are suddenly here and are well. What does it mean?'

They stared at each other. Then Arianna glanced

uneasily around the café. The barman seemed to be looking quite interestedly in their direction. 'There are too many people in here. Someone might recognize me. Let's go.'

'Why are all the women wearing masks?' asked Lucien. 'Is it for another festival?'

'Not all of them are,' said Arianna. 'Only the unmarried ones. I am supposed to start wearing one as soon as I'm sixteen, in a few months. It's another of the Duchessa's rules. Not this one's though. It's been going on for years. She has to wear one herself.'

'She's not married then?' asked Lucien, but Arianna only snorted in reply.

She was leading him away from the square and to a quiet backwater of the city. The houses were washed in pink and sand and ochre and little gardens sprouted from some of the roofs or from terraces halfway up. The sky was very blue and between houses he sometimes glimpsed more bell-towers with birds wheeling round them. Little canals crossed their path so often that they had to zigzag and use the bridges; there was no walking in a straight line.

'It's very beautiful, your city,' he said at last.

'Yes, that's why it's so rich,' said Arianna, matter-of-factly. 'Beauty is cash – that's the Bellezzans' motto – *Bellezza è moneta*.'

'Where are we going?' asked Lucien.

'We might as well take a look at the Scuola,' said Arianna, shortly.

They walked across another small canal, through a passageway, and arrived on the pavement alongside a much broader canal. Across a stone bridge was a grand building with 'Scuola Mandoliera' written on it, carved into the stone above the entrance. In front of it bobbed several black craft and people were coming and going in busy groups as if something important were happening.

'Mandoliers,' said Lucien. 'Those are the people who row the boats, right?'

Arianna gave him a withering look. 'Scull, not row. And they're mandolas, not boats. It's because they're shaped like almonds – *mandole*. It makes them very tricky to steer.'

'Have you tried?' asked Lucien, looking at the slender boats. He was thinking about how he'd been punting on the river in Cambridge with his uncle Graham, his mother's brother. You had to stand on the stern of a punt too.

'Of course,' said Arianna impatiently. 'We have canals on the islands too. And I've handled mandolas all my life on Torrone. Both my brothers are fishermen on Merlino.'

Her forehead creased.

'I've got them into the most terrible trouble – and all for nothing! Our parents will be worried sick because they came back without me last night. I gave them the slip, you see. My parents don't know where I am.'

Lucien said nothing but he was thinking the same about his own parents. 'At least Arianna knows where she is,' he thought. 'Which is more than I do.'

Arianna clutched his arm. 'It must be time for the selection,' she hissed. 'That's the Duchessa's mandola.'

An elaborately decorated mandola slipped smoothly through the water, sculled, Lucien couldn't help noticing, by an extremely handsome young man. It had a covered section in the middle, hung with silver brocade. The mandolier brought his craft in skilfully to the landing stage and an official of the School, in an ornate uniform, handed out first a waiting-woman then an elegant masked figure, which could only be the Duchessa.

'Quick!' said Arianna. 'Let's go in.'

'Is it allowed?' asked Lucien. 'Won't we get caught?'

'It's a public selection,' said Arianna defiantly. 'And they won't be expecting anyone to disobey the ban. I was banking on that. We'll be all right as long as you don't speak to anyone.' Then she hurried across the bridge and Lucien had to run after her.

The wooden gates under the stone entrance were indeed wide open and Lucien soon found himself in a courtyard filled with smartly dressed people. He felt a bit shabby in his borrowed clothes but no one was looking at him. At one end of the courtyard was a raised platform. At that moment the Duchessa was ascending the platform and seating herself on a carved wooden chair. A queue of nervous-looking young men was forming to the right of the stage.

Arianna had pushed her way to the front of the crowd, no longer worried about being recognized. When Lucien had managed to squeeze his way through to her he found her enthralled, violet eyes shining and hair escaped from her scarf. This was what she had been waiting for for a year, even if it hadn't worked out the way she meant, and she was thrilled to be here.

What was happening on the stage was a bit like a beauty pageant. The young men were led, one by one, for inspection by the Duchessa. She didn't quite open their mouths and look at their teeth, but it was almost as bad. After each inspection, the Duchessa spoke to the School official and the unlucky candidates were led off the stage, while the successful ones were lined up sheepishly at the back.

It was clear where their families all stood in the crowd; groans and cheers greeted each decision. Lucien wasn't at all sure that Arianna's plan would have worked. No one seemed to have come without supporters. The eagerness of the families was causing the crowd to surge forward, pushing Lucien and Arianna closer to the stage.

Lucien found himself at the front, a few feet from the Duchessa. The line of hopeful mandoliers was coming to an end. Of the last two young men Lucien thought, going by the Duchessa's previous choices, one was too short and one was distinctly bandy-legged. They were dispatched so quickly that Lucien was already turning to go when the Duchessa's voice rang out.

'That young man there. Bring him up.'

Heads turned, Lucien's with them. Fingers pointed. At him. 'No, it's a mistake,' he protested. 'I'm not here to be a mandolier.'

But strong hands were guiding him up on to the stage. He looked round wildly for Arianna. He caught a glimpse of her face, looking absolutely furious. And then she was gone. He was pushed towards the Duchessa and found himself hypnotized by her presence.

Her eyes, glittering through the holes in her silver butterfly mask, were violet, like Arianna's. 'Must be common here,' thought Lucien. Her voice was low and caressing and she smelt absolutely wonderful. Lucien, whose mother hardly ever wore scent, and who had had very little experience with girls, felt quite faint.

The Duchessa held out a hand to him, a favour she had bestowed on only one or two candidates. 'Tell me your name, young man,' said the Duchessa.

'Luciano,' said Lucien, remembering Arianna's version.

'Luciano,' said the Duchessa slowly, savouring the syllables like a particularly delicious cake.

Lucien felt himself blushing. What had Arianna said? Everyone knows what she does with the handsomest ones. He felt completely out of his depth. He didn't want to be a mandolier or one of the Duchessa's favourites. At the moment, he just wanted to be at home, with things around him he could understand. But even as he thought about it, he realised he *could* be a mandolier; he was strong enough, here, and it couldn't be so very different from punting.

'You remind me of a young man I selected many years ago,' said the Duchessa, and from the sound of her voice, he knew she was smiling. 'Yes, I think you will make a fine mandolier. Welcome to the Scuola.'

The crowd was quite silent. If Arianna was still there she made no sound as Lucien was led to join the other successful candidates and the Duchessa descended from the stage. Strong as he felt in this dreamlike city, he thought he might pass out.

All the young men chosen to train as mandoliers – and they all looked a fair bit older than Lucien – were shepherded off to their new quarters. The others all had families to hug them and give them tearful but proud farewells. Lucien even found himself hugged a couple of times by over-enthusiastic mothers and sisters.

At last he was alone in a little room with a wooden bed, old-fashioned carved wooden chest and a china jug and bowl. The friendly guide who had shown him in had said, 'See you in the morning at first light,' then left him. Lucien sat on the bed and put his head in his hands. He couldn't begin to make sense of his situation and all of a sudden a great weariness overtook him. He swung his legs up on to the hard mattress and rested his head on the pillow. Trying to get comfortable, he felt something digging into him and, reaching inside his woollen jerkin, pulled the Venetian notebook out of his pyjama pocket.

Lying there with the notebook in his hand and wondering if he would ever see his own home again, he soon fell into a deep sleep.

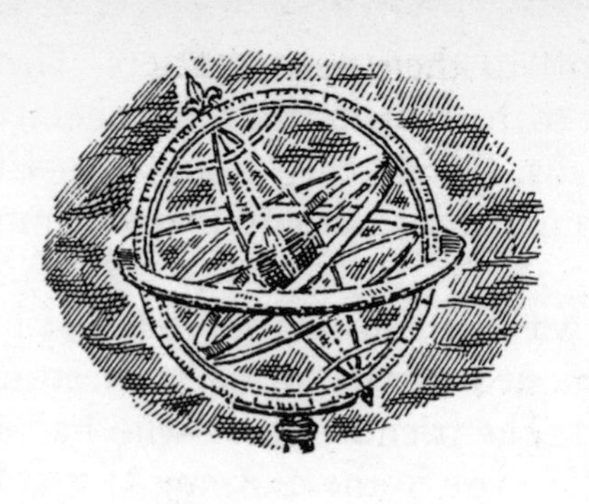

Chapter 3

A Garden in the Air

Lucien returned to his body with a jolt. At least, returning to his body was what it felt like. He was immediately weighed down by his exhaustion. If he hadn't already been lying in bed, he would have fallen. His throat was dry and sore. He put his hand up to feel his hair and met his bare scalp. Tears seeped under his eyelids; it was somehow much worse losing his hair the second time.

So it had been a dream. But an amazing dream. So real. And how could he have invented Arianna and the Duchessa and the whole incredible city, that was and yet wasn't Venice? It still felt so much like the reality, and his life confined to bed like the dream, that Lucien almost believed he would still be wearing Arianna's jerkin and trousers. But of course he wasn't. Just the blue pyjamas in which he had been transported to Bellezza.

There was a knock and his father came in.

'Morning, son. You're looking a bit better. Got some colour back.'

Lucien was astonished. He felt like hell. But he had to admit that was in contrast to how alive and well he'd been in Bellezza. Perhaps he *did* feel a bit better than when he'd last been in this body. Or in this bed. Whichever it was.

'Throat still hurting?' asked Dad sympathetically. 'You can write in the book, don't forget.'

The book! Lucien slid it out of his pocket and wrote, 'Tell me some more about Venice.'

Arianna's parents were furious with her but she scarcely noticed. After the Duchessa had called Lucien up on to the stage, she had run, cheeks burning, back through the side streets to Santa Maddalena and the Piazzetta, where a few boats were moored. There she had bribed a boatman to take her back to Torrone, with the money she had saved to pay her entrance fee to the Scuola Mandoliera.

It took all of that to persuade any native-born Bellezzan to leave his city on the day after the Marriage with the Sea. He had grumbled all the way to the island, but Arianna hadn't paid any attention to him. She gripped the side of the boat with one hand and stuffed the knuckles of the other into her mouth to stop herself from screaming with frustration.

It was so unfair. That boy, that Luciano, had

thwarted all her plans and then coolly stepped in to take her place. She knew with a part of her mind that it had not been his fault, that he hadn't deliberately set out to catch the Duchessa's eye. He was such a simpleton, knowing nothing about the Duchessa, or mandoliering, or Bellezza even.

But another part of her brain was fiercely jealous of him. He, with his dark eyes and curly hair and shy smile, would soon be sculling tourists along the Great Canal, making his fortune, his future assured. She didn't have a moment's doubt that the Duchessa would have chosen him. Though he looked barely old enough to meet the Scuola's entry criterion of fifteen and his build was slight, his looks would have assured him a place. And he wasn't even Talian, let alone Bellezzan!

Arianna relaxed her grip and dipped her hand into the water, splashing her face with it. They were out in the open lagoon now, far from the brackish waters of the canals. Luciano said he was Anglian and that she believed, though he spoke Talian, but she no longer trusted the rest of his story. How could she? He said he was ill when he was clearly healthy, that he was bald, when— bah! She snorted at the thought. He must have been deceiving her. His story didn't make sense. Perhaps he wasn't simple, but very cunning.

By the time the boat pulled into the landing stage at Torrone, Arianna's blazing fury had subsided into a dull, bitter misery. The lookout posted to watch the sea for her return hared off along the bank of the main canal after raising a hand in greeting and Arianna trudged homeward.

She knew better than anyone what turmoil her

absence would have caused on Torrone. She was their *Figlia dell'Isola* – Daughter of the Island. The only child born there in the last twenty years.

Everyone on Torrone was old. Arianna had no playmates except her parents and her two much older brothers. There were few families left on Torrone at all. Arianna's father, Gianfranco, had lived on the island all his life and was now curator of the tiny cathedral museum. The cathedral on Torrone was the most ancient building in the whole lagoon, built centuries ago while Bellezza was still a swamp. Tourists came from all over the world to see it and the magnificent silver mosaics it contained.

But there were no shops and no school. Arianna went by boat to a school on Merlino, the big island where her brothers worked and lived in their cottage by the shore. There, too, were markets, selling food and luxuries from the mainland. And every day in summer traders came to Torrone from the smaller island of Burlesca, bringing cakes and wine and lace and glass to sell to the tourists. But in winter Torrone had only fish from Merlino and whatever it could grow itself. It was through the winter months that Arianna had dreamed most of her escape.

Arianna's mother, Valeria, rushed out of their little whitewashed house near the cathedral and embraced the runaway roughly, crying and laughing with relief that soon changed to scolding and threats. The lookout had gone on to the cathedral to find Gianfranco and give him the news.

'Where have you been?' Valeria kept asking. 'We were worried sick. Tommaso and Angelo are out of their minds. They should be enjoying a good holiday today but do you know what they are doing? They're out in their boat getting as close to Bellezza as they dare.'

Arianna mumbled something about having needed to answer a call of nature and then getting lost in the crowd. She didn't really expect to be believed. She could have begged a ride on any boat going back to any of the islands, if she hadn't been able to find her brothers. The imperative was to get out of the city.

She hadn't really thought about what to tell her family if she had been accepted at the Scuola. Her plans had all stopped at her admission to the school. Perhaps, once she had been trained, she would have taken off her disguise and the Duchessa would have been forced to agree that girls could train in future. But, if she were honest with herself, Arianna would have to admit that she hadn't expected that the school would be flooded with applications from girls after her. Her plans were all for herself.

The scoldings poured over her and went on all day, added to by her father, rushing home, and her brothers when they came back in the middle of the afternoon, hungry and upset. Neighbours, too, dropped in to see that she was safe then shake their heads in sympathy with her parents over her wickedness and disobedience.

Arianna was heartily sick of being the centre of attention and wished, as she had so often before, that there were other children on Torrone, to take some of the pressure away from her.

'... and no one knows how long it can survive,' finished Dad. 'The water is rising every year and if the flood barriers aren't built, the whole city could disappear under the sea – like Atlantis.'

So it wasn't Bellezza. Lucien was sure that the city of his dream hadn't been sinking, though he didn't know how he knew it. Bellezza was as unlike a doomed city as it could be, bustling, prosperous, full of its own importance. And he couldn't see the Duchessa, from the little he knew of her, letting the sea take her city from her.

'Are you interested in Venice?' asked Dad. 'I could get you some books from the library.'

Lucien nodded, and wrote, 'Have you ever been there?'

Dad looked a little embarrassed. 'Only once,' he said. 'Before I met your mum.'

Lucien immediately guessed Dad had been there with a previous girlfriend.

'Did you visit any of the islands?' he wrote.

Dad looked at him oddly. 'How did you know about the islands? I didn't think I'd mentioned them. Yeah, we went to them. I mean I did. The one where they make the glass and the one where all the houses are painted different colours and the one with the old cathedral and the gold mosaics.'

'Torrone?' wrote Lucien.

'I thought that was a sticky sweet,' said Dad, puzzled. 'But it is a name a bit like that. I'd better get you those books.'

When he had gone, Lucien's mum brought him breakfast. He managed a few spoonfuls of soggy cornflakes and half a cup of tea, then sank back exhausted on to his pillows. He heard the door click as she took the tray away, then dropped into an uneasy doze.

And woke, sweating, from a dream in which he stood at the end of a sleek black boat, holding a long oar. The Duchessa sat far away in the other end, making notes in a book as if she were marking his performance.

'If you don't beat the record,' she was saying, 'I shall take my mask off.'

In the dream this had been the most terrifying threat. Lucien had forced himself awake rather than confront the horror he knew lurked behind that mask. But as he lay there, hot and damp with fear, a curious certainty settled on him. If this had been a dream, then the other hadn't. This was ordinary B-movie nightmare stuff, with none of the logical reality of his night-time visit to Bellezza. The city where Arianna and the Duchessa lived was real; he was sure of it.

Now all he had to do was to find out how to get back.

The next day was Sunday and, though her parents were now not talking to Arianna, they didn't deny her the annual visit to Mass in Santa Maddalena. The whole family rowed over to Bellezza early in the morning, mooring their boat at the Piazzetta, along with many other lagooners.

Inside the hushed cathedral, Arianna let her gaze wander up to the gallery that led to the Loggia degli Arieti, where she had spent the night before last so uncomfortably, with the rams. A brown-robed figure caught her eye, on one of the many wooden walkways that criss-crossed the cathedral just beneath its roof. She realized that she had seen the same figure, or one just like it, as she had climbed up to her hiding-place.

She had scarcely noticed it then, in her hurry to carry out her plan, but now, with the service droning on around her, she had time to reflect. Why had a monk been in the cathedral then and not out in the square watching the fireworks like everyone else?

Everyone in Bellezza paid more attention to state ceremonies and celebrations than they did to religion, even the priests and monks. Tradition was what mattered in the lagoon. Tradition and superstition. That's why her family were here today, because traditionally all islanders forsook their churches, even the special one on Torrone, and came to Mass in the basilica of Santa Maddalena on the Sunday after the Marriage with the Sea. The Duchessa herself was seated prominently in the front row, slender as a new bride, dressed all in white, with a silver mask in the shape of a cat's face.

Arianna had done this for every one of her fifteen years and it had always been the same. But today was different. As they left the cathedral, her parents steered her away from the Piazzetta and into the little streets to the north of the main square.

'We're going to see your aunt Leonora,' was all the explanation offered.

They got to the house of Gianfranco's sister-in-law, off the Campo San Sulien, which Arianna had always loved visiting because of its unexpected garden with its stone fountain. Water in the heart of the water-surrounded city was always a surprise. But it was clear this visit was to be no treat.

Leonora invited them in warmly and poured red wine for them. But the atmosphere was tense. Arianna's brothers were perched nervously on the edge of Leonora's spindly chairs. Gianfranco cleared his throat.

'Since you disobeyed not just us, Arianna, but the laws of the city,' he said, 'putting yourself in danger and causing us so much worry, we have asked your aunt to have you here with her for a while. Perhaps this will get Bellezza out of your system. Perhaps you will learn to value your home, which, though it isn't exciting, is safe and filled with people who love you.'

He blew his nose after this speech, which was a long one for him, and Arianna wanted to fling her arms round him. But she was too amazed to move. What kind of punishment was this? This was like condemning a child who steals marzipan to a whole week in a sweet shop. Arianna didn't know Leonora at all well and she had no children. But her husband, Gianfranco's older brother, had died a few years ago and left her his considerable wealth, made from selling trinkets to tourists. So the house was comfortable and Leonora herself was kind. And it was in Bellezza! Arianna knew she had got off lightly.

But when her parents and brothers said goodbye, the tears gathered obstinately in her eyes. Much as life on Torrone bored her with its endless tedium of few people and fewer adventures, she felt desolated by homesickness and clung to her mother, begging to be forgiven.

*

Lucien woke in the hard little bed to see sunlight pouring in through the window. He looked out and saw a green canal under a bright blue sky.

He was back. It seemed to be the next day in Bellezza, though it had been night-time when he left his own world. He'd had an interminable dreary day in his bed in London, enlivened only by the colour pictures in Dad's library books about Venice.

Lucien put his hand to his head, hardly daring to believe it when his fingers sank into thick curls.

There was a soft knock at the door then a rather ugly old man put his head round it. 'Quick,' he hissed. 'We must get you away before they realize you've gone.' Without waiting for a reply, he led Lucien by the elbow out of the room, across the courtyard and down to the Scuola's landing-stage where a sleek black mandola was moored. He bundled Lucien into the boat, then skilfully turned it in mid-canal and set off at an impressive pace.

'Where are we going?' asked Lucien, not sure if he was being rescued or kidnapped. As with his last experience of Bellezza, he found himself just going with the flow, luxuriating in the feeling of being ordinarily well in the middle of this extra-ordinary setting.

'To the laboratory,' said the mandolier shortly. 'Signor Rodolfo is expecting you.'

Since he could make nothing of this, Lucien remained silent until the mandola glided to a halt by a landing stage that must have been back near the big Piazza where he had found himself the day before. He could see the silver domes of the cathedral quite close above the roofs.

His guide led him up some marble steps, straight off the canal, and in through heavy wooden doors which seemed to be kept permanently open. It was dark inside the house, or palace, or whatever it was, and Lucien stumbled, having trouble adjusting his vision after the bright sunlight on the canal.

On, up many steps until he was sure he must be at the top of the building. The mandolier stopped by a thick dark wooden door and knocked before thrusting Lucien through it in front of him.

Lucien stood on the threshold, trying to understand what he was seeing. It was a mixture of a workshop, a chemistry laboratory and a library. It didn't quite have a stuffed alligator hanging from the ceiling but one certainly would have looked right at home there. It was filled with leather-bound books, shelves full of jars, and glass bottles containing coloured liquids and nameless objects. There were huge globes and a weird collection of metal circles on a stand. And a model of the solar system, which Lucien was sure was moving.

In the corner by a large window with a low sill sat a man dressed in black velvet. His clothes looked expensive and Lucien immediately knew he was someone important, though this had less to do with how he was dressed than his own aura. He had silver hair and he was tall and thin. He sat hunched in his armchair like a hawk roosting.

But there was nothing frightening about him, in spite of his air of controlled power. The man told his servant, Alfredo, that he could go and Lucien heard the door close heavily behind him.

'Welcome,' said Rodolfo. His eyes were glittering with excitement. He looked as if he might rub his hands together with glee. 'I have been expecting you.'

'That's what that man said,' said Lucien stupidly. 'But I don't see how. I mean, I don't know how I got here myself. Or why.'

'But you must have worked out it was something to do with the notebook,' said Rodolfo. 'I mean, you've done it twice now.'

'Yes, but...' Lucien stopped. How did this man know about the book and how did he know it had happened twice? It had taken him all day back at home to try falling asleep with the notebook in his hand – and sleep had been reluctant to come. He had put the book back in his pocket before the strange man had burst in and it was still there now, although hidden under Arianna's Bellezzan boy's disguise, which he had been glad to see again.

'I didn't know it was you I was expecting,' said Rodolfo. 'But I knew it was you when I saw you at the Scuola Mandoliera.'

'I didn't see you there,' said Lucien.

'I wasn't there to be seen,' said Rodolfo, simply.

He stood up and motioned Lucien to follow him to a dark corner of the room, where a silver brocade curtain hung on the wall. When Rodolfo pulled it back, Lucien wasn't sure at first what he was looking at. He would have said it was a bank of television screens, except that sounded modern and high tech and this was anything but.

Six small oval mirrors, ornately framed in what might have been ebony, showed moving pictures of scenes, some of which Lucien recognized. There was the Scuola and the Piazza where he had first seen Arianna, something that might have been the interior of the great cathedral and three other places, all richly decorated rooms, which he didn't know but which were obviously Bellezzan.

Under them was a complicated collection of knobs with knurled edges and brass levers aligned with what looked like signs of the zodiac, though some of them were new to Lucien. He gave up trying to understand. It was easier really to go back to thinking of Bellezza as a dream.

Rodolfo pointed to the mirror which showed the Scuola Mandoliera and Lucien realized how he had been seen the day before. And even as he watched, fascinated, he saw a tiny mandola glide into the frame and an elegant miniature figure step lightly out of it and into the School amid much bowing and scraping of officials.

'Is that the Duchessa?' Lucien asked.

'She has come to inspect her new recruits,' said Rodolfo. 'She will wonder what has happened to you.'

'Mirror, mirror, on the wall,' said Lucien. Rodolfo looked at a loss.

'Magic,' said Lucien.

'Not at all,' said Rodolfo, with an expression of distaste. 'Science.'

'So that's how you saw me,' said Lucien. 'But how did you know I was the person you were expecting? Is it because I don't look Bellezzan?'

Rodolfo scanned his face hard. 'You really don't know, do you?' he said. 'Come with me and I'll show you something.'

He strode over to the deep window, opened the casement and swung his long legs out over the sill. Lucien was startled until he realized there was some sort of roof garden outside. Rodolfo beckoned and the boy followed him out.

It was an oasis in the heart of the city. But Lucien saw immediately that it took up more space than it should have done. It covered an area much larger than the roof of the building they were standing on. It stretched away into the distance and Lucien thought he could see peacocks at the far end.

Huge pots held full-size trees and there were flowers everywhere, filling the air with their heavy scent. In the middle of the roof garden, a fountain played – more science, thought Lucien. Most of the garden was shaded and there was even a hammock slung between two orange trees, but close to the stone balustrade that enclosed it, the sun beat down on a tiled terrace.

Rodolfo stood in the sunshine and waited for him. When Lucien came up to him, he took the boy gently by the shoulders and encouraged him to look down.

'What do you see?' he asked.

Lucien looked first through the balustrade at the incredible beauty of Bellezza, its silver spires and bell-towers dazzling against the blue sky, but Rodolfo didn't mean that. He directed Lucien's gaze on to the tiles, with their intricate astronomical patterns. Just the sort of garden you'd expect a magician to have, thought Lucien.

And then he saw what he was meant to see. At their feet stretched out the black silhouette of only one figure.

'I have been waiting for someone without a shadow.'

Chapter 4

The Stravaganti

Time seemed to have stood still on the roof garden. Or at least slowed to a sluggish trickle. Lucien was still staring at where his shadow should have been. Rodolfo had gone back inside and now came out holding two glasses of a sparkling blond drink.

'Prosecco,' he said. 'You've had a shock.'

Lucien started to say he didn't drink but then realized he was very thirsty and had no idea what the water was like in this city. Where he might be was one thing, but the time he was in was clearly not the twenty-first century and all the city's beauty could not disguise the bad smell coming off the canals.

He drank the prosecco. It was cold and a bit sharp and to Lucien quite wonderful. Alfredo, the old mandolier who had brought him from the Scuola, had followed Rodolfo out of the window, with the bottle in one hand and a tray in the other, laden with untidy ham sandwiches. Lucien discovered he was ravenous. When had his last meal been? Pastries in the café with Arianna? Or the few spoonfuls of scrambled egg he had managed to get down before bedtime in his other life?

Whichever, it now seemed long ago and he had eaten three sandwiches and drunk two glasses of the sparkling wine before he asked Rodolfo any of the questions crowding his brain.

The silver-haired scientist, or magician, or whatever he was, sat in companionable silence while Lucien finished his meal, though he ate nothing himself.

'Feeling better?' he now asked.

'Yes, thanks,' said Lucien. 'Actually, I feel great.'

He put his glass down on the terrace beside him and stretched, taking conscious note of how each limb, each muscle felt. There was no tiredness, no weakness, no aches. It might have just been the wine, but he felt energy coursing through him.

Rodolfo was smiling. 'Tell me about yourself and your life in the other world.'

'You don't know then?' asked Lucien, who had assumed Rodolfo must be a powerful all-knowing sort of magician.

'Only where you must have come from and approximately when,' Rodolfo answered. 'Nothing about you personally, not even your name.'

'Lucien,' said Lucien. 'But it seems to be Luciano here. At least that's what I told the Duchessa.'

'Then Luciano it had better be,' said Rodolfo gravely, with just a hint of a smile.

'I don't know what you want to know,' said Lucien. 'In my real life, I've been very ill. I'm having some treatment which might eventually cure me but in the meantime it makes me feel a lot worse. I feel wonderful here, though. Nothing wrong with me at all.'

Rodolfo was leaning forward, listening carefully to every word. He spent the next hour questioning Lucien about every detail of his ordinary life, even quite trivial things like what his family ate at mealtimes and where they did their shopping. His dark eyes glittered at Lucien's descriptions of quite mundane things, like supermarkets, the Underground, football matches. Even pizza, which Lucien assumed he would know all about, caused Rodolfo's brow to wrinkle in puzzlement.

'A round flat bread with cooked tomatoes and cheese on top?' he asked. 'Are you sure?'

Lucien smiled. 'Or chicken tikka, or Christmas dinner, or even haggis, for all I know. Anything goes these days.'

Rodolfo looked blank. 'We do not have these things you mention in Talia. Are they good to eat?'

'Yes – some of them – but not necessarily on a pizza,' said Lucien.

Rodolfo leaned back in his chair and stretched, cracking his knuckles.

'Now it's your turn,' said Lucien. 'Tell me about Bellezza, about Talia.'

'What do you want to know?'

'Everything.' Lucien gestured around him. 'I don't understand any of it. I mean, why am I here and why don't I have a shadow and why were you expecting someone like me?'

Rodolfo got up and walked over to the stone parapet. He looked out over the silver roof of the cathedral. Then he turned and gazed at Lucien.

'To answer your questions, I have to start further back. Some time ago, a traveller came from your world to mine. It was hundreds of years ago in your time, though not in mine. He was the first to discover the secret, the first member of the brotherhood I belong to. He was the first Stravagante.'

'What's that?'

'A wanderer. For us, a wanderer between worlds. He was a powerful scientist from your country. You may have heard of him. His name was William Dethridge.' Rodolfo paused and looked hopefully at Lucien, who just shook his head.

'Ever since Doctor Dethridge made that first journey,' Rodolfo continued, 'there have been Stravaganti working on the principles by which such journeys are made. It is difficult work and sometimes dangerous. As time has gone by, we have discovered the risks of crossing from one side to the other.'

'Like in *Star Trek*,' said Lucien, and saw immediately he was going to have to explain himself. 'It's a TV programme about the future. They mustn't tamper with the time/space continuum or there are terrible consequences. And they mustn't interfere with alien cultures. That's the Prime Directive.'

'I do not understand most of that,' said Rodolfo slowly, 'but the spirit sounds right. Every journey between your world and ours is fraught with hazards and is not to be undertaken lightly. It can be done only by those who have studied the science of stravagation and familiarized themselves with its pitfalls and restraints.'

'Hang on,' said Lucien. 'I haven't done any of that. I just held the book and thought about the city. Only the first time it wasn't Bellezza. I was thinking about Venice, which I think is like Bellezza in my world.'

'Ven-iss,' said Rodolfo, thoughtfully. 'It doesn't sound like a Talian word, but I have heard it before. It was what Doctor Dethridge called our city.'

'Anyway, I haven't done any of that training.'

'And yet you are a Stravagante,' said Rodolfo. 'And that puts you in great danger here.'

'Why?' said Lucien. 'You haven't really explained why I'm here at all.'

'It is very hard for you to understand,' said Rodolfo, pacing the roof terrace. 'I don't claim to understand it all myself and yet I have been studying this science for years. You say you "held the book". May I see it?'

A little reluctantly, Lucien drew the book from the pocket of his blue pyjamas, which he still wore under his Bellezzan clothes, and handed it to Rodolfo.

Rodolfo held it reverently, like a Bible, turning it in his hands. 'Do you know where this came from?' he asked.

'My father found it in a skip on Waverley Road,' said Lucien.

'No. Whatever that means, it did not come from there. It was made in the workshop of my brother Egidio, here in Bellezza.'

'Then how did it get to London, to my world?'

'I took it there myself.'

Lucien gasped. 'You've been to my world?'

'Of course,' said Rodolfo. 'Did I not tell you I am a Stravagante?'

The thought of Rodolfo striding round London in his black velvet made Lucien smile. But he'd probably just be put down as an ageing hippy and not raise an eyebrow; people would assume he'd wandered over from Hampstead, not another dimension.

Rodolfo handed the swirly red and purple notebook back to Lucien.

'Look after it. Don't show it to anyone else. There are those who would take it from you.'

'But why?' asked Lucien. 'What good would it do them?'

'It might help them to discover the secret of travel to your world. More importantly, if you lost it, you would not be able to get back,' said Rodolfo, gravely.

'Who do you mean?' asked Lucien. 'Other Stravagantes?'

'*Stravaganti*,' corrected Rodolfo. 'No. Even if someone else's talisman fell into his hand a true member of the brotherhood would not take such a shortcut. But we have enemies. People who would like to plunder your world and bring its magic here.'

'Magic?' said Lucien. 'There's no magic in my world. It's completely ordinary.'

'And yet you can move large numbers of people in metal boxes under the ground and on the ground and even above the ground!' said Rodolfo. 'You have machines you can talk into to order your dinner and other machines to bring it to you. You have many ways of communicating with people miles away from you and reading books in libraries in other countries. Is not all of this magic?'

'No,' said Lucien. 'I understand why it seems that way to you, because you haven't got things like aeroplanes and the Internet and mobile phones. But they're not magic – they're inventions. You know, technology – science.'

Rodolfo seemed unconvinced. 'What I do in my laboratory is science,' he said. 'But let that pass. It is your kind of science, which I would call magic, that the Chimici are after.'

'The "kimmichee",' repeated Lucien. 'Are they your enemies?'

Rodolfo nodded. 'They are one of the oldest families in Talia. A big family, always marrying and breeding. Every city but one in Northern Talia is ruled by one of them. Even if not officially. They are the power behind every dukedom and principality in the country, except this one, the city of Bellezza. Even the Pope himself is one of them.'

'The Pope?' said Lucien, surprised. 'You have a Pope?'

'Of course,' said Rodolfo. 'Don't you? Ours rules, technically, in Remora. But his older brother, Niccolò di Chimici, is really in charge.'

'What would they do if they got into my world?' asked Lucien.

'If they got not only into your world but into your time,' said Rodolfo, 'they would bring back all kinds of magic – cures for illnesses, spells to make inanimate objects move, mystical weapons which can kill and maim from long distances away... Need I go on?'

'And the Stravaganti?' asked Lucien. 'What do they do? They don't take any of those things?'

'No,' said Rodolfo, quietly. 'They – or I might say "we", since you are now one of us, whether you like it or not – do not bring anything from your world to ours except what ensures a safe return. We have become guardians of the secret of this kind of travel. Ever since Doctor Dethridge made that first journey, by accident, it has needed someone to watch over any comings or goings between worlds.'

Lucien frowned. 'Hang on. There's something I don't follow. I mean all of it, really, but didn't you say this doctor was from hundreds of years ago in my world?'

'Yes, the sixteenth century. The time of your Queen Elizabeth.'

'We've got another one now,' said Lucien. 'Queen Elizabeth the Second. But if you don't know anything about supermarkets or the Tube and you all wear these old-fashioned clothes, what century is this?'

Rodolfo sighed. 'Still the sixteenth, I'm afraid. That is why the Chimici are so eager to get their hands on your twentieth-century magic.'

'Twenty-first now,' said Lucien absent-mindedly. His thoughts were racing. He was beginning to grasp something of the situation, even though there were huge gaps in what he understood. 'You mean the Chimici don't want to wait till all those things are invented here. They want to sort of speed up civilization?'

Rodolfo looked at him sadly. 'If it is civilization to kill vast numbers of people at a stroke, then yes, that is what they want.'

'But it's not all like that,' protested Lucien. 'You said yourself, there'd be cures for illnesses, things like that.'

'Are they harmless? Would the Chimici know how to use the magic that is supposed to be making you better?'

Lucien had a vision of some sort of crazed villain in a velvet cloak trying to inject chemicals into a Bellezzan who might or might not have cancer. 'No. You'd have to be a trained twenty-first-century doctor, I suppose.'

'And if they did have these cures and the skills to apply them,' persisted Rodolfo, 'do you think they would be made available to all? No. The Chimici want to help only the Chimici. They would steal whatever made them strong, made them live long, made their women have easy childbirth and healthy babies. And the devil could take everyone else.'

He was striding up and down the terrace now, angry and rather frightening. For all that Lucien was still grasping the rules of the game he was caught up in, he was glad he was playing on the same side as Rodolfo. The Stravagante would make a terrifying enemy.

Suddenly, Rodolfo stopped, as Alfredo came struggling through the window.

'Master,' he panted. 'The Reman Ambassador is downstairs. He wants an audience with you.'

Swiftly, as he spoke, the servant pressed the thumb and little finger of his right hand together and touched brow and breast with the middle fingers.

'Tell him I am not here,' said Rodolfo, frowning.

'I tried that, Master, but he has seen your mandola moored below,' said the old man. 'And he says "his man" hasn't seen you go out today.'

'His man?' said Rodolfo, outraged. 'So, they set spies on me now, do they?' He turned quickly to Lucien. 'Quick, into my laboratory. If their spy has been watching my door, he will have seen you come in. But there is more than one way of leaving. We must get you away.'

Lucien followed Rodolfo over the low window-sill but he was confused. How was he to get away? And what was the Reman Ambassador to him? Rodolfo strode over to the wall and grasped a candle-holder in the shape of a peacock with its tail at full spread. It was the most beautiful piece of workmanship and Lucien wondered that he hadn't noticed it when he first entered the laboratory. It was made of silver, with every colour of every feather picked out in bright enamels. The blue of the peacock's breast and the greens and purples of its tail shone in the darkness of the room like a beacon signalling a safe harbour.

Rodolfo wrenched the peacock's head round and the wall behind it swung back. Lucien couldn't believe his eyes. A secret passage! 'Just like *Cluedo*,' he murmured. But Rodolfo was already hurrying him into the passage and grasping the peacock's head again. Lucien could hear footsteps outside the laboratory door.

'Just follow the passage,' he said to Lucien. 'It will bring you to the Duchessa's palace. Push lightly on the door when you come to the other end and you will find yourself in her private apartments.'

Lucien stopped on the threshold at this alarming information. He had absolutely no intention of being alone with the Duchessa in her private apartments! He'd rather come face to face with a tigress in her cage. The Duchessa was definitely the most alarming person he had ever met.

'Whoa!' he said. 'Why would I want to do that?'

Rodolfo leaned close, his large dark eyes fixing

Lucien's like a hypnotist's. 'Because the person coming up the stairs is Rinaldo di Chimici,' he said softly. 'And if he ever finds you, he will happily kill you for that book. Now go. And I will follow as soon as I can. Take this firestone to light you on your way.' Here he searched inside his robes and thrust something into Lucien's hand about the size and shape of a large egg.

'Tell Silvia I sent you.'

Then he pushed Lucien inside the passage and the wall closed up behind him before he could ask, like the Elizabethan poet, 'But who is Silvia?'

Lucien stood inside the secret passage, letting his eyes grow accustomed to the dark. It was pitch black inside. Then he held up the 'egg' and watched, fascinated, as it started to glow. Soon it was warm to the touch and glowing red. It gave out a soft light but enough for him to see that he was in a narrow stone corridor with an uneven floor. It smelt musty but not damp. After listening for a while at the door behind the peacock sconce and finding he could hear nothing through its thickness, he shrugged and headed down the passage, the firestone making weird patterns on the walls as he went. Again he saw that he cast no shadow.

'Duchessa, here I come,' he muttered.

*

'Ambassador, what can I do for you?' Rodolfo greeted Rinaldo di Chimici with icy politeness but inwardly he was seething at the audacity of this aristocratic spy and his lesser spy at the gate.

'Senator,' said di Chimici, bowing formally but his eyes darted round the room. He had received information that a boy had been brought from the Scuola Mandoliera to Signor Rodolfo's laboratory and was intrigued. But he could hardly ask where the boy was.

'I am giving a dinner for the Duchessa at the embassy next week,' he improvised, 'and I was hoping you would join me.'

'It would be my pleasure,' said Rodolfo. 'but you do me too much honour to issue your invitation in person.'

Both men were saying one thing but meaning another, and their meeting did not last long. Rodolfo got rid of the Ambassador as quickly as he politely could but did not follow Lucien down the secret passage immediately.

Instead, he adjusted the setting of his mirrors and focused one on the canal outside his apartments. There, on the nearest bridge, slouched a figure in a blue cloak, apparently idly watching the murky waters. As Rodolfo murmured under his breath the figure looked up, startled, as if he was aware of the magician's gaze on him. And then the bridge was empty. Rodolfo smiled. 'So much for their spy,' he said.

*

Lucien inched cautiously along the secret passage, bathed in red light. At times he thought he heard music but it was very faint. The stone walls were massively thick. At last he reached the far end and found a door very like the one at the laboratory end. Here he stopped to think.

Silvia must be the Duchessa. Was she friend or foe?

She was clearly Rodolfo's friend, so that made her on the right side. Then, she was a much more alarming person than Rodolfo. Perhaps he should just hide in the passage until the Reman Ambassador had gone.

Thinking of the Ambassador, though, recalled Rodolfo's words: 'If he ever finds you, he will happily kill you for that book.' Suddenly, Lucien felt not just afraid but very vulnerable. Life here in Bellezza was certainly more exciting than lying in bed feeling sick but he didn't want to be stranded here for ever, which he would be if the book were stolen. And what would happen to the other Lucien if he were killed here?

These thoughts were enough to propel him through the door. He had to screw up his courage all the same and his eyes were closed as the door swung round.

'Well, well, what have we here?' asked a voice he recognized.

Lucien opened his eyes and blinked, dazzled by the opulence of the room he found himself in. Seated opposite him, without her mask, was the Duchessa. Her face wasn't terrifying at all; she was stunningly beautiful, although not young. Her large violet eyes pierced him as he gazed at her and her lips curved in amusement at his open-mouthed admiration.

'Do you like what you see, boy?' she said in a soothing tone. Then, rapidly changing: 'Is it worth dying for?'

She clicked her fingers at her waiting-woman. 'Call the guards. Tell them we have an intruder.'

'No, wait!' stammered Lucien. 'Rodolfo sent me here.'

The Duchessa gestured to the woman to wait. 'I

didn't imagine you'd be using his secret entrance without his knowledge. But who are you?' She got up and took his chin in her hand. He found himself looking slightly up at the tall woman. 'Aren't you one of my new mandoliers?'

She didn't wait for an answer.

'Whatever is Rodolfo thinking of? He knows as well as anyone that it is death for any outsider to see me without my mask.'

Lucien was panicking. It seemed as if death waited at both ends of the passage. 'He told me to come here because Rinaldo di Chimici was coming up the stairs. He said he would kill me.'

The Duchessa froze. 'That will be all,' she said imperiously, dismissing her waiting-woman.

'The guards, Your Grace?' she asked tentatively and was rewarded with a stare that would have turned a lesser woman to stone.

'Tell them to polish their weapons,' said the Duchessa finally.

When the woman had left the room, the Duchessa pointed to a chair next to hers.

'Any foe of the Chimici must be a friend of Bellezza's. And I *am* Bellezza. Now tell me who *you* really are.'

Chapter 5

Lagoon City

Much to her surprise, Arianna was bored. True, she was off the island and away from the prying eyes of its tiny population. But here on Bellezza she was nothing special, just another young girl. As she queued with her aunt at the fruit and vegetable stall, a basket on her arm, no one greeted her by name or asked after her grandfather's bad leg. Arianna's eyes roved towards the cathedral. This was all her big adventure had led to. Instead of sculling rich tourists round the canals of the big city, she was acting like a housewife, with no more thrilling prospect than choosing the shiniest aubergine.

Arianna sighed. Not for the first time, she wondered what would have happened if she had stayed with Luciano. She could have said she was his sister and then perhaps taken his place once the Duchessa had gone. The Duchessa! It simply wasn't fair that she had so much power when Bellezzan women had so little. Arianna hated her.

There was a sudden flutter in the queue as the women made way to let a tall, black-clad figure pass. 'Good morning, sir,' 'Greetings, Senator,' they murmured, curtseying and nodding. Arianna looked up, mildly intrigued as the Senator paused to talk to her aunt. Leonora looked quite flustered. Perhaps she had a new beau? He was handsome enough and a fine match for a wealthy widow, but weren't there rumours about him and the Duchessa?

'This afternoon then. Good-day. Good-day, ladies,' and he was off, striding across the Piazza, leaving many hearts beating faster behind him.

'What was that about?' asked Arianna, on their way back to Leonora's house. 'I didn't know you knew Signor Rodolfo.'

'Only slightly. He helped my husband once,' said her aunt, glancing furtively around to make sure they were not overheard. 'It's you he seems to be interested in.'

Arianna was astonished. 'Me? Why ever?'

'I have no idea. But he's coming to visit us this afternoon and he told me to tell you especially that he will bring news of your friend, Luciano.'

Arianna snorted. 'Some friend!' But she wouldn't say any more and as Leonora knew no more, they passed the next few hours in anxious anticipation. Leonora worked off her curiosity by cleaning every inch of her already immaculate house and polishing a treasured silver coffee-pot. Arianna did what she was asked to do but her mind was elsewhere.

As the great bell of the campanile struck three, the Senator was shown into the courtyard garden. He looked round with approval before seating himself and greeting Leonora. Then he turned his penetrating gaze on Arianna. In spite of herself, she blushed. He was such a very composed and distinguished figure and she had the strangest feeling that he knew all about her ill-fated attempt to become a mandolier. Luciano must have told him, the unfeeling brute! But Arianna's embarrassment soon turned to fear as she realized that it was dangerous for anyone to know what she had tried to do.

When the coffee and pastries had been brought out, Rodolfo leaned forward and addressed Arianna courteously.

'I believe you are familiar with my young apprentice, Luciano?'

'Your apprentice, sir? I thought he was to be a mandolier.' Arianna couldn't keep the bitterness out of her voice. 'Didn't the Duchessa choose him?'

'Yes,' said Rodolfo. 'But I persuaded her of her error. A natural mistake, but he had not come to the Scuola to enrol. He was on his way to see me.'

What is he playing at? thought Arianna. Luciano wouldn't have known Senator Rodolfo from a dish of herrings when she had rescued him a few days ago. As for becoming his apprentice... But she realized that she was happy to hear he wasn't going to be a mandolier, happier than she had been for days. Now she could stop being cross with him.

'Would you like to see him?' asked Rodolfo, turning immediately to Leonora to add, 'I mean, if that is acceptable to you, Signora. He knows no people of his own age in Bellezza and I thought your niece would be a suitable friend for him. He is new to the city and she could perhaps show him around?'

Leonora looked thoughtful as she said goodbye to their visitor an hour later. She fixed Arianna with a thoughtful stare.

'So Signor Rodolfo's apprentice is not a Bellezzan and yet he was at the Scuola on the day after the Marriage with the Sea? That makes two of you in the city on the forbidden day. Would you like to explain to me how you met him?'

Lucien woke to find his mother looking into his face. This was so startling that it took him a while to register that he was no longer in Bellezza.

'Oh, Lucien,' she said, biting her lip. 'You gave me such a fright. I couldn't wake you. How are you feeling?'

It was a question he couldn't answer. On one hand he was feeling just as wretched as he always did nowadays in the real world. But he was also wildly elated and the adrenalin was making him strong. Bellezza was real and he had safely negotiated his first voluntary journey there and back. He had practised 'stravagation', as Rodolfo called it, and it had been surprisingly easy.

He smiled at his mother. 'Fine. Really. I've had a really good sleep. A deep one – I suppose that's why I didn't hear you.' He stretched and yawned elaborately and saw the fright recede from her expression. She smiled back at him.

'Would you like some breakfast?'

'Yes thanks. Could I have a bacon sandwich?'

She went off happily. He hadn't asked for anything like that for weeks and it would be a pleasure to make it for him.

Lucien fell back on his pillows, his head whirling. He had thought his time was up when he had come face to face with the Duchessa, but fortunately Rodolfo had soon followed him through the doorway and explained everything to her. It was amazing how much less alarming she seemed when Rodolfo was around. They had obviously known one another for a long time and Rodolfo equally obviously wasn't intimidated by her.

Together, the three of them had worked on a cover story for Lucien. He was Luciano, a young cousin of Rodolfo's, from Padavia, who had come to be his apprentice. He would be given Bellezzan clothes in keeping with his position and a room in Rodolfo's palazzo. But in order to protect him, he must genuinely learn from Rodolfo. Quite apart from anything else he mustn't disappear back to his own world involuntarily and must be taught the science of stravagation.

There was much that Lucien still didn't understand. He had worked out for himself how to get to Bellezza from this world and it seemed to involve falling asleep clutching the book and thinking about the floating city. The first time he had made the journey back home it had been a matter of chance, but it seemed that if he lost consciousness in Bellezza, he would return to his own world – but only if he had the book in his hand.

'Does this mean I can't sleep in Bellezza?' he had

asked, when he was back with Rodolfo in the laboratory.

'Not if you are touching the book,' said Rodolfo, who had questioned him hard about the mechanics of his previous journeys.

'And I can only get here when I'm asleep in my own world?' pursued Lucien. 'I've noticed it seems always to be day here when it's night at home.'

'So it would seem,' said Rodolfo. 'It worked that way for Doctor Dethridge too, although even he did not know why. All we know is that it is easier for Stravaganti from your world to enter and leave ours than it is for us to travel in either direction. Perhaps because the first of the brotherhood, Doctor Dethridge, opened the way through and he was from your world. We still know very little about the time differences between the two worlds.'

For whatever reason, Lucien had been able to get back by holding the book and concentrating on his home. He had even returned briefly to Bellezza that same night, to report to his new master on how the journey had gone. It seemed to be the rule that he arrived in the same place he had departed from and after the lapse of only a few moments, although it had taken him hours to get back to sleep in his own world.

Perhaps that was why he was so exhausted now. But when the bacon sandwich came, he was able to eat almost all of it, to his mother's delight. Lucien had a secret hope that all the activity in Bellezza – walking, eating, behaving normally – might carry over into his everyday life and strengthen him there. Now all he could think of was going back to the city and being there every night.

'You must learn everything you can about Bellezza,' Rodolfo had said, just before Lucien returned home at dawn, as the evening candles were being lit in Rodolfo's house. 'I shall arrange for someone to take you around and teach you everything you need to know.'

How on earth was he going to fill the time in his world before nightfall?

Arianna was at a loss. In the end she told her aunt exactly what had happened. 'And when I saw the Duchessa was going to pick him, I ran away and went back home,' she finished.

Leonora paced up and down the small courtyard. 'I don't like it,' she said. 'None of it makes sense. And I'm afraid to let you get caught up in it. Politics always mean trouble in the lagoon, in all Talia come to that. And if this has anything to do with the Duchessa, then there's bound to be politics behind it. Still, Senator Rodolfo is a respectable man and if he has taken this strange boy under his wing, I don't suppose there is any harm in your spending time with him.'

Leonora seemed much less concerned about Lucien's being from another world than about his being involved in one of the Duchessa's schemes. Then she remembered the rest of the story.

'But the risk you took being in the city on the forbidden day! If you had been caught you would have been arrested and put on trial for your life! Your mother was quite right to worry about you. Be a mandolier, indeed! I never heard anything like it.'

Arianna started to argue but stopped herself. At least Leonora was going to let her see Luciano again and now that she knew he was Rodolfo's apprentice, she was even more fascinated by the idea of him. 'He must be a good scientist himself,' she thought, 'or Signor Rodolfo wouldn't take him on. And he wants me to show him round the city, which is bound to mean adventures. At least I'll have more chance of something interesting happening than if I'm sitting here polishing silver!'

*

In a bar in the north of the city, a man in a blue cloak was knocking back glasses of Strega. He felt he deserved it after his recent experience. One minute he had been spying on Senator Rodolfo's house – the next he had found himself in Padavia. It had taken him days to walk back to Bellezza and he was in a thoroughly bad mood. In future he was going to charge his masters a lot more if he was to spy on a powerful scientist like Rodolfo – at least enough to pay for his coach fare back if he were to be spirited away from the city again.

'Ancora!' he ordered the barman. He had no thought but to get very drunk indeed and then perhaps he would go and call on his fiancée, Giuliana.

*

'You!' said Lucien when Rodolfo's servant let Arianna into the laboratory.

She laughed at his discomfiture.

'You seem very much at home in Bellezza

now, baldy boy,' she taunted. 'Do you know how many natives would give their eyes to be in your shoes? Signor Rodolfo is a very important man, you know.'

'Thank you,' said the tall Senator, stepping out of the shadows. 'I'm glad you approve.'

Arianna fell to her knees in a clumsy curtsey and made the sign of the 'hand of fortune'.

'No need for that,' said Rodolfo, disapprovingly. 'There is no place for superstition in a place of scientific enquiry.'

'I had no idea my guide was going to be you,' said Lucien. 'Let me explain what happened at the Scuola.'

'I know what happened,' said Arianna, still a trace bitterly. 'The Duchessa saw you and liked what she saw. That's the way it works here in Bellezza. Appearances are everything. I know it wasn't your fault.'

'It's the way things work in Bellezza that I want you to teach Luciano,' said Rodolfo. 'We are giving it out that he comes from Padavia, but I think you know that is not the case?'

Arianna nodded slowly and turned to Lucien. 'So it's true. You are from another world?'

'Yes,' said Lucien. 'I'm a Stravagante.'

Arianna couldn't help herself; her curled hand went immediately to her brow. Everyone in the lagoon had heard the word but few knew what it meant. Only that it signified power and mystery and danger. Here was her adventure without looking further.

'Will you do it?' said Rodolfo. 'Will you teach Luciano to pass as Bellezzan?'

*

The next few weeks were the happiest Lucien had ever known. His days passed slowly and painfully as before. But at night he slipped easily back into his Belezzan life. He wore velvet, drank wine, spent the morning in science lessons unlike any he had known at school and passed every afternoon with Arianna, roaming the streets and bridges of the wonderful city. The only worry he had was remembering to keep out of full sunlight in case anyone saw that he didn't have a shadow.

In his waking life, he read everything he could get hold of about Venice. His dad was really pleased with this new interest and brought him volumes from the library and bought others from the local bookshop.

'You'll be quite an expert when you get back to school,' he said. 'Should help with history and geography.'

But the more Lucien learned about Venice, the more Luciano knew it was different from his Bellezza. For a start, in Bellezza it was silver that was valued, way above gold, which was considered an inferior material. All the domes and mosaics of the great cathedral were made of silver in Bellezza. When he pointed this out to Arianna, she gave her characteristic snort.

'Of course, what do you expect? Gold tarnishes. You know, goes black. It's the 'morte d'oro'. Doesn't that happen in your world?'

'No,' said Lucien. 'It's silver that goes black if you don't clean it. Gold never needs cleaning.'

'We don't clean silver here,' said Arianna. 'Just polish it sometimes.'

Lucien began to wonder what would happen if he took some gold, which was readily available and cheap in Bellezza, back to his world.

'Now you are beginning to think like a Chimici,' said Rodolfo, when he asked him about it.

Lucien was horrified but realized it was quite true. 'So it works both ways?' he asked. 'I mustn't take anything back from here?'

'Only the book you brought with you,' said Rodolfo. 'And, much later on, when you are an adept, you might be chosen to take another talisman, some object which would help a future Stravagante make the journey from your world to ours.'

'Like you taking the book?'

Rodolfo nodded. Lucien sighed. He couldn't imagine ever being as much of an adept as Rodolfo. The lessons were hard. There was a lot about matter and geology but that was as close to what Lucien might have described as science as they got. Mostly it was more like meditation. Rodolfo was very keen to develop Lucien's powers of concentration.

'Empty your mind,' he would say, which Lucien found impossible. 'Now focus on a point in the city. Visualize it. Describe it to me. Colours, smells, sounds, textures.'

This was an exercise which Lucien got better at over time, thanks to his afternoon wanderings with Arianna. There came a day when he was as familiar with the calles and campos and sotoportegos of Bellezza as he was with the streets and parks and alleys of his bit of North London. But it never lost its strangeness for him.

The city was like a net. Its hundreds of little waterways were what held it together. The odd-shaped patches of land, linked to one another by a myriad of little bridges, of wood or stone, were packed with tall thin houses, some grand and palatial, others poorer and more functional. Every tiny square had its own well, the natural meeting-place for all the locals. And much more of life was lived outdoors than in Lucien's London.

He had to remind himself that this city was functioning more than four hundred years in his past. There were no motor-boats on the canals, no electric lights, no proper toilets. He got very used to hanging on till he got back to his own world, rather than tangle with the Bellezzans' primitive plumbing. He knew that however fascinating he found the city, he was a tourist, in time and space.

One thing that convinced him of how long ago it was in Bellezza was the newness of some of the grand buildings. And everywhere in the city there were new buildings going up; mandolas and barges carrying blocks of stone thronged the waterways. Arianna's world was a busy one, full of new schemes.

'You don't say!' was her perpetual exclamation when he tried to tell her about his world. 'Everyone has a box with moving pictures in it in their living-room? And people of our age have one in their bedrooms too? And lots of them have a bedroom to themselves? And they can talk to their friends on the other side of the city without leaving the room? You don't say!'

Some things he never managed to explain to her. *GameBoys* for one, which she simply couldn't see the point of, and football. The more Lucien described the rules and the rituals, the more ludicrous they sounded in his own ears. 'But why do they pull their shirts over their heads?' Arianna would ask, to which he had no reply.

The more he learned about her world, the more remote his life in London seemed. Arianna told him about the city's many festivals. The carnival, of course, he knew about from his own reading about Venice, and she had told him about the Marriage with the Sea on his first visit. But there were also mandola races, rowing competitions, festivals of light when all the mandolas carried torches, special bridges where ritual fights were staged between local gangs, the list went on and on. It seemed as if almost every week held some cause for celebration for the superstitious and volatile lagooners. And every festival was marked by huge feasts and wonderful displays of fireworks.

'It all sounds so much fun,' said Lucien. 'You Bellezzans really know how to enjoy yourselves.'

'It's not all like that though,' said Arianna, looking serious for once. They were sitting on a stone bench within spitting distance of the Great Canal, eating plums. Arianna gestured across the water to where a fine building was nearing completion. 'That new church is called Santa Maria delle Grazie – St Mary of the Thank-yous.'

'Thank-yous?' asked Lucien, puzzled. 'What sort of a name is that?'

Saint Mary of the thank-yous,' said Arianna. 'Twenty years ago, before I was born of course, there was a plague in the city. It killed almost a third of the people living here.'

'That's terrible,' said Lucien, thinking of a third of his classmates or one in three of his neighbours.

'It was,' said Arianna. 'But it might have been worse. The church has been built in thanks that it wasn't. That it stopped at a third and left the other two thirds alive.'

When she talked about the plague, Arianna constantly made the gesture with her hand that Rodolfo called the *manus fortunae*, the hand of fortune. He regarded it as common superstition and rebuked his servant Alfredo whenever he caught him doing it. Lucien had noticed that citizens of Bellezza did it all the time, spontaneously, a bit like touching wood for luck, but much more often. Now he asked Arianna about it.

She looked at her hand, suspended in mid-air, surprised to find she was doing it. It was instinctive.

'It means "may the lady goddess, her king consort and her son aid us" and "may the circle of our life be unbroken",' she said, reciting it like a school lesson.

'The lady goddess?' queried Lucien. 'But that's a church going up over there. I thought this was a Christian country?'

Arianna shrugged. 'So it is. But it doesn't hurt to keep in with the old gods, does it? I know who I'd rather have on my side if the plague came again.'

Lucien remembered what Rodolfo had said about the Chimici bringing medical cures back from his century and then keeping them for their own people. It would be only a step from that to importing twenty-first century illnesses in test tubes. Lucien thought of AIDS and shuddered. Secretly, with

Chapter 6

Doctor Death

Lucien was feeling better. He was between treatments now and really beginning to think he would be normal again one day. His best friend, Tom, came to see him – the first time Lucien had been up to visitors since the treatment began.

After an embarrassed few minutes while Tom got used to Lucien's changed appearance, they were chatting as if they had never been apart. Lucien let Tom do most of the talking, limiting himself to questions and reactions. After all, as far as Tom was concerned, Lucien *hadn't* been doing anything worth reporting – only lying in bed for weeks.

Tom, on the other hand, was full of stories about school – the new supply teacher, the exploits of the swimming team, of which he was captain, and lots of gossip about who fancied whom. Tom had been keen on a girl called Katie ever since year eight and was now wondering if he could pluck up the courage to invite her to the year eleven disco at the end of term.

Lucien smiled, listening to Tom. He had visions of himself walking into the disco with Arianna. With her long legs and tumbling brown curls it would be a bit like taking Julia Roberts. His smile widened at the thought of what all his friends would say. Then he imagined what Arianna's face would be like when she heard the music and had a distant picture of her making the hand of fortune and saying 'Dia!' It would be like taking a Martian. He found himself chuckling and turned it into a cough.

Tom was contrite. 'Sorry, Luce. It's crass of me to bang on about the disco. I don't suppose you'll be up to coming?'

Lucien shook his head. 'Don't think so. Besides, who'd go with me? I'd need to take the Bride of Frankenstein.'

Tom punched him ever so gently, on the arm.

*

Lucien's parents were delighted with his progress. He got up and was dressed for most of every day now. He could even go for short trips away from the house, though he still got tired. On less good days, when he wasn't up to outings, he sat at his computer and trawled the Internet for good sites on Venice.

His favourite was *VirtualVenice.com*, where you could cruise the canals and walk the streets of a city so like his Bellezza that it almost took his breath away.

He would spend hours doing that every day. Another one had street maps of the city and he often pored over those, noting the similarities and differences in the names of places where he walked with Arianna every night.

One day, he typed William Dethridge's name into the Search box and was rewarded by a list of several sites. Once he had eliminated the inevitable non-matches – a modern musicologist, a mountain range in Alaska, several Australian mathematicians, a coin dealer, a bike shop in the Lake District – he found three sites that really did deal with Rodolfo's Elizabethan doctor. But there was nothing about his being a Stravagante.

Nevertheless, Lucien read the entries with mounting excitement, downloaded them and printed them out. He dared not take the pages to Bellezza, which would mean breaking one of Rodolfo's rules, but he set to work memorizing everything he could.

The first was an academic site – *www.histdocs.ely.ac.uk/mathematicians/dethridge.html* – which listed the bare facts:

DETHRIDGE, William (?1523-?1575)
Born: ?April 20, 1523
Died: ?November 1575
Datainfo: Dates uncertain; no independent confirmation
Lifespan: ?52 years

Nationality: English, but spent many years studying in Italy.
Education: Oxford 1538-42. Bologna 1543-6. In

1547 became lecturer in mathematics at Wadham College, Oxford, a post which he retained until his disappearance in 1575.
Religion: Anglican. But, like John Dee, often viewed with hostility as a practitioner of the occult. He was tried for witchcraft in 1575 and condemned to death by burning, but there is no record that the sentence was ever carried out.

Scientific disciplines: Mathematics, calendarism, alchemy, astrology.
Marital status: married, 1548, Johanna Andrews. Six children, of whom three survived to adulthood: his sons Bruno and Thomas and daughter Elizabeth.

For more information, open these links:

Publications / Bibliography / Related Websites

Despite the dry tone, Lucien found these sparse facts fascinating. So William Dethridge had really existed and been some sort of magician, with a connection to Italy, though it was a bit of a surprise to find he had been a mathematician. Alchemist and astrologer sounded more like it, though goodness knows what a calendarist did. But what had happened to him? The site referred to his 'disappearance' and said there was no record of his execution but gave the date of his assumed death anyway.

The next site had been much more chatty: *www.williamdethridge.org* claimed to be the official homepage of the 'William Dethridge Society', which was a weird sort of fan club. It offered links to its newsletter 'The Magus', a chat room for followers of the 'Master' and, after a list of facts much like the one on the previous site, gave a further list, of Unsolved Mysteries about Doctor Dethridge:

> *When was he born?* Dethridge gave his own birthdate as 20th April 1523 in the village of Barnsbury, but no parish register for the period records any such information. In the light of what followed, it has to be asked 'was William Dethridge a mortal man at all?'
> *What arts did he practise?* He was an astrologer at a time when the Queen had her own Royal one, and an alchemist, which was a legal profession. What exactly did he do that cost him his life? (If indeed it did – see below.)
> *When did he die?* He was condemned to death by Elizabeth I in 1575 but apparently disappeared before the sentence could be carried out. What happened to him? He was never seen in England again. One theory is that powerful friends engineered his escape to the continent but there has been no further mention of him found in any document. Besides, where would he have gone? Italy was not safe for someone with his reputation; burnings for witchcraft were common there at this period. His disappearance remains a mystery, with some explanation perhaps based in the occult.

This was even more exciting. Lucien couldn't wait to tell Rodolfo about it. The third site was quite amateur, put together by someone called Paul Evans, who had written an article on William Dethridge for an obscure journal called *Natural Philosophy*. *www.paul-evans.co.uk/william dethridge* just said:

> Doctor Death: the strange absences of William Dethridge, an article by Paul Evans in *Natural Philosophy*, volume 43, issue 2, September 2001. Synopsis: local people in Dethridge's home village of Barnsbury used to call him 'Doctor Death', because he was, on more occasions than one, found in a sort of trance from which he could not be roused. Tradition has it that he was transported to the undertaker on at least two occasions and subsequently sat up in his coffin. Could this be the reason he was arraigned for witchcraft? The author investigates the evidence for the popular belief that William Dethridge was in communication with the devil.

Lucien felt a thrill down his backbone when he read that one; surely these 'absences' must have been times when Doctor Dethridge had been on his travels to Talia? It was disturbing to think that he might have been put to a horrible death for doing what Lucien now did every night.

Giuliana was uneasy. It had never occurred to her that she was doing anything dangerous when she had accepted an invitation to the Duchessa's Palazzo. The work had not been difficult, although she had had a dreadful cold for the next week. And the money had come in very useful. She was getting married in a few weeks, to her handsome Enrico, and now they would be able to afford so much more for their household.

That was when the trouble began. She couldn't help herself, in her pride at bringing more to their union than might be expected of a poor peasant-girl; she told him about the money. From then on he showed her no mercy till he had wormed the whole story out of her. His eyes shone when he found out that the Duchessa used a substitute on some State occasions.

To Giuliana, he said, 'Just think, my own darling in the water! All the people of Bellezza waving and cheering my Giuliana without knowing!' But to himself, as a professional spy, all he could think of was how to make the most out of this information. And as a true Talian, he hugged his blue cloak around him and said, 'And since it was you who really made the marriage with the sea, it is you who will reap the rewards of prosperity. This money is just the beginning, Giuliana. We shall be rich!'

That was what was frightening Giuliana. She begged him to understand that he must tell no one, that the story was to end there. But she knew Enrico and in her heart she wished she had never told him.

*

Rodolfo was fascinated by the information Lucien brought him on his next visit. Lucien had to begin by explaining the Internet again because Rodolfo kept seeing 'the web' as something like a huge network spun by spiders. And if it were that, it was all too easy to imagine a sinister presence at the heart, a member of the di Chimici family trying to entrap unwary users.

'No, it's not like that,' Lucien insisted. 'It's neutral. In fact people complain that it isn't regulated enough. Anyone can post up any sort of silly stuff on it. Dancing guinea-pigs, whatever.'

Rodolfo gave him what Lucien thought of us one of his 'puzzled alien' looks.

'I can't understand why anyone would want to see pigs dance,' he said gravely, 'but if anyone can put "silly stuff" in this web, then how do you know what they say about Doctor Dethridge is true?'

'I don't,' said Lucien patiently. 'But I think you'll be interested.'

Then he had told him all he could remember: the academic, university site, the fan club and, most interesting of all, the article about 'Doctor Death's' occasional trances.

Rodolfo was completely gripped and made Lucien repeat it all several times. He was particularly interested in the mystery surrounding Dethridge's disappearance.

'What do you think happened to him?' asked Lucien.

'I don't know,' said Rodolfo slowly, 'but I hope it means he is here, somewhere safe in Talia.'

Lucien had a sudden thought. 'What year is it? I mean now, here in Bellezza.'

Rodolfo turned his large dark eyes on Lucien, as if reluctant to answer, but in the end he said, 'It is 1577.'

Although Lucien had known it must have been something like that, it was still a shock. And now he felt excitement fizzing through his veins.

'So he disappeared only two years ago. Less, if it

was in November. It's only June now. When did you last see him?'

Again the reluctance and then it was as if Rodolfo had made up his mind to tell Lucien a story he had so far withheld.

'It was about two years ago,' he began. 'We in the brotherhood have accepted that we will not see him again. We believed him to be dead. He did say, last time, that he was in danger.'

'But why didn't he come here then?' said Lucien. 'Surely, if he planned to escape the death sentence, he would have stravagated to Bellezza?'

'No,' said Rodolfo. 'This was not his city. He came to and from Bellona, to the University. Although of course he travelled to other cities when he was here.'

Lucien was by now used to the way that Talian names were variants on the ones in his world. Bellona must be Bologna, he decided. But he hadn't realized that each Stravagante was limited to one city for his departure and arrival. It was like only being able to use one airport. He supposed that he, Lucien, always arrived in Bellezza because that was where his purple and red notebook had come from.

'Did William Dethridge use a – a talisman, like my notebook?'

Rodolfo nodded.

'Yes, but to explain it, I must tell you about the way in which he came to Talia first. You have read that he was an alchemist. Do you know what that is?'

'Someone who tries to make gold from lead?'

'In your world, yes. Here of course our natural philosophers are striving to create silver. Getting gold is easy enough.'

Lucien remembered the name of the magazine that had carried the 'Doctor Death' article.

'Is a natural philosopher what you call a scientist?'

'A scientist, yes, like myself. But not all of us are striving to make silver, any more than all are Stravaganti. Anyway, Doctor Dethridge was trying to make gold, not from lead but from earth and salts and various minerals. He had been to university in your world's version of Talia, in the city we call Bellona. When he was conducting one of his experiments late at night in his laboratory in Anglia – your England – there was an alchemical accident – an explosion affecting time and space. When he came to he found himself still clutching the copper dish he had been using in the experiment. Imagine his excitement and amazement when he saw that the dish now contained gold!'

'So he did it!' exclaimed Lucien.

'Yes and no,' said Rodolfo. 'It was indeed gold, but he hadn't made it in your world, where it is valued, but in our world, where it is not. When he looked around him, he found himself, even more to his amazement, transported to Talia, in Bellona, in the laboratory of one of our greatest scientists, Federico Bruno. From that day on, Doctor Dethridge gave up his interest in alchemy and dedicated himself to the science of stravagation.'

'And did he never take any gold back with him?'

Rodolfo shook his head. 'He tried. He took the copper dish back, but when he returned to your world, it contained only earth and salts. And his laboratory had been half destroyed by fire. Still, the dish was now his talisman, his most precious possession, which carried him back and forth between worlds. From then on he wasn't interested in gold or in making his fortune; it was the pure science of stravagation that consumed him. It was Doctor Dethridge himself who established the rules about taking nothing between worlds except talismans.'

'Talismans in the plural?' said Lucien. 'He brought something else to Talia besides the dish?'

'Yes, over the years, on his many travels. Slowly, cautiously, he introduced other objects to enable other Stravaganti, whom he trained in many Talian cities, to make the perilous journey to his world. And in time he took objects from our world to yours to enable journeys in the other direction. It was only ever the dish, forged in one world but transmuted in another, which brought a Stravagante to Talia without being from Talia itself.'

Lucien remembered something.

'It wasn't him who brought the notebook to my world though, was it? You said it was you – and it was in my time too.'

Rodolfo sighed. 'There is still so much we do not know. Ever since Doctor Dethridge's first journey, twenty-five years ago, whenever one of us has made the journey to your world, it is a world that has moved on in time much faster than ours. It didn't work like that for him; he always returned to his own time and place. The gateway he opened is clearly between your England and our Talia but there is no clear explanation about how the time changes between our two worlds. We are still working on how to travel to a parallel time as well as a parallel space.'

Lucien took a while to digest all this. In the end he

hung on to the easiest bit. 'But if he stravagated to avoid being killed, then where is he now?'

'You are right,' said Rodolfo, suddenly decisive. 'I am sure he is not in Bellona. There is a strong cell of our brotherhood there and news would have reached me. It is vital we find him. He can help us against the Chimici.'

He strode over to the magic mirrors and, working the levers, focused them on all sorts of places Lucien hadn't seen before, walled and turreted cities, palazzos and piazzas that were still recognizably Talian but not in Bellezza.

'This is going to take time,' he said. 'I think we should abandon our lessons for this morning. Do you want to go and find Arianna?'

*

Arianna was trailing her hands in Aunt Leonora's fountain when Lucien was shown out to the garden. Her eyes brightened and she jumped up from the stone ledge when she saw him.

'Good!' she cried. 'Have you been let out early?'

'Sort of,' said Lucien. 'Rodolfo is too busy to teach me today.' He looked warily at Leonora as he said it. He was never sure how much she knew about him.

'Then we have the whole day?' asked Arianna. 'That's wonderful. What shall we do?'

'May I make a suggestion?' said Leonora. 'If you're supposed to be showing Luciano round Bellezza, he ought to see more of the lagoon. Why don't we take a boat to the islands?'

Arianna was delighted. 'But do you think my parents would allow it?' she asked, suddenly doubtful.

She hadn't seen them for weeks, since they brought her to Bellezza for her 'punishment' and she still wasn't sure of its terms.

'I will be with you,' said Leonora firmly. 'We'll start in Merlino, and if we can find your brothers, we'll ask them if you'd be welcome on Torrone.'

Lucien's heart sank. He wouldn't be able to tell Arianna what he had discovered with her aunt around. But Arianna's enthusiasm was infectious. She was suddenly homesick for the islands, and to swap the rank Bellezzan canals for the clean smell of salt water. She bounced round Leonora as her aunt organized a hasty lunch basket and they set off to the Piazzetta to find a rowing-boat and a willing oarsman.

*

In the Reman embassy, Enrico had to wait a long time to be seen. The Ambassador was suddenly very busy when he heard who it was in the ante-room. Enrico shrugged; he could wait. He understood that the Ambassador was annoyed with him. He probably thought that Enrico had abandoned his post when Rodolfo had spirited him miles away. But di Chimici's tune would change when he heard what his spy had to tell him. Curling up on the hard wooden bench as comfortably as if it had been a feather bed, Enrico wrapped his blue cloak around him and went to sleep.

*

In the rose-coloured palace, the seamstress had finished measuring the Duchessa for her new dress and was backing out of the room, her arms full of violet satin. The Duchessa yawned and stretched in a very un-ducal fashion and drifted over to the window.

Below, in the square before the cathedral, she saw Luciano, carrying a large basket for a plump, respectable-looking Bellezzan woman. But it was the third member of the party that caught her eye, the leaping, laughing brown-haired girl with them. She must be under sixteen, since she was unmasked. And she looked intolerably familiar.

'So,' breathed the Duchessa. 'That is the little companion Rodolfo has chosen for our young friend.'

She summoned her youngest waiting-woman, Barbara, the one who had been so excited about the Marriage with the Sea.

'You see that group crossing the square? The woman and the boy and girl. I want them followed. See to it immediately. And I want all the information that can be found about the girl.'

As the woman ran from the room, the Duchessa leaned her forehead against the cool glass. Her head throbbed. At that moment she would have given anything to change places with the light-hearted girl dancing her way down to the Piazzetta.

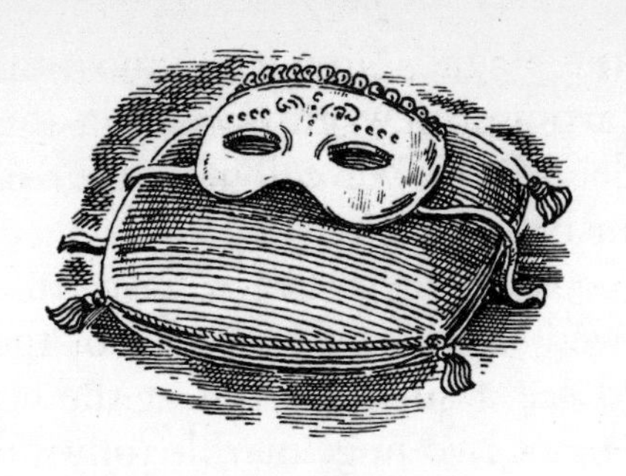

Chapter 7

Where Beauty Wears a Mask

Arianna's heart sang as the oarsman rowed them out into the salty water of the lagoon. Fascinated as she was by the beautiful city which hovered like a dream on the edge of her childhood, she was a true daughter of the islands.

They had to skirt round the south of the city and up to the north-east where Merlino lay. But first they had to pass a cypress-veiled island and Arianna was quiet for the first time since Lucien had come to her aunt's house that morning. He noticed the change in her mood.

'What is it?' he whispered.

But it was Leonora who answered. 'That's where we bury our dead. The whole island is a cemetery now. It wasn't always so but we needed many more graves at the time of the plague. Now it is almost full and there is talk of starting a new graveyard on the mainland. The Isola dei Morti, we call it – the Island of the Dead. My husband is there.'

They all bowed their heads instinctively as the oarsman rowed slowly under the lee of the cypresses. Lucien could see a small church at the centre of the island and one or two huge marble tombs between the trees. He shuddered involuntarily, although the island itself was quite calm and peaceful.

Their spirits lifted as they left the sombre island behind them and could see the larger shape of Merlino ahead of them. The boat nosed into the small harbour, its oarsman glad to rest. Leonora spoke to him about their plans and he nodded as they set off into the town.

'We might as well let Luciano see the sights before we look for Tommaso and Angelo,' she said.

There seemed to be a lot of people seeing the sights. The harbour was packed with boats, some quite large ones. The main street of Merlino was thronged with people who were clearly visitors to the lagoon. Lucien didn't know how he knew that. They were dressed in clothes of four hundred years ago, not wearing shorts and carrying cameras, but they still didn't look as if they belonged.

For a moment Lucien wondered if he looked that way too; after all, he was more of a tourist than any of them. He was glad to be with two lagooners, who knew the islands like the back of their hands.

'Where are they all going?' he asked.

'To the museum,' said Arianna. 'Everyone comes to see the glass. We should go too.'

Lucien had read about Murano glass in his Venice books but that was nothing like what he saw in the Merlino glass museum. Coloured glass there was, all the colours of the rainbow, but what was spectacular was the shapes. You could buy vases and paper-weights and cheap ornaments from the many stalls in the street, but the objects in the museum were true works of art.

The finest were in the rooms dedicated to the anonymous Glass Master of the fifteenth century. There were turreted castles, fully rigged ships, winged rams, peacocks and whole gardens of glass trees and flowers, with delicate spider webs, accurate right down to the dewdrops on them.

Lucien had to be dragged away.

'Come and see the beastly mask,' said Arianna.

In a corner of the Glass Master's main room was an ornate glass case, displaying on a black velvet cushion an intricate mask. It was so elaborate and beautiful that it was hard to believe it had all been made from glass. It had a faint pearly blue sheen and should have been quite exquisite. But something about it was sinister. Lucien shifted uneasily.

'You feel it?' asked Arianna. 'This was the cause of our horrid custom of masking all women. Well, not this one but its partner. Come outside and I'll tell you. It's too crowded in here.'

As they left the museum, Arianna pointed out the motto carved in stone above the doors – *Ove Beltà porta una Maschera*.

'Where Beauty Wears a Mask,' she translated from the Old Talian. 'That's the real Bellezzan motto, ever since the Duchessa's accident.'

They walked to a little grassy square near one of the canals – for Merlino, like Bellezza, was an island made of numerous smaller ones. Leonora unpacked their lunch basket and sat on the stone wall round the central well, while Lucien and Arianna stretched out on the grass. Lucien let the sun warm the chill out of him brought on by the mask.

'The Glass Master made the mask at the request of the Duchessa,' said Arianna, munching on a radish. 'Not this one of course. It happened about a hundred years ago. It was his masterpiece, created to her own design, and she was going to wear it at Carnival.'

'It must have been very uncomfortable,' said Lucien.

'More than that in the end,' snorted Arianna. 'She was wearing it at the great ball that comes at the end of Carnival, in the Piazza Santa Maddalena, outside the cathedral. Her partner was the young Prince of Remora, Ferrando di Chimici. Faster and faster he whirled her round the square, all the people watching and cheering. And then, she tripped. Tripped and fell and the mask shattered.'

'Ouch!' winced Lucien.

Arianna nodded. She was taking a ghoulish delight in this story.

'The Duchessa's screams nearly started a war. Her guards were sure the young Chimici had tried to assassinate her. There was total panic and confusion.'

'What happened to her face?' asked Lucien, not really wanting to know the answer.

'No one ever saw it again,' said Arianna dramatically. 'She wore a mask in public ever afterwards. And made it law that all unmarried women over sixteen must wear one too. I suppose she thought that young girls and married women were no rivals. She was very vain before the accident apparently. And she made the Senators and Councillors wear masks when the Senate and Council are in session. I don't know why.'

'So that the arguments themselves carry sway, not the reputations of the speakers,' said Leonora mildly.

'Huh!' said Arianna. 'You think you wouldn't know Senator Rodolfo if he wore a mask over his big black eyes?'

'But why is there a mask in the museum?' asked Lucien. 'Why did the Glass Master make another one?'

'Because the Duchessa made him do it,' said Arianna. 'And then,' after a dramatic pause, she added gleefully, 'she murdered him!'

'Really, Arianna,' said Leonora. 'There is no proof of that.'

Arianna shot her a scornful look. 'All right then. By a great coincidence, the day after the replica mask was put on display in the museum, the Glass Master was taken ill with a violent stomach disorder, which looked just like the symptoms of poisoning. He died in agony.'

Lucien didn't like to admit it but Arianna's interpretation did sound convincing. Maybe all Duchesse were ruthless egomaniacs; perhaps they had to be.

'What happened to the young Prince?' he asked.

'He died too,' said Leonora. 'Of a fever.'

Arianna swung round in astonishment. 'I didn't know that! I bet that was the Duchessa's doing too.'

'Possibly,' said Leonora. 'Or possibly the idea of

one of her courtiers. Or possibly he just had a fever. Bellezza was very unhealthy at the time. It was a legacy of the old swamps she was built on.'

'So all this mask business started a hundred years ago?' asked Lucien. 'It isn't the present Duchessa's idea?'

'No,' said Arianna. 'Before the accident, people only wore them at Carnival. But this one could change it. It's only a law, like the one about mandoliers, and she makes laws all the time.'

'I dare say she has her reasons for not changing this one,' said Leonora. 'You will soon get used to wearing the mask, Arianna. And you know we marry young in the lagoon. I wore it only two years myself.'

They stood up and brushed the crumbs from their clothes. 'Let's go and find my brothers,' said Arianna.

They went down to the shoreline and walked along the shingle till they got to where the fishing-boats were moored. The smell was terrible. Fishermen lounged around, eating their lunch. The morning catch had been cleaned and sold and they would spend the afternoon mending their nets and in other occupations while they waited for the evening catch.

Lucien could not distinguish one fishing-boat from another and even the fishermen all looked much the same to him, but Arianna ran straight to a pair of them and was caught up and hugged in their strong arms.

Lucien hung back a bit shyly with Leonora until Arianna beckoned them over and introductions were made. He liked the brothers straightaway; they were brown-skinned and hearty and they shook his hand with healthy vigour. They were obviously devoted to their little sister and very pleased to see her.

'What are all those bones?' he asked after a while, noticing the small white piles lying round on the beach. Some fishermen were whittling them.

'Those are the bones of the merlino-fish which we find washed up on the beach,' said Tommaso, making the hand of fortune. 'Worth more to us than any live fish we catch.'

'You make daggers from them,' explained Angelo, unsheathing a terrifyingly sharp example from his own belt and giving it to Lucien to inspect. 'Very highly valued in Bellezza. We pass the time between catches sharpening them into blades and then ship them to the mainland to have the handles fixed on.'

'And they're very expensive,' said Arianna, eyeing the dagger with envy.

'We wouldn't be able to afford them if we weren't part of the business,' said Tommaso.

'And you know,' teased Angelo, 'that you're not going to get one till you're sixteen and can be trusted to handle it.'

Arianna pouted.

'A dagger *and* a mask,' whispered Lucien. 'You're going to be even more dangerous in a few months' time then.'

Arianna smiled. Leonora began negotiations with the brothers about how welcome the party would be on Torrone. Lucien and Arianna walked away from the shore to get out of the overpowering presence of the smell of fish.

'It's sad, really,' said Arianna. 'The dagger I get may be one of the last. Still, it'll make it more valuable.'

'Why?' asked Lucien.

'The merlino-fish seems to be dying out,' she replied. 'Or rather, the supply of bones is running out. No one has seen a live merlino for years. The fishermen think it may be extinct. It's a pity, because my brothers make more money from the trade in merlino-blades than they do from the fishing.'

'Who buys the daggers?' asked Lucien.

'Tourists,' said Arianna. 'And assassins of course,' she added.

*

The Reman Ambassador was more interested than he wanted to show. If the Duchessa used a substitute on State occasions, then she would be at her most vulnerable and unguarded wherever she herself was during the impersonation. But he wasn't going to take the word of this scruffy spy for it.

'Bring me the girl,' he said. 'I want to hear all about it from her own lips.'

*

Instead of going straight to Torrone, Leonora asked the oarsman to take them next to Burlesca. Tommaso and Angelo both thought it would be better if the whole family were there when the family reunion took place and suggested the Bellezzan party could pass the time on that island until the brothers had finished work on Merlino.

'So we're going to see your Nonna first,' said Leonora.

Arianna clapped her hands. 'Goodee! We'll get some of Nonno's cakes. We're going to see my grandparents,' she explained to Lucien. 'They are my mamma's parents and they live in the funniest little house on Burlesca. You'll see.'

As the boat neared the next island, Lucien could see it was a riot of colour. As soon as they were close enough to make out the houses, he could see that every one was painted a different colour – bright blues and pinks and oranges and yellows jostled side by side. It would have looked awful in a London suburb but somehow, under the blue skies of the lagoon, it seemed perfect.

'Look! There's their house,' shouted Arianna, when the boat had moored. 'Isn't it funny?'

Lucien suddenly saw what she meant. Amid all the greens and turquoises and purples there was one pure white house. It stood out from all the others like the white chocolate in a continental assortment. Various tourists stopped to look at it as they passed and Lucien guessed that, in his world, this would be the house to feature on the most popular postcards.

Outside the front door sat an old woman dressed in black. She had pure white hair and on her lap on a small black cushion rested a heap of snowy white lace. She was working it with her crooked fingers, so fast that they seemed to blur, but all the time saying hello to passers-by and chatting to her neighbours, who were similarly occupied. She never looked at the work once.

'Nonna!' cried Arianna and launched herself at the old woman, whose face lit up at the sight of her granddaughter.

How alike they are, thought Lucien. The old woman had a twinkle in her eye and a look that would mean mischief in a younger person, even though she seemed so respectable in her black dress.

'Arianna! How lovely to see you! And your aunt Leonora too. And who is this young man?'

Chattering all the time, the old woman abandoned her lace and led them into her house. Lucien stopped a minute to look at the work. It must have been going to be a tablecloth or something like that. In the centre was a peacock, with its tail at full spread, which reminded him of the Glass Master's finest work. All round the edge a pattern of leaves and lilies was being worked.

'Glass and lace,' said a voice, echoing his thoughts. 'That's what the islands are all about.'

Lucien looked up and saw Arianna's grandmother had come back to usher him in. She was looking at him with a very intelligent expression and suddenly he felt seen through and acutely aware of his lack of a shadow.

'It's beautiful,' he said, blushing. He had a terrible pang at the thought that he could never take such lovely lace home for his mother.

'Beautiful and useful too,' said the old woman, nodding. 'It has its own language, you know.'

Before he could ask what she meant, Arianna came bouncing back.

'Never mind lace,' she said. 'What about cakes?'

Arianna's grandmother dispatched her to the cake shop, where her husband worked.

'Tell him to come and join us,' she called. 'He'll be shutting up for the afternoon soon, anyway.'

Arianna was soon back, with a wrinkled brown-skinned old man. He walked with a stick and Arianna bounded alongside him balancing a huge tray of cakes.

'Luciano, this is my grandfather,' she said. 'He makes the best cakes on the island. Some of his recipes go back for generations and they're great secrets, aren't they, Nonno? You're going to leave them to me when you die, aren't you?'

'So, you're going to be a cake-maker, are you?' asked her grandmother. 'I heard it was a mandolier.'

Now it was Arianna's turn to blush and she was quite subdued for a while. It made her uneasy to think that Leonora had told her family about her adventure on the forbidden day. How much did they know about Luciano, in that case?

But she was the only one not at ease. They were all sitting at a great stone table in the grandparents' back garden, which was full of terracotta pots of red flowers and overflowing greenery. They made a pretty sight against the white walls. Lucien had a hunch that if Arianna's grandfather had lived on Merlino, where all the houses were white, he would have painted his bright pink. He was that sort of a person. He wasn't tall and his crooked leg made him seem even shorter, but he was an impressive figure, with his bushy white eyebrows. And he did make the most delicious cakes.

'Try this kind,' he said to Lucien, pointing to some crumbly, sugary ones in the shape of crescent moons. 'I make them with lemons.'

The cakes, some of which were more like biscuits, were served with glasses of prosecco. Lucien stretched out his legs and drank the sharp wine with the sweet cakes, enjoying the scent of the garden and the warmth of the afternoon sun. He couldn't remember ever feeling happier.

*

Giuliana was terrified. 'You will get me into such trouble, Enrico! Not just me but my family too. I made a promise. And that Duchessa meant what she said. If she finds out I told anyone, then we'll be banished from the city.'

'You worry too much, cara,' said her fiancé, smoothing her dark hair back from her forehead. 'This Duchessa is an old woman. She won't live for ever. And how can she hurt you when she is gone?'

Giuliana was not completely reassured. Behind her mask, she still looked worried. The Duchessa was not that old and she was suspicious that Enrico had so casually brought up the subject of her possible death. Giuliana had never been quite sure what her fiancé did for a living. He had trained as an ostler, but then come to Bellezza, where horses had been banned two hundred years earlier. She knew he now did some work for the di Chimici family, which often involved absences from her, but she didn't know what sort of work and now she was frightened.

At the embassy, officials waved them through much more quickly than on Enrico's last visit. His name was now worth something to the Ambassador and it didn't hurt that he was with a young woman with a fine figure.

'Ah, my dear,' said the Ambassador when Enrico introduced his fiancée to him. 'How good of you to come. Would you like some wine?' He poured wine into the most expensive silver goblets for them. 'Now,

I'd like you to tell me all you can remember about this year's Marriage with the Sea.'

*

Torrone was a great contrast to the other two islands. While they had been bustling with life and activity, the smallest island was quiet and tranquil. There were visitors there, as everywhere in the lagoon, and there were a few stalls to sell them food and drink and lace and glass and even a few merlino-daggers. But the greatest number of people were streaming down the path by the main canal towards the church. 'It's a cathedral really,' Arianna told Lucien, 'but it's no bigger than a church.'

All the bounce had gone out of her and, instead of skipping ahead of him down the path, she dragged back, unwilling to come face to face with her family. Her brothers led the way, chatting to Leonora and leaving a waft of fishiness in their wake. They stopped at a little whitewashed house and a comfortable middle-aged woman in a green dress came to the door.

In moments, she had made her way to Arianna and gathered her in her arms. It made Lucien quite homesick and he turned away. What was he doing here, hundreds of miles away in space and hundreds of years in time, and who knew how distant from his own family?

But Valeria, Arianna's mother, made him welcome too. She seemed a bit in awe of him when she was told he was under Senator Rodolfo's protection, but she was a hospitable woman.

'Run and get your father, Tommaso,' she said. 'He'll be closing the museum soon.'

'But, Mamma, I'd like Luciano to see our cathedral,' said Arianna, now her old self since her mother was obviously so pleased to see her.

'All right. You two go with him and I'll start my cooking. You'll all stay and eat with us, won't you?'

As Lucien and Arianna carried on down the path with Tommaso, people kept stopping to greet the 'daughter of the island'. Her escapade had obviously been forgiven if not forgotten and every islander wanted to give her a kiss or a pat on the back. Arianna was in her element. Lucien could see how she had become so confident. Every person on the island treated her as special and took an interest in her. But they were all much older than her. The only other young people Lucien saw were among the visitors milling round outside the tiny cathedral.

But they went first to the museum, where a calm, grey-eyed man welcomed them, embracing Arianna with even more affection than the rest of the islanders had. Gianfranco was pleased to see them all and wanted to show Lucien the cathedral himself. Since it was almost time for it to close, they waited till the last tourists had been ushered out and then went in alone, Gianfranco jangling the keys on a large heavy ring.

The cathedral was cool and still, in spite of the tide of life that swept through it every day. Before the altar was a marble screen, carved with birds and flowers, as fine as Paola's lace. And through it, behind the altar, was a huge mosaic of a woman. It was made of silver and blue and towered up into the dome of the building.

'Our Lady,' whispered Arianna, making the hand of fortune.

'Mary?' asked Lucien.

'If you like,' she shrugged. 'Or the goddess. It doesn't matter. She is the Mother of the Lagoon and everyone comes to see her. Not just the tourists. All lagooners come to ask the Lady's help in times of trouble.'

Lucien could see a whole constellation of candles burning at the feet of the mosaic figure. And there were flowers and beads and all sorts of trinkets laid at its base too.

'Do you see that stone slab behind the altar?' Gianfranco asked him. 'Under there lie the bones of a dragon. The Maddalena, patron saint of the lagoon, is said to have killed it by the touch of one of her tears. The sheer holy power of it shrivelled him up.'

As they completed the guided tour of the cathedral, Lucien felt more and more confused. On the one hand it was a church and he felt he ought to recognize what went on in it. On the other hand the lagooners seemed equally happy with stories of goddesses or dragons, which seemed to belong to an earlier, pagan time.

They went back to Arianna's house, where Valeria had cooked the fish that her sons had brought with them and a big dish of pasta, with herbs and olives and garlic. It was completely unlike anything Lucien had ever tasted in Italian restaurants in North London.

After the meal, which was eaten on a little vine-covered terrace, Valeria made coffee. Leonora had paid the boatman off in Burlesca, as the two brothers had offered to bring them back in their fishing-boat.

'We should go when we've drunk this, Mamma,' said Angelo. 'Fishermen have to start early in the morning,' he explained to Lucien.

It was then that Lucien noticed for the first time that it was getting dark and the first stars were coming out. With a horrible jolt, he realized that, back in his world, it must be morning.

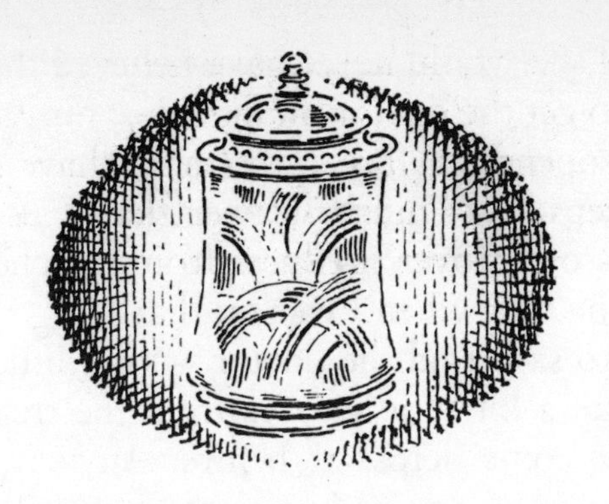

Chapter 8

A Jar of Rainbows

This time when Lucien came round, it was much worse. It wasn't just his mother peering anxiously into his face; their local GP, Doctor Kennedy, was there too, with her stethoscope on his chest. When Lucien's eyes fluttered open, his mother collapsed in tears. He felt dreadful seeing her so upset.

'It's all right, Mrs Mulholland,' said Dr Kennedy, when she had taken his pulse and shone a torch into his eyes. 'Lucien seems to be perfectly well – as well as he can be at this stage of his treatment.'

'Mum, I'm sorry,' said Lucien. 'I didn't mean to frighten you. I was having a dream about some beautiful lace I was going to buy for you. And I just couldn't seem to come out of the dream.'

He was lying but he couldn't bear to see her so

upset and she would never have believed the truth. He decided to get the doctor on his side.

'It's happened before. I seem to have these very heavy sleeps now, much heavier than I used to. Is it the illness or leftover tiredness from the chemo? I was tired all the time when I was on that.'

'Hard to say,' said the doctor, with a little frown. 'It sounds like a bit of a leftover from the treatment, but I've never come across it before. Anyway, you seem fighting fit now. You've just slept in a bit late. And he isn't the first teenager ever to do that, you know,' she added to Lucien's mother, who managed a watery smile.

'I'm sorry I called you out for nothing,' she apologized. 'But I was so frightened when I couldn't wake him up. Last time it was only a matter of minutes, but as I said, this time I'd been trying for about half an hour.'

After the doctor had gone, Lucien got up and dressed and behaved as animatedly as he could, though in fact he was now dog-tired. It was almost as bad as when he had been having the chemo, and he had forgotten what it was like to feel so drained. For the last few weeks he had begun to feel almost normal again. When his mother decided he was well enough to leave him on his own and went to the supermarket, Lucien immediately lay down on his bed.

But not to sleep. He fell into unconsciousness clutching the book, wishing himself in Talia, desperate to get back to the boat, from which he had made such a sudden disappearance the night before.

Lucien had drawn Arianna aside, as soon as he realized how late it was.

'I'm going to have to get back. It's daytime in my world and if I don't wake up there, there'll be the most almighty scare. It's happened before. I must stravagate soon.'

Arianna looked at him in disbelief. 'You can't just disappear! What can I tell everyone?'

'If it's like other times, I'll be gone for only a few moments – the blink of an eye,' he told her.

'Are you sure?' asked Arianna doubtfully.

Lucien hesitated. 'No, I'm not entirely sure. I've only done it in Bellezza before, in Rodolfo's laboratory. But I'll wait till we're on the boat. It's getting darker and you can cover for me – take everyone's attention from me.'

It had been decided that Arianna would return to Bellezza to continue her stay with Aunt Leonora but no one referred to it now in terms of punishment. Arianna felt forgiven and as if she could now enjoy her holiday in the city. But she was worried about Lucien.

As soon as the goodbyes had been said, which seemed to Lucien to take forever, and the brothers had rowed their boat out into the waters of the lagoon, he signalled to Arianna that he was ready. It seemed as good a chance as he would get, although theirs was not the only boat in the water. The nearest one was far enough off for nothing to be noticed in the dark.

'What's that over there?' asked Arianna excitedly, pointing towards the city. Everyone craned their necks to see what she was talking about – and Lucien disappeared.

She had been going to make something up about a

shooting star or a flying fish, but the sudden sense of Lucien's absence froze the invention in Arianna's throat. One minute she could feel the warmth of him next to her, his side lightly touching hers, and the next he was gone. It left her trembling.

'What?'

'Where?'

Fortunately, there *was* something. A rocket or flare launched into the night sky above the cathedral, sending out a shower of red sparks to illuminate the curves and lines of its unmistakable rooftops. At the same moment, Arianna felt the warmth of Lucien return. She gasped.

'You have very good eyesight, niece,' said Leonora. 'What is there to see *before* a firework goes up?'

'Wasn't it pretty?' said Tommaso.

'Signor Rodolfo must be preparing his next display,' said Angelo, 'For the Maddalena's day.'

'It's not like the Senator to be so careless, is it, Luciano?' asked Leonora.

'No indeed,' said Lucien, who was also trembling. 'He must have meant to set it off.'

Arianna said nothing. She was so stunned by having witnessed a stravagation that she didn't say anything else for the course of the journey.

As soon as they were back on Bellezza and he had escorted Leonora and Arianna home, Lucien raced to Rodolfo's palazzo. It was very dark now and he didn't see that not one, but two figures watched him from the shadows.

Alfredo let him in and Lucien ran up the stairs two at a time. The laboratory door opened before he could knock and he fell into the room panting.

'Can't stay ... got to get back before Mum ... supermarket ... stayed too late on islands ... big hoo-ha.'

He sank into a chair and Rodolfo looked at him seriously.

'So my mirrors told me. I told you to miss your morning lessons, not disappear for the whole day and forget to return to your home world. I sensed you were still here. That's why I sent up the flare.'

'I didn't see the flare, but I heard about it,' said Lucien. 'Look, never mind. I'm dying to ask you all sorts of things – about Doctor Dethridge and Arianna's grandmother and the merlino-fish and the glass mask, but I must go. I'll be back tonight – I mean tomorrow morning.'

He clutched the book and hurled himself into meditation. His whirling thoughts steadied and settled like sediment in a glass and he found himself sinking with them, away from the laboratory, from Bellezza, from Talia.

Rodolfo stood for a long time looking at the empty chair and sighed. 'Remarkable, most remarkable.'

*

The two shadows in the street outside Rodolfo's palazzo moved away and headed for the nearest tavern. One had a blue cloak and walked with a swagger. The other was dressed in rough workmen's clothes. They had both got off little boats at the Piazzetta mooring and found themselves trailing the same party. Now it was time to share a few glasses of Strega and some information.

Lucien awoke as he heard his mother's key in the door. He ran down the stairs, almost as fast as he had run up the others in Bellezza, and greeted her in the hall.

'Let me help you unpack,' he said.

'Well, you certainly seem well enough now,' said his mother, and he was relieved by her sunny look.

But lugging the bags in from the car and distributing the contents into cupboards, fridge and freezer left him exhausted. As soon as he felt he could risk it, Lucien yawned elaborately and said, 'I do feel just a little sleepy. Mind if I lie down for a bit?'

'No,' said his mother, without suspicion. 'You go on up and have a nice nap. I'll bring you some tea in about an hour. You don't want to spoil your night's rest.'

Rest was something that Lucien never had now. Every night was passed awake in another world. All the exercise he was getting there, and the fresh food, was in one way doing him good. He was putting on weight and getting his muscle tone back in his own world. He was even beginning to grow a dark fuzz of hair. But one way and another, he was still exhausted. Now he took the precious notebook out of his pocket and put it carefully on his bedside table. This time he wanted to be sure of a proper sleep.

Guido Parola was at his wits' end. He should have been going to university in Padavia but there was no money for that now. His older brother had drunk and gambled all the family fortune away and had now disappeared. Their father was very sick and there was no money to pay for a doctor to cure him or even a woman to help with his nursing. Guido's mother had died when he was still little.

It was touching to see the tall gangling red-haired boy tending his father so gently. But they were down to their last few scudi and he had to buy good-quality nourishing food to keep his father alive. He was in the market when a schoolfellow of his called out to him. Within a few minutes, they were in a local tavern and Guido was drinking heady Bellezzan red wine, paid for by his friend, and pouring out his troubles.

*

'Today we are going to make fireworks!' announced Rodolfo as soon as Lucien returned to Bellezza the night after the near-disastrous trip to the islands. The sunlight streaming into the laboratory gave Lucien the strangest feeling that Rodolfo could turn night into day. Perhaps he could. Lucien still had no idea how powerful Rodolfo might be. But today they were going to make fireworks.

'For the Maddalena,' explained Rodolfo. 'Her feast day is on the twenty-second of July and, since she is the patroness of the lagoon, I always have to do something special. But this year's must be even more special than usual because the Feast will coincide with the opening of the church in thanks for recovery from the plague.'

'Arianna says your display was something special at the Marriage with the Sea,' said Lucien. 'I wish I'd seen it.'

'You won't be able to see any of my displays,

Luciano,' said Rodolfo gently. 'You can't have fireworks by day. There are some things that need the dark.'

It was a bitter realization that took some of the joy out of making the fireworks, but as the morning wore on, Lucien became absorbed in what he was doing. A lot of it was what he would have described as science even in his world, mixing gunpowder with various chemicals that would produce different colours when ignited. But for the set pieces, Rodolfo used techniques that were much closer to what Lucien would have called magic.

On his workbench were glass jars containing all sorts of glittering substances in unearthly colours and strange objects, which only a magician would have in his possession. Lucien watched in amazement as Rodolfo unstoppered a jar that seemed to contain a miniature skeleton of a dragon and muttered words over it. It crumbled instantly to a fine green powder, which Rodolfo tamped down into the shell of the firework they were working on, adding a swirl of red and gold glitter which moved in his hands as he poured it in.

He glanced up at Lucien's face, amused. 'A cheap effect, but it always goes down well with the crowd,' he said. 'Now, let's take a break before the next one.'

Lucien dragged his mind away from the world of night-time explosions and fire in the sky.

'Did you find out anything about Doctor Dethridge?' he asked, as they stepped out into the roof garden.

'Not yet,' said Rodolfo. 'I have sent messages to my fellow-Stravaganti in Bellona, Remora, Giglia, all the big cities. It took all yesterday. I wished I had your magic to do all this by the cables you told me about. But I had to use the science of mirrors instead and it was a tedious search. Everyone is now looking for evidence of a man without a shadow, but there is no news as yet.'

'Rodolfo,' asked Lucien suddenly. 'Why did you bring me here?'

Rodolfo looked surprised. 'I didn't bring you here, Luciano. I merely left the talisman. I did not know who would find it. The talismans have a way of finding the right person.'

'But why then?'

'Every month at full moon I use various methods of divination. A few months ago I was reading cards and casting stones to see if I could see into the future and a pattern emerged which I didn't understand. It involved the Duchessa and danger and a young girl. It also showed a book and I had already chosen your notebook to be the next talisman. It seemed as if it might be time to take it to your world.' Rodolfo did not mention the Death card.

'And why did you take it there, so close to where I live and go to school?'

'I didn't know anything about you at the time. I went back to where Doctor Dethridge lived, in Barnsbury. In his time it was a country village. Now it seems to be part of North London. The site of his house and laboratory are unrecognizable. I saw what I now know must have been your school, but I did not know what it was then. It was big and full of people, so I left the talisman in a house next door and hoped it would be near enough.'

'But how did you get it into the house?' asked Lucien.

'I pushed it through a rectangular hole in the front door,' said Rodolfo.

'I still don't understand why you bring talismans into my world, though,' said Lucien. 'I mean, is it to make more Stravaganti?'

'In a way,' said Rodolfo slowly. 'That was how Doctor Dethridge did it in the first few years. But there have been only a few visitors from your world since him. It seems as if they come only to help when we have a crisis.'

'Are there a lot of crises?' asked Lucien.

Rodolfo sighed. 'Too many. The Chimici want to rule all Talia. Oh, they call it a Republic now, but you can be sure that once it is all in their grasp, it will become a Kingdom, an Empire even, as in the old days when Remora ruled over all the Middle Sea and beyond. But Bellezza resists them.'

'They want you to join?' asked Lucien.

'They want the Duchessa to sign a document committing Bellezza to join their Republic,' said Rodolfo. 'They have been trying to annex the lagoon for nearly a hundred years.'

'But you're not at war with them? I mean, the Reman ambassador is here and *he's* a Chimici,' said Lucien.

'Not at war, no,' said Rodolfo. 'There has been mutual hatred between us ever since the night of the glass mask – I think you've heard that story? – but we have been very civilized about it. Poisonings there may have been, the odd stabbing. But not all-out war. That's not the way the Chimici like to work. They have grown strong in Talia by plotting, political marriages and stealth.'

'Is it true that the Duchessa poisoned the Glass Master and then killed the Reman Prince?' asked Luciano.

Rodolfo shrugged. 'Possibly. It's the sort of thing a Duchessa might do. Duchesse are dangerous enemies. They are fiercely protective of their city. Silvia would have no mercy on anyone who tried to take Bellezza from her.'

'But the Prince was only dancing with her,' protested Lucien. 'I mean with the other Duchessa.'

'And perhaps tripped her while she was wearing the glass mask?' suggested Rodolfo.

'But the Glass Master? He didn't mean to hurt her – he made that mask on her orders. Why did she poison him?'

'His work damaged her beauty. And she was Bellezza. It was like blowing up the cathedral,' said Rodolfo. 'All Bellezzans think that way. They wouldn't have been shocked.'

'But you don't approve, do you?' asked Lucien.

'Not really,' said Rodolfo. 'He was my ancestor, you know. I base a lot of my fireworks on his glass designs. Now, it's time we worked on the centrepiece of the Maddalena's display.'

*

Rinaldo di Chimici was running out of patience. He had been visiting Bellezza for months and was tired of it. Every journey was uncomfortable; he had to leave his carriage on the mainland, because of the ridiculous Bellezzan laws about horses, and then take a boat, which made him feel sick.

His apartments were sumptuous but just being in the city made him ill. He kept a scent-soaked handkerchief pressed to his nose almost the whole time, because of the smell from the canals, and he had all his food tasted for him before he would touch it. He did not trust the Duchessa. And he did not think he was going to prevail against her by argument.

So he had sent, reluctantly, for a tall red-headed young man with a merlino-blade hidden under his cloak.

'Why can't she just sign?' the Ambassador complained, thinking aloud. He was trying to justify his next course of action. The Duchessa was a woman, after all. 'What is so special about this overgrown swamp village that she insists on keeping it independent?'

Guido Parola remained silent. Remora was paying him handsomely for what they wanted him to do. But the Duchessa was Bellezza and Bellezza was his city. Large sums of money might persuade him to strike it down, but no one could pay him enough to criticize it – that would be treachery.

'Anyway, you know your orders. The Feast of the Maddalena. Ignore the Duchessa that the crowd will be applauding. The real one will be in the State mandola. There won't be room for guards – just a waiting-woman or two. And, according to my information, Senator Rodolfo, who hardly ever leaves her side, will be busy with his fireworks.'

Parola nodded. It would be easier if there were two Duchesse. Easier to succeed and easier to convince himself that the real one was out there on the bridge of boats and the one in the mandola was just an ordinary, middle-aged woman.

*

'Now, with this one, we will work together,' said Rodolfo. 'Then you can make some more of the Reman candles and rockets by yourself tomorrow.'

He uncovered a huge wire structure in the corner of the laboratory. It was in the shape of a woman, with long hair.

'Here she is,' said Rodolfo, 'our patron lady and saint. The hair is the most important part. You know the story of how she anointed the Lord's feet and dried them with her long hair?'

'I know that's what Mary Magdalen did in my world,' said Lucien. 'At least I know there's that story in the Bible.' He still had no idea what the Bellezzans believed in. Their churches seemed such a strange mixture of his world's Christianity and an older, pagan religion.

'Maria Maddalena,' nodded Rodolfo. 'It is the same story. Our saint was once a sinner, who served the Lord. She was redeemed and became almost as important in the Middle Sea as our Lady goddess. Have you heard the story of how she destroyed the dragon by weeping over him? Now, hand me that jar.'

They worked for the rest of the morning in companionable silence. By lunchtime the framework of the body was filled with packets of explosives and minerals which would outline it dramatically against the sky.

'Now for the hair,' said Rodolfo.

Lucien remembered something. 'In my world, I

think Mary Magdalen has golden hair, but you don't think much of gold in Bellezza.' Rodolfo looked surprised.

'Golden hair is unusual in Talia, but we wouldn't disprize it – it is not the element, after all. Still, it doesn't arise with the Maddalena. Our patron lady had black hair,' he said. 'But you're right that there is a problem. Black hair doesn't show against the night sky. He went to a high shelf and took down a glass flask they hadn't used before. It shone in his hands, sending prismatic colours dazzling through the laboratory. Lucien had to shield his eyes.

When he could focus again, he saw that the jar was full of rainbows. Rodolfo smiled at his apprentice's amazement.

'We shall wreath her hair with moonbows,' said Rodolfo. 'It will be full moon on the night of the Maddalena's feast, and the silver light will shine through each arc of colour. And every red-blooded Bellezzan will dive into the canal to find the real pots of silver at the end of each lock.'

That was the moment that Lucien decided he would be in Talia for Rodolfo's firework display no matter what it cost him.

Chapter 9

Twelve Towers

The Duchessa had spent the morning presiding over her Council. The two hundred and forty Councillors found it difficult to reach a consensus on the seven criminal charges brought before them and the Duchessa had found it even harder not to yawn.

Perhaps I'll invent a special new large mask for Council meetings, she thought, one that covers the mouth as well as the eyes. She could hardly use a substitute for such important criminal proceedings, where she sometimes had to give a casting vote and always proclaimed sentence.

Only one convicted criminal had been led off across the Bridge of Sorrow to her dungeons today. 'I must be getting soft in my old age,' the Duchessa said to no one in particular.

'Surely not, Your Grace,' said her youngest waiting-woman, who then put her hand to her mouth, fearing that she had been rude. 'I mean, milady, that you are not old, not that you are not soft, I mean...'

The Duchessa chose to be amused. 'What is your name, child?'

'Barbara, milady,' said the young woman, curtseying.

'Well, Barbara, aren't you the one I sent to find out about the girl in the Piazza? Is there any news?'

'Yes, milady. There is a man waiting to see you downstairs.'

'Then why hasn't he been sent up?'

'Milady, your dressmaker is waiting to give you a final fitting of your gown for the Maddalena Feast,' said another of her women. 'We did not think you would want to postpone that.'

The Duchessa thought for a while. 'Very well. Send down to make sure the messenger is well entertained and I'll see him as soon as the dressmaker has gone. I hope she has made both dresses.'

*

Arianna couldn't wait to see Lucien again. Ever since the incident on the boat, she had been dying to talk to him about it. As soon as they were on their own, exploring the back streets of Bellezza, she said, 'What happened? Did you get into trouble?'

'Almost,' said Lucien. 'It was a close thing.'

'We mustn't ever let that happen again,' said Arianna seriously. 'I mean, we were lucky to be out on a boat in the middle of the lagoon, with hardly any others on the water. Or you could have caused a sensation and word would have got back to the Chimici.'

Lucien hesitated, then decided to take Arianna into his confidence. 'Of course we mustn't let it happen by accident. But I'm going to try and stay a whole night on purpose.'

Arianna stopped walking and stared at him.

'How are you going to manage that? And why?'

'I'm going to persuade my parents to leave me on my own. And I'm going to be here. I'm not going to miss the festival. I've been making fireworks for it all morning.'

'Does Rodolfo know?' asked Arianna.

'I'm not going to tell him,' said Lucien calmly, although he didn't feel altogether comfortable about this decision. What if Rodolfo detected his presence still here on Bellezza, like last time? He was sure the magician would not approve.

*

The dressmaker had remembered to make two dresses, although she had no idea that one of them was for the substitute the Duchessa would use for her appearance at the feast of the Maddalena. She believed, like all the other dressmakers in Bellezza, that the Duchessa was extremely vain. The second dress, like all the ones worn on important occasions, would be preserved in a room in the Palazzo that was open to the public. The dressmaker understood that it must have a tiny waist and fall in slender folds about the hips. She never went to festivals herself, so she would not see how youthful the Duchessa would look as she stepped lightly from boat to boat, over the improvised bridge of boats across the Great Canal to the new church.

The dress and its companion were beautiful. Indeed the Duchessa's gown was only one size larger than her substitute's, though no one would mistake her for a young girl any more. She didn't use a substitute out of vanity, although she had that in abundance. She had started the practice more than fifteen years ago, for good reasons of her own. Now she found she rather enjoyed the risk of being discovered.

Silvia was restless. She had been Duchessa for two and half decades and she longed to do something more active for her city than wear beautiful dresses, particularly now that it was under such threat from the Chimici. Still, this one was rather fine; the violet satin matched her eyes, which shone from the lavender mask, decorated with silver sequins and trimmed with purple feathers, that she would wear with it. She looked like an exotic bird as she preened before her looking-glass.

'Excellent! Help me out of this now though. I am anxious for my next appointment.'

The dressmaker was ushered out rather hastily but was mollified by the cakes and wine she was plied with in the outer room. She was curious as she watched the Duchessa's next visitor enter her private apartment in his rough working clothes. He didn't look like a mask-maker, or a hairdresser or any of the other dozens of people dedicated to the Duchessa's beautification and adornment.

'Come in, come in,' said the Duchessa, adjusting her plain green silk mask, for which she had changed the State one as soon as the dressmaker had gone. 'Tell me about the girl.'

'Why don't you and Dad get back to normal?' suggested Lucien. 'I'm so much better now. You could go back to teaching in the schools, Mum.'

Vicky Mulholland was a violin teacher. She visited several schools in the borough and, after school and in the holidays, she taught pupils in her own home. But ever since Lucien had been so ill, all this term, she had almost stopped working.

'I don't know,' said his mother. 'Isn't it a bit soon to leave you?'

'Don't be silly, Vicky,' said his father. 'Perhaps Lucien is trying to tell us, ever so tactfully, that he'd like to spend some time on his own or with his own friends. There's no need to mollycoddle him, you know.'

Lucien was grateful. The old Dad wouldn't have noticed something like that.

'As a matter of fact, I was thinking of spending some more time with Tom,' he said. 'We still have a lot to catch up on. But I'll be fine on my own too. I know I'm not ready to go back to school but it's nearly the holidays and I can amuse myself for a week or two.'

'Well, as long as you always have my mobile number and call me the minute you feel worse,' said Vicky.

'Mum!' said Lucien, in an exasperated tone, though he felt guilty about the deception he was planning. 'I'm not made of glass, you know. My last check-up showed I'm stable and the tumour's gone way down. The doctor even said I could go back to school after the holidays. Surely I can spend my days vegging out at home without you worrying?'

His mother sighed. 'You're right. I fret too much, I know.'

She smiled and ran her hand across his fuzzy head. 'But I'm going to write my mobile number on the noticeboard all the same.'

When Lucien returned to Bellezza, Rodolfo was in a state of high excitement and it was clear that all thought of firework-making had gone out of his head. He was dressed for travel, in leather boots and a cloak, and had prepared a similar outfit for Lucien.

'Good, you're early. We have a good few hours' journey ahead of us,' he said as soon as Lucien materialized in the laboratory. 'We're going to Montemurato – I think I've found Doctor Dethridge.'

There was no time to ask questions. Alfredo sculled Rodolfo's mandola up the canal and past the Scuola Mandoliera, to the far end of the island where a boat waited to take them to the mainland. As they cut through the water, Rodolfo filled Lucien in on developments.

'One of our brotherhood did see Doctor Dethridge in Bellona about two years ago and it must have been after the last time I saw him. But since then he has not made contact with any other Stravaganti. However, news has reached one of our number in Remora of an Englishman living in Montemurato. It is worth investigating.'

'And where is that?' asked Lucien, feeling adventurous in his pantomime boots.

'About an hour's ride once we get to the mainland,' said Rodolfo.

Lucien swallowed. He had never sat on a horse in his life. But he couldn't bring himself to admit it. Still, once they had disembarked and he saw the huge animal waiting on the quay, Lucien's heart sank. There was no way he could pretend to ride something like that.

When an ostler came forward with a wooden mounting block, Lucien opened his mouth to explain, but Rodolfo spoke first.

'I'll mount and then you can sit in front of me. This beast is strong enough to carry both of us. Just hang on to the front of the saddle and you will be quite safe – even if not comfortable.'

Lucien was so relieved that he wasn't too frightened, even though Rodolfo did ride extremely fast. The horse was very powerful and yet Lucien was sure that Rodolfo had whispered some sort of spell into its ear before they set off. No ordinary horse could have travelled so fast; the landscape blurred as they rode through it.

Then gradually their surroundings seemed to slow down and clarify. Lucien saw a hill in the distance with a walled town on top of it. As they got nearer, he could see that in among the walls were set many towers.

'Montemurato,' said Rodolfo, reining the steaming horse in to a walk. 'The walled mountain. There are twelve towers altogether surrounding the city. Each one is a watchtower – a very safe place for someone hiding from a death sentence, wouldn't you say?'

The watchtowers were evidently occupied, since

guards suddenly appeared at the gate below the nearest one. Rodolfo dismounted lightly, helping down the stiff and aching Lucien from the horse's back. It was his job to hold the horse by the reins, while Rodolfo explained their errand to the city watch.

'We are looking for an Anglese,' he said. 'A learned man, a scholar, with a white beard. No, I don't know what he was calling himself. Gugliemo, perhaps, with a family name beginning with D.'

'Don't know anyone of that name and description,' shrugged the guard. But if it's a scholar you're after, you'd better try the university.' He made a mark on a scrap of vellum and gave it to Rodolfo. 'This allows you and your companion to stay in Montemurato till sundown. After that you're in breach of the law.'

'Thank you,' said Rodolfo, with a reassuring look at Lucien. 'We'll be gone long before that. Now I need stabling and provender for my horse.'

The guard told him where to go and the travellers walked up the steep cobbled street into the city. They stopped and bought a flask of wine, some bread, olives and peaches from a wayside stall. Then they sat and ate their lunch on a stone bench under a fig tree outside the door of the university.

Scholars came and went, in robes, some splendid, some patched and grubby. One or two had white beards, but in the full midday sun they all clearly had shadows. Lucien pulled himself further into the shade of the tree, feeling conspicuous again. Rodolfo frowned.

'This doesn't feel right,' he said. 'I don't think he's here.'

'Couldn't he be inside?' asked Lucien, 'giving a lecture or conducting an experiment?'

'It is perfectly possible,' said Rodolfo in a low voice, 'but we Stravaganti can usually tell when another of us is in the vicinity. We are drawn to one another, just as my mirror was to you. You would probably have found your way to me even if I hadn't sent Alfredo to fetch you. Come, you are a Stravagante yourself – can you sense another of the brotherhood nearby?'

Lucien had to admit that he couldn't. Rodolfo stood up and as he did, a bell struck one. That was the time when Lucien usually finished his morning lessons in the laboratory.

'Arianna!' he said now, suddenly aware how late it was. 'She'll be expecting me!'

'There's no need to worry,' said Rodolfo. 'I sent a message to her aunt that we had been called away today. Now come, we must look for our quarry elsewhere.'

As they set off through the town, Lucien smiled. He could imagine how frustrated Arianna would be to miss this trip. Fond as she was of Bellezza, she loved the idea of travelling and there didn't seem to be much scope for girls to do that in the lagoon.

Montemurato looked like a film set to Lucien. The streets were all cobbled, the houses tall and crooked, the whole town dominated by the formidable bulk of the twelve towers that encircled it. It was easy to imagine swordfights, assignations in the dark, treachery, chivalry and intrigue. He noticed that the ordinary houses had two doors: one massive wooden affair with iron hinges and knockers and a smaller, newer one set higher in the wall, about three feet square. He asked Rodolfo about it.

'The smaller ones are the doors of death,' said Rodolfo, matter-of-factly. 'A lot of people put them in during the Great Plague twenty years ago. They are for the coffins.'

Lucien shuddered in the warm sunshine. Someone walking over my grave, he thought. People were so practical about death here in the sixteenth century. It was all so hushed up somehow in his own world and time. He tried to shake off his morbid thoughts as they searched for Doctor Dethridge.

They tried the university library, the museum, the many churches and the small observatory at the top of one of the towers. No one had heard of anyone like the Stravagante. As it got later, Rodolfo reluctantly turned back towards the tower at which they had come in.

'I'm sorry, Luciano,' he said. 'I seem to have brought you on a wild goose chase.'

'It's OK,' said Lucien. 'I don't mind. It's been very interesting.'

As they went to retrieve the horse, Rodolfo suddenly clutched Lucien's shoulder. 'It's him,' he whispered.

A white-haired but cleanshaven man was grooming a horse out in the stableyard, hissing through his teeth in a companionable way. He wasn't old by Lucien's standards, only a bit older than his own parents, but he was stooped and his teeth were crooked and discoloured.

'That can't be him,' Lucien whispered back. 'Look!' He pointed at the stable floor. The afternoon sunlight slanted across the yard, casting shadows of horse and man clearly across the straw and cobbles. But Rodolfo advanced towards the groom anyway.

'Dottore,' Luciano heard him say softly, and the man dropped his brush in surprise. A minute later the two men were embracing and the 'doctor' was brushing a none-too-clean shirtsleeve across his eyes.

'But what are you doing here?' Rodolfo was asking. 'We looked for you up at the university.'

Dethridge, for it did seem to be him, looked anxiously at Lucien.

'Nay, al that is behinde mee,' he said in a strange old-fashioned-sounding tongue, with a country burr.

Rodolfo looked round quickly, to see if they were alone.

'Do not worry about the boy; he is one of us. Come, Luciano, step into the sunshine. See!'

Lucien felt shy as he stepped forward. He heard the Englishman gasp and felt hideously exposed standing there without a shadow – it was like being naked in front of a stranger.

Dethridge shook him by the hand, solemnly. 'Well met, yonge mann. And wel ycome to the Brethrene. Me thought not to mete anothere suche as my selfe.'

*

The Duchessa was hungry for information, though the man in the rough clothes told her little that she did not already know. She was aware of the girl's family circumstances already and just wanted to check that Arianna was who she thought she was.

'They went to the islands you say? She has brothers on Merlino, grandparents on Burlesca and her father is curator of the museum on Torrone? You are sure about all this?'

'Absolutely sure,' said the man. 'And she is staying here on Bellezza with her aunt Leonora, in the house with the fountain off the campo San Sulien.'

'Leonora,' mused the Duchessa. 'That must be Gianfranco's brother's widow.'

'Signora Gasparini, *sì*,' said her informant.

There was a silence. 'Milady?' he asked hesitantly. 'Shall I continue to find out more?'

The Duchessa gathered herself together. 'No. Thank you. I have all I need. You have been very helpful.'

And she gave him a purse, heavy with silver.

'So,' she said to herself, after he had gone. 'A new piece has entered the game. One I have been waiting for ever since that night Rodolfo came to me with his strange readings. Will she be a pawn or a queen? We shall see.'

*

Rodolfo, Lucien and Doctor Dethridge were in a tavern. They had little time to talk before Lucien had to stravagate back and no one understood that better than the Elizabethan. But he wouldn't go back to Bellezza with them.

'I canne not,' he said. 'Bicause this Citie pleaseth me and kepeth mee sauf.'

It was strange; Lucien supposed he must have been speaking Talian like all the other people he had met in this world. He had no more trouble understanding the old man than he had listening to Rodolfo or Arianna. But he definitely sounded as though he came from four hundred years ago, even though he was living in the same time that Lucien was visiting. And, when he thought about it, Dethridge seemed to be speaking an old form of English, rather than Talian. Lucien shook his head; it was too difficult to analyse. He just concentrated on what the two men were saying.

'But tell us what happened,' Rodolfo was asking. 'How have you become a citizen of Talia?'

Dethridge was obviously fearful. He looked over his shoulder before speaking in a low voice. 'I was condemned to dye by fyre. They sayed I had mayde Magicke and was in converse with Devyls. There was noe waye to escape and so I stravayged to Bellona. What happened to mye erthly bodie I doe not knowe.'

He drank some wine with a shaking hand.

'I had to hide my selfe in the Citie. I hadde no moneye and noe worke and I was stil afeard for mye life. So I travelled here and toke a lowly job and kept mye selfe hid, lest any one should see my Conditioun. Then my shadowe riturned to mee. On that daie I knew that I moste bee dede in mine olde Body and translated here for alwaies.'

He looked at Lucien. 'You are of goode fortune, yonge mann. You may cum and goe bitwene the Worldes by the waie I opened. But I may travel that road no more. This is my onlye worlde now.'

Chapter 10

A Bridge of Boats

Lucien was more disturbed by meeting William Dethridge than by anything else that had happened to him in Talia. Until that moment, he had always been able to half pretend to himself that the time he spent in Bellezza was a fantasy – a kind of waking dream. His two lives were so different that it was easy to go along with each without thinking about the other. But meeting another Stravagante who travelled in the same direction as himself was a big shock. And not just any Stravagante but the man who had created the whole process more than four centuries ago. And now that man was stranded for the rest of his life in another world.

The time before the Maddalena Feast passed swiftly in both worlds. 'Luciano' made fireworks, talked obsessively to Rodolfo about Doctor Dethridge and continued his afternoon wanderings with Arianna, who was consumed with envy about his trip to Montemurato. Lucien used all his remaining energy to behave as much like his old self as possible, so that his parents would get used to leaving him on his own during the day.

But there was a problem in Talia too. Lucien was sure he was being followed. He had seen the man in the blue cloak several times on his explorations with Arianna and had not thought much about it. But he was sure he had glimpsed him in Montemurato too, and after that he had been keeping an eye out for him.

At the moment it made him no more than slightly uneasy, but being trailed was like having a mouth ulcer; he couldn't ever be unaware of it. He wondered whether to say anything to Rodolfo about it, and when. He still hadn't told him about meaning to come back for the Feast.

On the day of the Maddalena, Lucien woke up tired after spending the whole of his night helping Rodolfo set up the firework display on a raft at the mouth of the Great Canal. The larger set pieces, like the Maddalena herself, had been removed from the laboratory by a mixture of magic and hard labour, Rodolfo having shrunk them enough to get them through the laboratory door and down the stairs. Once on the waiting barge though, he had returned them to their monumental size.

Lucien had agreed with Arianna that he would collect her from her aunt's house as soon as he had left Rodolfo and stravagated back to his home to check on what day it was there. Leonora had given approval for the two young people to go alone to the Feast. Although she had been told about Lucien's belonging to another world, she had never referred to it and seemed to think him a very suitable companion for her niece.

It was a Sunday in his own world and Lucien was worried that his parents wouldn't go out, but he persuaded them to visit a stately home with a fine garden. Now he struggled to keep his eyes open and fixed an animated smile on his face all through breakfast, while they took ages eating grapefruit and croissants and even reading the newspaper. At last they were gone, and he crawled back to bed to sleep for an hour. In order to convince his mother that he wouldn't be alone all day, he had phoned Tom and invited him over later that morning.

The Reman Ambassador was nervous. It was his job to accompany the Duchessa across the bridge of boats to the Chiesa delle Grazie, knowing that the sylph on his arm was some peasant with a pretty figure. There would be no conversation because of the noise of the fireworks and that would also help to keep his mind off what was happening in the State mandola.

When Enrico called at the embassy to give his regular report, the Ambassador was glad of the distraction. He hadn't taken the spy into his confidence but he was a useful tool; without him tonight's plot would never have been conceived.

Now he could see the man had information he thought was going to be worth silver. He was big with it, like a woman in her ninth month.

'All right, man, spit it out. I can see you have something to tell me,' he said.

'It's the boy, Excellency, the Senator's apprentice. I have been following him on your orders ever since that day I saw him go into Signor Rodolfo's palazzo. There are things about him that can't be explained.'

'Take a seat and tell me more,' said the Ambassador, pouring Enrico a large goblet of wine.

'Well, they say he's from Padavia, a cousin or something. But no one there has ever heard of a Luciano in the Rossi family. I checked it myself. Then, he's never around after dark, only by day.'

'These things are of mild interest I suppose,' said the Ambassador coolly, 'but not inexplicable. I expect he goes to bed early. Senator Rodolfo must be an exacting teacher.'

'How about this then?' said Enrico. 'I followed him when he went out on a boat with his little girlfriend. They went to the islands, saw the glass museum, chatted to some fishermen, visited the cathedral on Torrone...'

'Fascinating,' said the Ambassador, 'but I don't see...'

'With respect, Excellency,' said Enrico, 'if you'll just let me get to the point. It was when they were coming back from Torrone. It was dark and the boy was in a bit of a state. It was the only time I'd ever seen him out in the evening and I was watching him carefully. Then suddenly he wasn't there any more. It was only a few moments but he definitely disappeared. Then he was back, just as if he hadn't ever been away.'

The Ambassador looked bored. 'Is that it? I mean,

it's all very interesting but it could have been the light playing tricks on you. You can't have been very close if you were in another boat. And you've admitted it was dark.'

'Maybe,' said Enrico. 'And maybe I wouldn't have noticed it. But there's something else odd about the boy. He has no shadow.'

The effect on the Ambassador was electrifying. He sprang out of his chair, all appearance of indifference gone, and grabbed Enrico by the throat, showing surprising strength. The spy spluttered, dropping his wine and falling out of his chair.

'What did you say?' hissed the Ambassador. 'Are you trying to play games with me?'

Enrico struggled to speak.

'Please ... Excellency ... no games ... 's true ... no shadow...'

The Ambassador released him. 'You had better not be making this up,' he said, pouring more wine for both of them. Enrico gulped his thirstily, massaging his bruised throat. But though his neck was hurting, he felt secretly elated. This had to mean good money.

When Tom rang the doorbell, Lucien was still asleep. He came down the stairs rubbing his eyes, but at least he was feeling more human.

'Hey!' said Tom. 'I thought you were feeling better.'

'I am, honestly,' said Lucien, though he now felt bad about what he was going to do to Tom. At least they had a few hours together. Tom had brought lots of CDs and some photos of the disco. He was very chatty, because he had taken Katie and they were now an item. It was lucky that Lucien didn't have to say much, because his mind was still on Bellezza, anticipating the night's revels.

If you'd asked him a year ago whether he'd be more interested in a disco or watching fireworks with a lot of adults wearing masks, there would have been no contest, he thought. And there was no contest now.

The Ambassador was pacing his room in high excitement. It was all within his grasp now – Bellezza, the Kingdom, and now the key to the mystery that the di Chimici family had been pursuing for years. Then he, Rinaldo, would be one of the most important members of the family. Perhaps he would even become head of it? His ambition was without limit. A vision of a silver crown floated before his eyes.

*

'Who is it this time?' asked the Duchessa, but immediately became bored with the subject. 'No, don't tell me. Just put her in the dress, wind her up and set her off across the boats.'

She adjusted the lavender and silver mask, and went to meet the Reman Ambassador in her most formal audience chamber. It was lined with glass and mirrors and had been designed to confuse visitors. Thus, Rinaldo di Chimici found himself bowing to a reflection of a gorgeous vision in violet.

'I'm over here,' said the Duchessa mockingly, and at that moment the Ambassador was so furious at her treatment of him that he didn't care any more about what was going to happen to her. By the end of the evening he would have Bellezza in the palm of his hand and a much greater goal within his reach.

The Ducal party walked the short distance to the Piazzetta, where the black and silver State mandola was moored, with an only slightly less ornate one behind it. Di Chimici handed the Duchessa formally into the first vessel, where she was instantly engulfed in a flurry of silver brocade, which was then tightly drawn around the cabin in the middle. Then he stepped into the second mandola and the two boats moved out towards the mouth of the Great Canal.

Lucien and Arianna were on the near side of the water, waiting for the fireworks. The Duchessa would step on to the bridge of boats and then, escorted by the Ambassador, walk across it to the new church and declare it open. At that moment the fireworks would begin. While the consecration service was being performed by the Bishop of Bellezza, the State mandola would glide across the canal to collect the Duchessa and bring her back to the square. A feast would be waiting in her Palazzo, for all the dignitaries of church and state. The people, in the usual manner of lagooners, would hold their own party in the Piazza.

'I can't wait to see the fireworks!' said Arianna excitedly. 'Aren't you thrilled to think you made some of them? What's the best one going to be?'

'It's a secret,' said Lucien, 'You'll have to wait and see.'

He was as jumpy as a cat with new kittens. He kept thinking that any minute now, Rodolfo would realize he hadn't stravagated back to his own world and come striding through the crowd to dispatch him home. He was also sure he had spotted the man in the blue cloak in the mass of people thronging the canalside.

He knew the sequence of fireworks and, as soon as the set piece with the Maddalena's rainbow hair had finished, he planned to disappear. He was still feeling mean about telling Tom he was too tired for him to stay on after lunch. He thought he would never forget Tom's face when he had sent him home, half disappointed and half what? Understanding? Lucien had a horrible feeling that Tom's other emotion might have been relief.

He pushed the thought to the back of his mind. If his best friend in one world was getting a bit bored with the company of an invalid, at least his best friend in this world was glad to be with him. He smiled at Arianna's animated face. She certainly knew how to enjoy herself. He decided that for the rest of the evening he was going to behave like a true Bellezzan and live for the moment.

*

Inside the State mandola it was a bit of a squash. The Duchessa, her double, and one serving-woman were squeezed together in a space only big enough for two. The second 'Duchessa' was obviously terrified, her eyes big behind the mask. The real one was merely bored, as she had so often been of late.

It had been getting worse since the day she had seen the brown-haired girl in the square. A restlessness and dissatisfaction with her own life had overtaken her. It was a torment to her to sit enclosed with a servant and another stupid peasant girl who would be able to enact the deception only by the thought of the purse of silver.

I don't know how many more of these charades I can endure, she thought to herself. But at least I shan't have to put up with that dolt of an Ambassador with his endless talk of the treaty and his horrible smelly handkerchief. Honestly, you'd think a di Chimici would have a more expensive scent, one from Giglia, where they have perfected the making of perfume.

And then he was at the cabin curtain and the Duchessa practically had to push the impostor out, so much was she trembling.

The young woman's trembling didn't show in the flickering light of the torches and Rinaldo di Chimici had to force himself to believe that this was not the true Duchessa he was leading carefully from boat to boat. Slowly and precisely, they stepped from vessel to vessel, the keels bobbing on the water. It was a progress that had to be undertaken with great care. A mis-step could land them both in the stinking canal. He shuddered at the thought and pressed his lace handkerchief more tightly to his nose. The crowd on either bank were cheering wildly. They loved their Duchessa and every time she appeared in public, she looked lovelier and younger to her people. The very sight of her made them feel their city was safe and the most important and splendid in the country.

When the resplendent pair reached the middle of the bridge of boats, the first rocket went up, exploding precisely above their heads, illuminating them and all the crowd with a shower of violet and silver stars.

Watching through a chink in the brocade curtains, the real Duchessa smiled. Rodolfo paid such attention to detail. He always found out what she would be wearing on State occasions when he had fireworks to make.

A little way behind the State mandola, Lucien swelled with pride. 'That's one of mine!' he yelled to Arianna across the roar of the crowd. She smiled at him, her violet eyes shining like the firework breaking over her. She squeezed his hand and he squeezed back.

A tall figure slipped through the crowd towards the State mandola. No one noticed him go. All eyes were on the procession across the bridge of boats and the galaxy of light and colour that illuminated their way.

A skein of silver birds flew across the sky. Then a peacock spread its blue and purple and green tail magnificently, till it filled the horizon. A phoenix laid a golden egg then glowed from gold to red and disappeared in a spray of stars. The egg hung in the air till a new phoenix hatched out of it in a new splendour of red and gold. A silver ram walked across the black night to the hoarse cheers of Bellezzans.

And then, at the climax of the display, a massive green dragon blazed across the sky. The set-piece of the Maddalena exploded higher against the night. A huge crystal tear fell from her eye and landed on the dragon, which dissolved into a million red and gold stars. At that precise moment the full moon came out from behind a cloud and shone through the Saint's rainbow hair.

Lucien thought his heart would stop. With the commotion of the crowd going mad about the effects he had helped to create, he didn't notice the State mandola gliding off through the water, nor the dark figure crouched at the opposite end from the mandolier. He saw only that Rodolfo had been right. As the last dazzling rainbow tresses seemed to fall into the water, Bellezzans began leaping into the canal.

A madness overtook Lucien. He knew he couldn't take any silver back to his world, even if he found it. He knew too that he should go now, should stravagate before the feast. But at that moment he was a Bellezzan through and through. In the blink of an eye, he had taken a sighting on where a lock of the Saint's multi-coloured hair had disappeared and dived into the canal himself.

*

'Exquisite,' murmured the Duchessa, feeling the mandola move beneath her as the Saint dissolved, leaving the moon bathing the city in silver, its citizens afflicted with one of their regular fits of madness. She wasn't bored any more but filled with a fierce tenderness for her silly, loyal, patriotic subjects. The thing they had in common with her was their passion for their city. The Duchessa had to suppress a tear behind her mask. It would never do to stain it.

Then the silver curtain was wrenched back and a tall red-headed young man put a dagger to her throat.

*

Lucien came up spluttering, having grabbed something from the canal. The water tasted filthy but the coldness of it brought him to his senses. He suddenly thought with horror that his notebook would be getting wet and he didn't know if he could stravagate with a soggy talisman. Real panic set in when, shaking the hair out of his eyes, he realized he had drifted into the centre of the canal. His one thought was to get out of the water and, seeing a mandola coming past him, he grabbed at the side and, with a huge effort, hauled himself aboard.

*

The Duchessa knew she was going to die. A thousand regrets flooded her mind but not for her personal safety; they were all to do with the city, Rodolfo and the brown-haired girl.

Inside the cabin all was silent. The assassin said not a word and the waiting-woman was frozen with terror. The mandolier obviously hadn't realized that anyone had climbed aboard and was calmly sculling his way across the canal mouth to the new church to wait, as he thought, for the Duchessa to come out after the consecration.

The assassin waited a long moment with the blade of his dagger at the Duchessa's white throat.

And then all was chaos and water as the mandola rocked dangerously and a very wet young man flung himself into the already crowded cabin. Lucien registered all at once that he was in the State mandola with the Duchessa and his instincts took over. He knew she shouldn't be there; he had just seen her walk across the bridge of boats. But there she was without

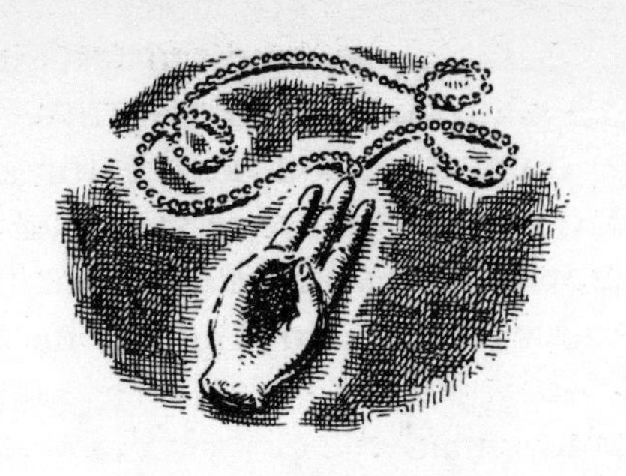

Chapter 11

The Hand of Fortune

The mandola rocked wildly on the water. There were too many people inside. The Duchessa's waiting-woman very sensibly put her head outside the silver curtain and shouted to the mandolier. He stopped trying to steady the vessel and looked in on the mayhem in the cabin. His eyes bulged when he saw the Duchessa, a fact that Silvia immediately noted as telling in his favour. He obviously hadn't been part of the plot.

The mandolier helped Lucien to bind the assassin with the silver cords used for holding back the brocade curtains. Lucien put the merlino-blade in his own belt. As soon as the assassin was safely trussed up, the Duchessa took command of the situation.

'You – Marco, isn't it?' she said to the mandolier.

'Yes, Your Grace,' he said, uncertain about the person he was addressing, but taking the safe side.

'You have done me good service tonight and you will be rewarded. But you are to say not a word about it until you appear as a witness in Council for the trial of this miserable traitor and whoever his masters are. Understand?'

'I understand, milady.'

'Good. But now, we must get the villain and this young hero who has saved my life back to the Palazzo. Can you do this and help us as discreetly as possible to get them into my apartments?'

'Yes, milady,' said the mandolier, quite convinced about the Duchessa's identity now. Then he hesitated. 'But what about the other lady, milady? The one who walked across the boats?'

Behind her mask, the Duchessa's lip curled in disdain. 'Let the Reman Ambassador bring her back in his mandola. I shouldn't wonder if he knows something of events here on mine tonight.'

Marco went back to the end of the State vessel and sculled for dear life back to the Piazzetta. No one noticed the black mandola slipping through the water, except a tall figure on the fireworks platform, who knew that it was not supposed to be returning to that shore without collecting the Duchessa. Rodolfo immediately ordered Alfredo to take him back too.

*

The substitute Duchessa, a baker's daughter called Simonetta, was very uncomfortable. The church service had been all right, if a bit long, and she had been drilled in when to stand and sit and kneel, which was useful, since she wasn't much of a churchgoer herself.

But when she came out of the church it was all wrong. She enjoyed the cheers of the crowd, just as she had on the walk across all those boats, but where was the State mandola? Getting back into that and being given her payment was the part that had kept Simonetta going throughout the deception.

The Ambassador was at her elbow in a moment. Suppressing the joy and fear he felt at the plot obviously having worked, he guided the fake Duchessa into his own mandola. 'We'll go back in mine, my dear,' he said, much more familiarly than he would have dared with the real Duchessa.

Once inside the cabin, the young girl's terror and confusion increased. She had not been coached for anything like this. Suppose the Ambassador wanted to talk to her?

But she needn't have worried. Rinaldo di Chimici was too full of his own thoughts to make conversation.

*

Some of the Duchessa's personal guard were waiting at the Piazzetta and were very surprised to see the State mandola back so soon. But they quickly snapped into action when they saw the trussed-up assassin and the dripping Lucien. The man was taken straight to the dungeons and the Duchessa's waiting-woman hurried her and Lucien up into the palazzo. Fortunately, there was hardly anyone about in the square. They were all down by the canal waiting for the return of the fake Duchessa. So they missed the real one.

Once the party had reached the safety of the Duchessa's private apartments, more women fussed around them. A hot bath was organized for Lucien and women dabbed at the muddy marks that he had made on the Duchessa's satin dress while struggling with the assassin.

'Take off those wet things,' ordered the Duchessa.

Lucien felt himself blushing as he stood dripping canal water all over the Duchessa's priceless rug.

'Oh, for heaven's sake! Someone give him a towel! Do you think I'm going to eat you, boy? Wine, please, and quickly.'

Wrapped in a towel and taking huge gulps of the red Bellezzan wine, Lucien began to feel a bit better. He hadn't let the waiting-women take the dagger, or the notebook, which was just a bit damp. They had giggled over his underwear, which he had made them promise to bring back as soon as it was dry.

The Duchessa drank deeply herself. If it hadn't been for the sudden arrival of Lucien, she had some doubts about what would have been the outcome of this evening.

The waiting-woman from the mandola held up a dripping wet bag. 'What shall I do with this, milady?'

Lucien remembered. When he had dived in after the rainbows, his hand had closed round the neck of a canvas bag. At the time he had been concentrating on getting back up to the surface without drinking more canal water than he had to. He supposed he must have dropped it over the side of the Duchessa's mandola when he climbed aboard it. Not that he had known it was hers. He was still totally confused about why she had been there, when he'd seen her walk across the bridge of boats only minutes before.

'So,' said the Duchessa when she saw the bag. 'You were one of the silver-divers. I'm glad the rumour of my largesse spread, though I hope I don't have to make it an annual custom. This is a special year, you know, with the Chiesa delle Grazie having been completed, along with twenty-five years of my reign. Go on, take it. You earned it.'

Lucien prised open the wet cord around the neck of the bag and saw the glint of silver inside.

'You know I can't take it home, don't you, Your Grace?' he said, confused.

'I don't mind where you keep it,' said the Duchessa, fixing him with her intense gaze. 'You shall have fifty times what is in that bag for the service you rendered me tonight. Let Rodolfo look after it for you,' she added, seeing that Lucien was about to protest.

'Now leave us,' she told her waiting-women.

Lucien had no time to feel nervous about being alone with her, because, as soon as he was, the door to the secret passage behind the Duchessa's peacock sconce swung out and Rodolfo stepped through.

'What has happened?' he asked, looking anxiously at Lucien, who stood naked apart from his towel, still holding the dripping bag. 'And what are you doing in Bellezza at this time of night?'

The Duchessa was looking at him too. 'Oh, do get in that bath before it goes cold! Look, there is a screen, you know. I must tell Rodolfo what happened.'

Lucien found the screen – a ridiculously elaborate

set of embroidered silk panels – and sank gratefully into the hot, scented water. He thought he would never get the smell of canal out of his nose or the taste out of his throat. He ducked his head under the water and soaped his hair. He stayed in the bath till it was nearly cold, having nothing to put on but the towel and desperately not wanting the Duchessa to offer him the loan of one of her dressing-gowns.

He listened to her and Rodolfo talking in fierce whispers and, when he put his head round the screen, saw that Rodolfo was pale with fright. His master saw him and strode over.

'You have saved Silvia and I am forever in your debt. So is all Bellezza, but the details must not be known.'

He stopped and looked at Lucien.

'Where are your clothes?'

'The women took them. And I'm not sure if I can get home – the book is damp. Look!'

Rodolfo looked thoughtful and took the book in his hands.

'I can do something about this,' he said. 'But you must tell me everything before you stravagate.'

He had run all the way from the Piazzetta and up through his own palazzo and was still wearing his black velvet cloak, which he now took off and wrapped round Lucien. Then he walked to the empty fireplace and set his firestone in it. Soon warmth began to fill the room.

The Duchessa got to her feet, rather stiffly and rang her little silver bell. 'Why don't you take him back to your side, Rodolfo? I can't stay here. I must go and rescue that poor child who impersonated me at the

Feast tonight. She must be petrified.'

Lucien understood at last. The Duchessa used a body double! And he saw from the expression on Rodolfo's face that he hadn't known about it until now either.

*

Arianna didn't know if she was more worried or furious. She hadn't been able to see Lucien surface after his impulsive dive. So she searched the canalside and later the Piazza Maddalena, but it was hard to find anyone in the crowds. In the end, she had to return home to her aunt, hoping that Lucien had managed to stravagate back to his home world before his parents got back. For now she must do what aunt Leonora always referred to as 'containing her soul in patience' – something Arianna was very bad at.

*

Simonetta walked across the Piazza on the arm of the Ambassador, as if in a dream. Cheering Bellezzans lined the short distance to the rose-coloured Ducal Palazzo and she managed to wave graciously to them, but inwardly she was quaking. Something must have gone wrong; the Duchessa's senior waiting-woman had been so specific about her duties and they should have ended half an hour ago.

How relieved she was to see that same waiting-woman inside the doorway of the Palazzo! The woman approached and firmly guided her away from the Ambassador.

'Excuse me, Excellency,' she said. 'Her Grace must have a few minutes to refresh herself before the feast.

Please await her in the reception hall.'

The Ambassador bowed. He didn't know that this was the waiting-woman who had been in the State mandola. He had given orders that whoever was with the Duchessa was to be dispatched, including the mandolier if necessary. Now he could hardly contain his excitement. It would not be long before the floating mandola and the bodies would be found and the assassin would be far away by now. Rinaldo di Chimici took a proffered goblet of wine and drank deep. To Bellezza, he made a mental toast, last city-state to join the Republic.

Lucien was relieved to find himself back on his bed. The clock said five and the house was quiet. His parents were not back. Anxiously he checked his clothes. He was back in what he had been wearing before he went to Bellezza this morning, apart from his boxers, which were still drying out somewhere in the Duchessa's Palazzo. He had given the merlino-blade and the bag of silver to Rodolfo to look after for him. The notebook was not much the worse for its immersion in the canal, though the colours on the cover had run a bit. Rodolfo had carried it over to the fireplace and dried it carefully in the warmth of the glowing red stone.

Anyway, it had got him back. He sniffed cautiously. No smell of canal, thank goodness. Carefully, he put the notebook on the bedside table and fell into a deep natural sleep.

The Duchessa swept down the marble staircase of the Palazzo, magnificent in her violet satin. She had diamonds in her ears and at her throat and was wearing a diamond tiara in her dark hair. A cheer went up from the guests at the feast, who were waiting for her arrival before moving into the dining hall. But her eyes sought out only one person, Rinaldo di Chimici.

She was rewarded by seeing him start and choke on his wine.

'Ambassador,' she called graciously in her unmistakable musical voice. 'Are you all right? We mustn't keep my guests waiting.'

Di Chimici approached her like a man who has not only seen a ghost but has been ordered to take it in to dinner. He had realized straightaway that this was the real Duchessa. Something had obviously gone wrong. But what? And did the Duchessa know about the planned assassination? As she glided beside him on their way into the dining-hall, the Ambassador knew he was in for several hours of exquisite torment.

And so did the Duchessa. All the terrors of the evening had been worth it to see the Reman Ambassador's discomfiture and she had no intention of letting him off lightly. If he had planned to have her killed by a paid murderer, she would make him suffer agonies of uncertainty and fear for his own life in the course of her celebration banquet.

'It was a lovely day. Thank you for encouraging us to go,' said Mum to Lucien when they got in about an hour later. 'Gracious, is that the time? You must be starving. Let me go and see what I can rustle up in the kitchen.'

'Certainly not,' said Dad. 'I bet Lucien and Tom have been living on snacks all day. Let's have takeaway Chinese.'

Lucien had rubbed the sleep from his eyes when he heard them opening the front door. He seemed destined to survive on catnaps today, but he knew he must go back to Bellezza as soon as he could reasonably get to bed.

Over the takeaway, his parents told him all about their day and fortunately did not ask much about his. They kept exchanging conspiratorial looks but Lucien was too tired to ask them what they were hatching. His eyelids drooped.

'Overdone it a bit today, have you?' asked Dad, gently taking Lucien's fork out of his hand.

'You could say that,' said Lucien, yawning. He had seen a fireworks display he had helped to make, dived into a stinking canal and recovered treasure and then foiled an assassination attempt on a country's absolute ruler. Out loud he said, 'Who'd have thought watching videos and eating popcorn could make you so sleepy?'

'Off up to bed with you then,' said Mum firmly. 'We want you fresh tomorrow. There's something we want to tell you.'

Normally, Lucien would have risen to such bait. But not tonight. He stumbled up to bed and groaned as his hand clasped the book. What wouldn't he give for a proper night's sleep!

An ordinary rowing-boat ploughed its way through the waters of the lagoon. It was rowed by a very good-looking young man, who carried one passenger, a plainly dressed woman, still handsome, though no longer young. She was obviously married, because she didn't wear a mask. She sat quietly, looking out towards the islands, as they came nearer to the colourful houses of Burlesca.

The boatman moored and offered to accompany his passenger but she refused. She let him help her out of the boat then, carrying her basket, set off for the only white house in town. The handsome boatman shrugged and went off in search of something to eat.

Paola Bellini came to the door, drying her hands on her apron, but they flew to her mouth when she saw who her visitor was.

'Can I come in, Mother?' said the woman in a low voice. 'There is something I must talk to you about.'

*

When Lucien materialized in Rodolfo's laboratory the morning after the Maddalena Feast, he was surprised by the warmth of his master's welcome. Lucien had expected him to be angry about his overnight stay, but the magician caught his apprentice in an affectionate hug, the first he had ever given him.

'You are all right?' Rodolfo asked, giving Lucien a long appraising look. 'Did you get into any trouble with your parents?'

'No, it was cool,' said Lucien, a bit embarrassed. They had not had long to talk the night before, because Rodolfo had been anxious to rejoin the Duchessa at the feast and make sure she was properly guarded. Now Lucien felt he should explain why he had stayed on in Bellezza.

'I know I shouldn't have taken the risk,' he said, 'but I wanted to see the fireworks.' It sounded childish and selfish as he said it.

'And what did you think of them?' asked Rodolfo, gravely.

'It was brilliant,' said Lucien. 'Even better than I had imagined. But I know I shouldn't have done it. I'm sorry.'

'Don't be sorry,' said Rodolfo. 'If you hadn't been here, Silvia would have been killed.' He shuddered. 'It might even be why you were sent here in the first place – why the talisman found its way to you rather than someone else.'

He drew the merlino-blade from his own belt and handed it solemnly to Lucien. Then he sat down beside him and, for the first time in Lucien's presence, made the hand of fortune. 'You see? By the power of the goddess, her consort and son, the circle of Silvia's life is unbroken.'

'Not really,' said Lucien, self-consciously hefting the dagger and remembering what it had been intended to do. 'Who is the goddess, and those others? And what does it have to do with me?'

'It's our old religion,' said Rodolfo, 'the one we had here before Christianity. All over the eastern part of the Middle Sea, people believed in a goddess and her consort.'

'He was a god too, presumably,' said Lucien.

'Yes, but not as powerful as her. Their son was more powerful than him too. Some believe that the consort originally *was* her son and it was only later, when incest became taboo, that a husband was invented for her and that is why he is such a shadowy figure. The son has always been almost as revered as his mother. When Christianity came along, all those pagan statues of the goddess and her son were allowed to stay. Only now they were supposed to be of Our Lady and the new Lord.'

He looked expectantly at Lucien.

'Sorry,' said Lucien. 'We're Church of England. I don't know much about well, your Lady – you know, Catholics.'

Rodolfo frowned. 'What is the Church of England? And what are Catholics?'

Lucien was surprised. 'You know, Henry the Eighth and all that. He wanted to marry Ann Boleyn and the Pope wouldn't let him, because he was already married, so he started his own church.'

It was Rodolfo's turn to look surprised. 'Doctor Dethridge never said anything about that. In our world your England, Anglia as we call it, has the same church as ourselves, ruled by the Pope.'

'Well,' said Lucien. 'In Doctor Dethridge's time it was a dangerous subject. After Henry died, and his son too, his daughter Mary had people killed for following the King's new kind of religion. And in Dethridge's time, Queen Elizabeth had people killed for believing in the other one, Catholicism.'

'Catholics is what you call the people who believe the old Christianity?'

'Yes. Roman Catholics, we say, because of the Pope in Rome, I suppose.'

'Fascinating,' said Rodolfo, musing. 'Here, the Pope is in Remora, the capital of the Republic. I must tell you some day about the founding of Remora by Remus, after he had defeated his brother Romulus. But now that we have found Doctor Dethridge again and he is a citizen of Talia, I must get him to tell me all about his England and its religion.'

'Anyway,' said Lucien. 'Go back to the goddess.'

'Lagooners are among the last people in the Middle Sea to cling on to their belief in her,' continued Rodolfo. 'They accepted Christianity because they had to. They build churches and go to Mass, as you've seen. But in their hearts they believe that it is the goddess who looks after them and after Bellezza too. That is why they have always been ruled by a woman, the Duchessa. They never really felt comfortable about a male god, or a male saviour, come to that. And least of all a male ruler.'

'They do seem almost to worship the Duchessa,' said Lucien, remembering the fanatical crowds last night and the infectious madness that had plunged him into the canal.

'They do,' said Rodolfo, simply. 'She is their idea of the goddess personified. That is why her wellbeing is so important to them.'

'So you don't think the assassin could have been a Bellezzan?' asked Lucien.

'I don't know; I haven't seen him yet,' said Rodolfo grimly. 'But if the people ever knew that you had saved the Duchessa's life, they would be sure that you were sent by the goddess. You would be a hero.'

'You said last night we mustn't let anyone know,' said Lucien. 'That's cool, I mean I didn't really think about what I was doing and I don't want to be a hero or anything. But don't you think people should know that someone wants to kill the Duchessa?'

'No one should know that it wasn't she who opened the church, or wasn't she, as I now suspect, who performed the Marriage with the Sea. Lagooners are deeply superstitious; they would believe that the prosperity of their city was in danger.'

'But somebody knew about the double,' said Lucien slowly. 'Or the assassin wouldn't have been aboard the mandola.'

'Precisely,' said Rodolfo. 'And I imagine Silvia's torturers are hard at work as we speak, finding out who that is.'

Chapter 12

Two Brothers

As it happened, the torturers were not needed. Guido Parola was ready to confess everything. From the moment that he had entered the State mandola, Parola had been a changed man. Brought face to face with the Duchessa, he knew he could not bring himself to kill her, not even for the silver which would cure his father. And Lucien's instinctive defence of the Duchessa had made him deeply ashamed. All his true Bellezzan feelings had resurfaced and he was ready to tell all. And, after that, to die.

Imagine his confusion when, after a day in which he was brought clean, soft bedding, ample warm water for washing and several excellent meals, the swishing of taffeta skirts and the glimpse of a silver mask announced the arrival in his cell of the Duchessa herself. Parola flung himself at her feet and begged forgiveness.

'Do get up,' she said coldly. 'No, do not offer me a corner of your mattress. As you see, my bodyguard has brought me a chair.'

She sat down, smoothing her full skirt, her well-muscled bodyguard standing behind the chair, and looked at the abject young man kneeling before her. He was very tall and had large dark brown eyes, unusually for a redhead.

'The Chief Inquisitor tells me that you are a Bellezzan,' she said.

'I am, Your Grace,' he said.

'And that you were willing to betray your city for money?'

Parola bowed his head and said nothing. He had no defence.

'What do you think is the appropriate punishment for such a crime?' asked the Duchessa.

'Death!' said the young man, looking up with eager, shining eyes. 'I deserve to die for what I tried to do to you, milady. The only remission I would ask is that you should hear my story and forgive me before I die. I am truly sorry.' And he wept, genuine tears of remorse.

Then he told her everything, the death of his mother, his brother's debauchery, his father's illness, his meeting with a schoolfriend, who just happened to know someone willing to pay good money to a man desperate enough to do anything.

'You were no more than an instrument,' said the Duchessa, more kindly. 'Just as much as that weapon you carried, you were guided by someone's hand.

Now, you have told the Inquisitor the name of the person who employed you.'

Parola nodded and would have spoken, but the Duchessa stopped him.

'We will not say his name out loud. I know who it was. Now, it may suit my purpose better not to have a public trial, in which you and he are accused and convicted. I prefer to judge and sentence you here and now.'

'Yes, milady,' whispered Parola, not doubting that his last hour had come and that the Duchessa's bodyguard would soon dispatch him with his sword. 'Only say you forgive me and let me send word to my father before I die. Then let me make my confession to a priest, before your sentence is carried out.'

'I do forgive you,' said the Duchessa, smiling slightly behind her mask. 'But it is not usual to go to confession before joining the Scuola Mandoliera. It's not like becoming a knight you know.'

Parola looked up, confused. 'You are releasing me, milady?'

'Not exactly,' said the Duchessa. 'I am retaining you in my service. You will train at the Scuola and become one of my mandoliers – you aren't over twenty-five, are you?'

Parola shook his head. 'I am nineteen,' he admitted.

'Then it's high time you had a respectable trade,' said the Duchessa. 'You can't go round knifing people for a living.'

Lucien's parents continued to behave mysteriously. Before going off to work, his dad gave him a wink as he hugged him and said, 'See you tonight.' The words and the hug were usual; the wink was not. His mother had an almost full day of lessons. But she said at breakfast, 'I'm going to be very busy today, Lucien, but we'll have a chance to talk at dinner.'

Talk about what, Lucien wondered, but he wasn't bothered about being left to his own devices. He needed time to himself, to think and to doze. His mother was out most of the day but he wasn't tempted to return to Bellezza and see what was happening there at night.

He was beginning to feel uneasy about his nightly visits to the city. The situation there was getting more dangerous. It was only a matter of luck and the element of surprise that had made Lucien the hero of the assassination attempt and not one of the victims. He wondered what would have happened to his body here in his own world if he had been stabbed in Bellezza. Would Mum or Dad have come into his room and found him lying dead in his bed with blood all over the sheets?

His imaginings became more ghoulish. Suppose they had started a murder hunt in London? No killer would ever have been found and he would have become a statistic; just one of many unsolved murder cases. And what about his body in Bellezza? Would that have just disappeared? If the assassin's attempt had been successful, would anyone have even known he had died in the Duchessa's defence?

The questions were all unanswerable so Lucien fell into a deep sleep till lunchtime, dreaming of a trial in which the Bellezzan assassin, still unaccountably holding the merlino-dagger, stood in a very twenty-first century witness box, saying, 'You can't prove I killed him without a body.' The dagger dripped blood all over the courtroom floor and, in his dream, Lucien knew the blood was his.

In the north of the city was a small canal where fledgling mandoliers learned their skills. No visitors or tourists ever came there; it was a backwater in every sense. It was such a narrow waterway that the houses on either side were quite close to each other. Two of them were joined by a private bridge, linking their top floors; the houses belonged to Egidio and Fiorentino, Rodolfo's older brothers.

They were both still handsome men, although Egidio, at forty-five, was quite old for a Bellezzan. When they were at home, in one house or the other, or walking over the canal by the little bridge that linked them, the two brothers often amused themselves with watching the efforts of the newly enrolled mandoliers.

In their day, they had been the best mandoliers in Bellezza, as well as the best-looking. They had rowed the Barcone to the Marriage with the Sea and had made good money taking tourists up and down the Great Canal. At twenty-five, like all other mandoliers, they had been generously pensioned by the Duchessa. For that, if for nothing else, they would have always been grateful to her.

Egidio had started a shop which sold paper and notebooks and pencils, all decorated with the swirly marbled designs that also covered Lucien's talisman. As years went by and Rodolfo set up his laboratory in the palazzo next to the Duchessa's, his designs and skills had improved Egidio's stock until it was the envy of all Europa. His shop, in a small calle near the cathedral, was always busy with tourists.

Fiorentino had a flair for cooking and, with his money from the Duchessa, he opened a café on the Piazza Maddalena. It started modestly but soon expanded; he bought the shops on either side of it and it was soon a flourishing and expensive restaurant. 'Fiorentino's' of Bellezza became a byword for fine cooking in the Middle Sea. Both brothers had prospered since they ended their mandoliering days but neither had married. It seemed that no woman held any attraction for someone who had once enjoyed the favour of Silvia, the Duchessa. They were still her devoted servants, prepared to do anything she asked. And if they were jealous of their little brother, who had scarcely left her side for nearly a score of years, they never showed it.

On this day, the two brothers were enjoying a glass of wine on the terrace of Egidio's house. They had been watching a young novice learning how to turn his mandola in mid-canal, while talking knowledgeably to a boat-load of 'tourists', who were in fact examiners at the Scuola. For every mandolier had to sit exams in Bellezzan history, music, literature and art, as well as pass a proficiency test on his water-skills.

This particular specimen, though undeniably handsome, was clearly finding his task difficult. The brothers slapped their thighs and whooped with laughter as the youth lost his oar and had to be paddled back to retrieve it by his cargo of examiners. Then Fiorentino spotted another mandola, much more expertly sculled, cutting through the canal and stopping at Egidio's landing stage.

'*Dia!*' said Fiorentino. 'It's Silvia!'

It wasn't her State mandola, just a black one, but with a curtained cabin, denoting a person of importance. The brothers didn't wait to see who was in it; they ran down the stairs like the young men they had once been.

On the landing stage a tall red-headed young man was handing out a well-dressed masked woman. He was obviously nervous. The black panelled door to the landing stage swung inwards and he escorted the Duchessa inside, where she was affectionately greeted by the two distinguished-looking older men. The whole party returned to the terrace, where she accepted a glass of prosecco and a plate of pastries.

'This is Guido,' she said. 'I am enrolling him in the Scuola Mandoliera.'

'Isn't it a bit late?' asked Egidio. 'The new recruits have been practising for weeks.'

'They owe me a mandolier,' said the Duchessa calmly. 'Besides, Guido is a special case. He tried to kill me.'

Guido hung his head and felt the blood rising to his cheeks. He wished she wouldn't talk like this but accepted it as part of his punishment. Both brothers had involuntarily put their hands to the hilts of the merlino-daggers they carried in their belts. Guido had noticed them straightaway, being something of an expert, and admired the workmanship.

'Don't be silly, boys,' said the Duchessa, looking at the serious frowns on the brothers' foreheads. 'He's a reformed character. The point is, I want him to lie low for a while. Let's say, it suits my purposes. He will be inconspicuous in the Scuola – you must agree he looks the part.'

There was no chance of Guido's regaining his composure while all three gazed at him, assessing his looks. He blushed to the roots of his red hair, which was unusual enough in Talia to ensure he was considered handsome, even without his slim figure and his regular features.

'Now, now, Fiorentino, don't be jealous. You know I've given all that up,' laughed the Duchessa. 'Besides, I do not find attempted murder an aphrodisiac.'

'What do you want of us?' asked Egidio simply.

'To give him a home under your roof,' replied the Duchessa. 'Yours or Fiorentino's. And to teach him the rudiments of mandoliering, so that he doesn't fall behind in his studies. And to keep him from all unwanted attention, especially from the Reman quarter.'

'For you, Silvia, if this is what you really want, you know we will do it,' said Egidio seriously.

'Now, let me have another of those cakes,' said Silvia. 'Do they come from your restaurant, Fiorentino?'

'Not directly,' he said. 'I get them made for me by a fellow on Burlesca – Bellini, I think he's called.'

'How interesting,' said the Duchessa thoughtfully, delicately licking the sugar from her fingertips. 'I thought they tasted familiar.'

*

Arianna was bursting to find out what had happened to Lucien the night before. She was agog during his description of the assassination attempt. Much as she had told herself she hated the Duchessa, she was horrified at the idea of the man with the merlino-blade.

'And she was in the mandola all the time?' she asked. 'That was a double on the bridge? I knew there was something fishy about the way everyone says she still looks as young as ever.'

Her eyes nearly popped out of her head when Lucien showed her the merlino-blade.

'You have the luck of the Lady!' she said enviously, sliding the blade appreciatively out of its sheath.

'You call it lucky to come face to face with a murderer?' said Lucien, smiling.

When Lucien had been over every detail of the assassination attempt several times, he astounded her again with developments in his other life.

'What?' she said in disbelief. 'They're bringing you to Bellezza?'

'Well, not Bellezza,' said Lucien. 'You know that it's called Venice in my world – at least it is by English people.'

His parents had been so pleased with their surprise. They obviously thought he would be delighted and he was. They were all going to Venice for a week and very soon. Lucien had a hospital appointment in late August and they needed to be back for that.

'I spoke to Doctor Kennedy,' Mum had said, 'and she seems to think you're quite strong enough to go, so we've booked the tickets.'

'Great!' Lucien had said. He couldn't wait to see the magical city in his own world and see in what ways it was like the Bellezza he now knew so well.

But he hadn't told Rodolfo yet. Somehow, he didn't think that he would be able to get back to Bellezza while he was out of his usual setting. And he didn't know whether he was going to be needed. Rodolfo obviously thought things were getting more dangerous too, and had asked Lucien always to return to the Palazzo before stravagating home.

'You're very quiet about it,' Arianna said. 'I would love to travel to another country, like your Anglia.'

'Perhaps you will one day,' said Lucien. 'Or to another world. Maybe you'll become a Stravagante and travel to mine. I don't see why Stravaganti should all be men.'

Arianna's eyes shone. 'You're right! It doesn't look as if I'll ever be a mandolier now, but I bet I could be a Stravagante. Maybe I'll ask Signor Rodolfo about it.'

They were sitting in the café near the boarded-up theatre, where they had drunk hot chocolate the day that Lucien had turned up in Bellezza. The man behind the bar had been watching them rather closely. When they had finished their drinks and left, he beckoned to a man eating apricot tart in the corner. He finished his mouthful, picked up his blue cloak and went to talk to his new friend at the bar.

*

Rinaldo di Chimici was suffering the torments of the damned. He had seen nothing of the young assassin since the night of the Maddalena Feast. Had he run away, with the half of his fee which he had already been given? The Duchessa's manner to the Ambassador had not changed, which seemed to indicate that there had been no attempt on her life, but she was such a slippery and subtle opponent that he couldn't be sure.

What was so agonizing was that he just didn't know what had happened and had no way of finding out. In the end he decided to take Enrico into his confidence.

The spy was flattered. It had taken him much time and effort to win the Ambassador's trust and now he felt puffed up with his success. Secretly, he felt nothing but contempt for di Chimici's clumsy attempt to eliminate the Duchessa. Enrico knew at least half a dozen men who would have done the job properly. He would have done it himself, for the right money.

Still, he was thrilled to think it had been his information that had enabled the assassination plan and he quickly decided to pass on something else he had just found out.

'There's another way of getting at her ladyship, Excellency,' he said now.

Di Chimici gestured at him to continue.

'You know the boy, Signor Rodolfo's apprentice?'

The Ambassador nodded. 'Go on.'

'Well, the Senator seems very fond of the boy. And we know her ladyship is very fond of the Senator, don't we?'

Enrico leered in a manner which caused di Chimici to shudder. In his way, he was quite fastidious and the idea of having to use this odious little man's information repelled him. But he could not afford to be proud. He nodded.

'So don't you think the lady would be upset if her fancy-man's favourite was under the death penalty?'

'Undoubtedly,' said di Chimici, 'but how could you arrange that?'

Enrico tapped the side of his nose. 'Trust me. I have a plan. We know that the boy doesn't come from Padavia. Well, he obviously doesn't come from Bellezza either.'

'What does that matter?' said di Chimici, who had a good idea that Lucien didn't come from anywhere Enrico would have heard of.

'You don't know about the forbidden day?' asked Enrico. 'That boy was in Bellezza the day after the Marriage with the Sea. I have a witness. If he wasn't born on Bellezza, then his life is forfeit.'

*

Now that she knew he was safe and the excitement over the assassination attempt had passed, Arianna decided that she really was very cross with Lucien.

'You know I was worried sick about you?' she said as they walked back to Rodolfo's. 'And all the time you were having adventures. I bet you're a hero to the Duchessa and you've got all that silver. And a merlino-blade,' she added, looking with envy at the assassin's dagger in his belt. 'While I had to go home on my own and tell my aunt you left me at the door.'

'I couldn't help it,' Lucien said, annoyed. 'I seemed to go a bit mad at the end of the fireworks, and when I found myself in her mandola, there was no time to think. I wasn't having fun, I can tell you.'

It was the closest they had ever got to a row, and they made the rest of their journey in silence.

*

Guido Parola moved his things into Egidio's house, the Duchessa having arranged a nurse for his father. He was relieved; he felt safe here. He was most unlikely to bump into the Reman Ambassador at the Scuola Mandoliera or in the brothers' houses overlooking the canaletto. He had been enrolled in the Scuola that day with Egidio and Fiorentino standing as his sponsors. Now they were like two extra godfathers. There had been one awkward moment after the Duchessa had gone, when Egidio had made it clear to the young man exactly what would be done to him if he should ever raise his hand against her again. But since then they had started to become friends.

And now he was to have his first lesson on the water, before the light failed.

'You're a natural!' said Fiorentino after an hour in his own mandola, with Guido sculling. 'Of course, you'll have to learn all the patter, but I think we'll make a mandolier of you yet.'

Egidio nodded. 'And now we'll all go and have dinner at your restaurant, brother.'

*

Rodolfo now kept one of his mirrors permanently fixed on Montemurato. It was focused on William Dethridge and followed him as he moved around the walled city. Ever since the attempt on Silvia's life, Rodolfo had been sick with worry for her safety and he thought that the old Stravagante might have some useful ideas. But Dethridge was terrified that, having escaped death for witchcraft in his own world, he might fall foul of the same prejudices in Talia. Now that he could no longer be given away by his absence of shadow, he seemed determined to act as unobtrusively as possible.

But before he and Lucien had left Montemurato, Rodolfo had given William Dethridge a hand mirror. The Elizabethan had accepted it reluctantly, but it was hardly an incriminating object if it should be found among his belongings, even if an unlikely one for an old man with no reason to be vain. Now, Rodolfo was trying to make contact with Dethridge.

He stood gazing into the Montemurato glass, murmuring formulae until the face of William Dethridge swam into view. Its expression was one of pure terror.

'Master Rudolphe,' gasped the old man. 'Thanke godnesse. You muste holpe mee!'

'What is the matter?' asked Rodolfo, alarmed by Dethridge's obvious fear.

'They are building a bone-fire,' he said. 'And I feare that it is for mee!'

Chapter 13

A Death Sentence

The trip to Venice was coming closer; Lucien had only a few days to adjust his mind to it and to prepare Rodolfo for his likely absence from Bellezza. He was genuinely excited at the prospect of seeing the real city and, if he were honest with himself, he had to admit that he wouldn't mind a rest from his nightly adventures. Whenever he did sleep during the day, without stravagating, he was haunted by nightmares about the man with the dagger on the Duchessa's mandola.

He couldn't believe it when Rodolfo told him that the assassin had been set free and was now in the Scuola Mandoliera.

'But why? Isn't he very dangerous?'

'Not any more,' said Rodolfo. 'Silvia has him eating out of her hand.'

'But isn't he going to be punished? And what about whoever hired him? It must have been the di Chimici, mustn't it?' Lucien was beginning to feel that his one act of heroism, albeit accidental, was being allowed to fizzle out.

'I think Parola *is* being punished,' said Rodolfo. 'If he is genuinely sorry, what could be worse than living with his own treachery? As for di Chimici, Silvia was going to have a show trial but I convinced her that there are more subtle ways of getting revenge on one's enemies. And she did agree that the people mustn't know about the doubles.'

'So you don't think she's in any danger now?' asked Lucien.

'I wouldn't say that,' said Rodolfo grimly, 'but perhaps not immediately.'

'The thing is,' said Lucien, 'after today, I don't think I'm going to be able to get to Bellezza for a while. My parents are taking me on holiday abroad. I won't be able to get to Talia unless I leave from England, will I?'

Rodolfo looked at him closely. 'So you are getting better in your own world?' he asked.

'I seem to be,' said Lucien.

'And where are they taking you?'

'To Venice,' said Lucien.

Rodolfo smiled. 'So you'll be in Bellezza all the time, in a manner of speaking. And when you come back, you can tell me if our city is still as beautiful in your time.'

*

William Dethridge left his horse on the mainland and

took the boat to Bellezza. He had left Montemurato in the middle of the night, still fearful that his life was at risk. Now he was going to stay with Maister Rudolphe, where he felt he would be more safe. Even after a year and a half, he still couldn't separate the Talia of this dimension from the Italy of his.

In Italy, as in Elizabeth's England, there was a hatred and distrust of anything magical. No matter that the Queen had her own astrologer, who had chosen her coronation day in accordance with the stars. Now the unexplained equalled the unlawful and anyone, like himself, who had a connection with Italy, was immediately under suspicion. That was where the great occult masters lived – something common to the countries in both dimensions.

Dethridge trusted Rodolfo and believed him to be the most powerful Stravagante in Talia. If Talia was turning away from magic, under the di Chimici, then association with Rodolfo might well be dangerous, but Dethridge preferred trusting in the magician's powers to staying alone in the walled city. Everywhere he went he heard the word 'strega', a word that he knew meant 'witch', as well as a strong drink. And in the centre of the town square a bonfire was being built.

The fear of death by burning was strong upon him since he had escaped the sentence in his own world. And regaining his shadow and being permanently stranded in Talia had further helped to unhinge his mind. He could not bear to think of the wife and children he would not see again, and he could not believe that he was safe from persecution. When he saw the fire being prepared, he immediately assumed that someone in Montemurato knew what he was – or what he had been.

Now, as dawn broke and the boat approached the shining silver city, he breathed easily for the first time in days. It was hard to believe that somewhere so beautiful could also be dangerous.

*

Enrico was consolidating his friendship with Giuseppe, the Duchessa's spy, over a glass or two of his favourite liqueur. The two men had met on several occasions since that first night when their assignments had led them both to Leonora Gasparini's doorway and they had pooled information. Now, the two men knocked back Strega in the little bar near the boarded-up theatre. As the evening wore on, they became more friendly with one another and with the normally morose man behind the bar.

'Ancora!' slurred Enrico. 'Have another one on me. And you too, my friend with the bottle. Have one yourself.'

No one in Bellezza ever said things like: 'Don't you think you've had enough?' There were no cars for drunken citizens to drive, not even any horse-carts. So they were no danger to anyone but themselves. The worse that could happen to an inebriated Bellezzan was to fall into the canal and, if he did, nine times out of ten the shock of the cold water was enough to sober him up.

Indeed, such things had happened to Enrico in the past. Now, however, he was not as drunk as he seemed. He needed information that only Giuseppe and the barman could provide and he was becoming too good a spy to miss the opportunity.

'You know that lad we were discussing the other day,' he now said to the landlord, judging the moment had come. 'The one you said was here on the Giornata Vietata,' lowering his voice.

'What about him?' said the landlord, looking nervously round the bar. This was dangerous talk.

'Well, you remember that girl he was with, both times?'

'The pretty one?' said the landlord. 'Yes, I know her. Lives with her aunt near San Sulien.'

Enrico looked triumphantly at his new friend. This was going to be easier than he thought. 'You see, Beppe? It is the same one. The one you followed to the islands. Now, tell our friend here what you found out.'

'She's only living with her aunt for the summer,' said Giuseppe. 'She was born on Torrone. Her parents still live there.'

'You see?' said Enrico in a whisper. 'Another traitor! That's both of them in the city on the forbidden day!'

The landlord was uneasy. A boy was one thing; that one was almost a man. But a soft young girl, and one as pretty as that – it didn't bear thinking of.

'You'd both be willing to testify before the Council, wouldn't you?' asked Enrico and he took out his purse to pay for the evening's drinks. Both men saw that it was heavy with silver. 'Same terms as with the boy,' he said to the landlord. 'Half now and half after you've given evidence.'

The landlord licked his lips. After all, it wasn't right to let the young people get away with such blasphemy. Everyone in Bellezza knew the rule about the forbidden day. He just nodded slightly, but that was enough for Enrico.

'Ancora!' he called at the top of his voice. He now had two witnesses who would seal the fate of Rodolfo's apprentice and his little girlfriend. And the best part was that the Duchessa, presiding over the Council, would have to pronounce their death sentences herself. The only way they could be reprieved would be if Bellezza joined the Republic. Then the Federal law would outweigh Bellezza's own poxy little rules.

So the Duchessa's greatest friend and admirer would be turned to the di Chimici side, persuading her to sign the treaty so the boy could be saved. And the boy would be persuading Rodolfo, because of the girl. Neat. Absolutely foolproof. Enrico tossed off another glass; there was no need to keep a cool head now. He would tell Giuliana she could order her trousseau tomorrow.

*

Arianna was feeling sad. There were only a few days left when she could spend her afternoons with Lucien and now that they had quarrelled, she didn't know if they would have even those. Of course he would only be away for a week, but she knew that everything would be different when he got back. The summer would be coming to an end and she would have to go back to her life on Torrone.

She didn't know how she was going to bear it. The pressure would begin to build up on her to marry once she was sixteen and she didn't know who in Talia could suit her after her friendship with the black-haired boy from another world.

She heaved a big sigh, then shook herself. This was not the Bellezzan way. Live for the moment. Enjoy the day. When Lucien arrived at the fountain, Arianna was waiting for him with the usual sparkle in her eyes and no hint of her previous dejection. She was so relieved to see him that she didn't refer to their quarrel.

'We are going somewhere different today,' she said straightaway and led him out of the garden and through the maze of calles down to a spot on the Great Canal where they could catch a ferry. The ferries were cheaper than travelling by mandola, just as they were in the Venice of Lucien's world. They criss-crossed the Great Canal like moving bridges.

And once they were across, Lucien and Arianna did not stop to explore the quarter on the far side of the Great Canal. They walked quickly through it and found themselves walking alongside another canal and crossing a stone bridge. On the other side was a boatyard where half a dozen black mandolas were drawn up out of the water.

'What is this place?' asked Lucien.

'The Squero di Florio e Lauro,' said Arianna. 'They were two saints. See – that big church over there is dedicated to them.'

'Who were they?' asked Lucien. He didn't know all that many saints and he certainly hadn't heard of these two.

'Oh, just some pair of twins,' said Arianna airily. 'They are supposed to have saved the island from invaders by praying. But some people think they were the Great Twins – you know, the Gemelli who are in the stars.'

'And are they the patron saints, or gods, of mandolas?' asked Lucien, who was getting used to the Bellezzans' belt-and-braces approach to religion.

Arianna shrugged. 'I don't think so. The Squero is just named after them because it's near the church.'

The mandolas were having their keels scraped and re-caulked. But behind them Lucien spotted a new mandola being built. It was the most beautiful vessel of them all. It was black, like all of them, but there was something extra graceful in its clean lines. Lucien was seized with a desire to stand on its stern and take it through the Bellezzan waterways. He turned and saw that Arianna had the identical expression. She grinned at him and he smiled back. Who knew? Maybe one day he would have a mandola in Bellezza, that one or one very like it.

*

When Lucien turned up for his last morning of lessons with Rodolfo before his trip to Venice, he found to his surprise William Dethridge sitting in an armchair.

'Gretinges, yonge Lucian,' said the old man. 'Thou didst not thinke to finde mee here?'

'No,' said Lucien, 'but I am pleased to see you.' Slightly awkwardly, he shook Dethridge's hand.

'Youre apprentiss hath godly maneres,' the old man said approvingly to Rodolfo, who was over by his magic mirrors.

Rodolfo turned and smiled. Then he bowed.

'It is an honour to me to have two Stravaganti from the other world in my laboratory,' he said.

'Nay,' said Dethridge. 'I am that noe more. Just a naturall philosophere now.'

'Has it occurred to you that you could go back as a Stravagante from this world?' asked Rodolfo.

Dethridge paled. 'I wolde not goe backe to that terrabyl worlde where they wolde burne mee.'

'No,' said Rodolfo, soothingly. 'As a Stravagante from this side, you would find yourself in the future of your old world. You would be in Luciano's time, a visitor to the twenty-first century. All you need is a talisman which originated from that world. And I suppose you still have the copper dish?'

Dethridge pulled it out of his jerkin. Such an ordinary object to have started the whole business of stravagation, thought Lucien. Now the Elizabethan was looking at it as if it were the most precious thing he had ever seen.

'I thanke ye, Maister Rudolphe. Ye have given me hope of escape if thinges goe not wele for mee hir. They doe not burn wyches in yonge Lucian's time?'

'No,' said Lucien. 'I've seen people who call themselves witches on daytime TV.'

The two men looked at him as if he spoke of arcane mysteries.

'But never mind that now,' said Rodolfo. 'I think I have found the reason for your fears in Montemurato, Dottore.'

He beckoned them over to the mirrors and showed them the one trained on the city of twelve towers. It was showing the bonfire in the main square. William Dethridge trembled at the sight of it. As they watched, tiny people were heaving what looked like a straw-stuffed scarecrow up to the top of the pile of brushwood.

Lucien understood. 'It's a guy!' he said. 'They're going to burn a guy, Doctor Dethridge, not a person. You know, just as we do in England on Guy Fawkes Night. "Remember, remember, the fifth of November" and then we have the fireworks – though they're nothing like as good as Rodolfo's.'

He looked up and saw two blank expressions. Lucien's knowledge of history was really being tested by all this stravagation. 'I suppose Guy Fawkes hadn't happened when you left England,' he said to Dethridge. 'He tried to blow up the Houses of Parliament. I think it was a Catholic plot.'

Dethridge was obviously amazed.

'Ah, yes, Catholics,' said Rodolfo. 'I wanted to talk to you about them, Dottore. But to return to Montemurato, the figure on the bonfire is indeed that of a witch as the Dottore surmised. It is a harmless festival – the Festa della Strega – always held in the walled city at this time of year. It is connected with a story of a witch, a 'strega' who flew over the walls a hundred years ago and brought a curse on the city. They keep the curse at bay by 'burning the witch' once a year and drinking a lot of the liqueur called Strega too. You must have moved to Montemurato shortly after the last Festa, Dottore. That's why you haven't come across it before.'

Dethridge relaxed. 'So ye doe not burn peple for magicke in Talia?'

Rodolfo did not answer straightaway. He obviously did not want to alarm the old man. 'We used to,' he said at last. 'And then things got better. There is so much of what you call magic in your world and what we call science in Talia. But the di Chimici have been stirring up fear and hatred against the kind of thing I do here. I think it will not be long before they start to persecute the Stravaganti, if only to wrest their secrets from them. But for now, you have nothing to be afraid of.'

'Come on – we'll miss the plane,' said Dad, as Mum checked for the umpteenth time on passports, tickets and money. Lucien havered for a long time about whether to take the notebook, but it didn't feel safe to leave it behind. He liked to have it with him.

At last, they were on their way to the airport. Lucien spent most of the flight dozing. He had had a busy day in Bellezza the night before, studying stravagation principles with two masters, one from each side, and spending his last afternoon with Arianna exploring the south of the city, before heading back to the laboratory to get home for an early start in his own world.

They landed at a much smaller airport than Heathrow and, using Mum's guidebook, went into Venice by a variety of means. As their bus travelled across the causeway, Lucien thought of his boat-rides with Rodolfo when they went to Montemurato. The causeway made travel to the city so much easier.

'Now we get a vaporetto!' said Mum triumphantly. She had done her homework and led them to a landing stage to catch the number 82. 'It will take us all the way down the Grand Canal to the Piazza San Marco,' she said confidently. And it did.

Lucien could not volunteer a word for the whole

water journey. His heart was in his mouth. This was, and was not, his city. The canal was so busy with vaporetti, barges and motorboats it took a while to notice the gondolas. But there they were, black and sleek. If Lucien concentrated on them alone, it seemed as if he really were in Bellezza. Except that most of the gondoliers were much too old and fat to please the Duchessa. It made Lucien laugh out loud.

'What's so funny, Lucien?' asked Dad.

Lucien just gave a big grin.

His parents exchanged contented looks. They didn't know what he was laughing about but they could see the happiness radiating out from him.

Lucien could see his shadow on the floorboards of the vaporetto and it filled him with joy.

The knock on the door was loud and urgent. The maid answered it and was roughly elbowed aside. The two city guards pushed past her and out into the water-garden, where Leonora sat attempting to teach her niece how to embroider a border of strawberry leaves. Arianna was almost relieved to see them, until one said, 'We have a warrant for the arrest of Arianna Gasparini on a charge of treason.'

Leonora dropped her frame. 'What nonsense is this?' she demanded. 'My niece is not yet sixteen. How could she be any threat to the dukedom?'

'By flouting one of its most ancient laws,' said the guard sternly. 'There is evidence that she was in the city on the Giornata Vietata and that she is not a citizen of Bellezza.'

Aunt Leonora coloured and her hand flew to her mouth. But Arianna stood immobile. She had always known of the risk, when she decided to hide in the Maddalena three months before. Now she knew she must face the consequences of her action.

*

Two different guards were hammering on the door of Rodolfo's laboratory.

'Open! In the name of the Bellezza City Watch! We have an arrest warrant!'

They were about to kick down the door when Rodolfo let them in. They looked round the room, expecting a boy, and found only a cowering old man.

'Where is the boy?' demanded the senior guard. 'We have a warrant for the arrest of one Luciano, surname unknown, on a charge of treason.'

'Yonge Lucian!' said the old man, uncurling from the armchair. 'What treasoun colde sich a yongling doe? Ye are mis-taken.'

'There is no mistake, old man,' said the second guard. 'Senator, you are in charge of the youngster?'

'He is my apprentice, yes,' agreed Rodolfo.

'Then where is he? Shouldn't he be here at his lessons?'

'He is somewhere in the city,' said Rodolfo, almost truthfully. 'Show me the warrant.'

He read the scrap of vellum and his heart sank when he saw the words 'Giornata Vietata', but he stayed outwardly calm.

'We do not have lessons in the afternoon,' he said, handing back the warrant. 'You cannot wait here.'

'Yes we can,' said the first guard.

'In that case, my friend and I shall go out,' said Rodolfo calmly.

'You can't do that,' said the second guard.

'Oh,' said Rodolfo, raising an eyebrow. 'Do you have a warrant for my arrest too? And for that of this eminent Anglian Dottore, Gugliemo Crinamorte?'

Dethridge gave the Senator a quizzical look, but stood up and walked to the door with him.

'Alfredo,' said Rodolfo to his manservant, who was just behind the door. 'Please take care of my guests. They will be here some time, so see they have everything they need. After you, Dottore.'

And the two Stravaganti swept out of the room.

It wasn't till they got to the bottom of the stairs that Rodolfo said, 'Quick, into my mandola. I'll scull us. We need to find Silvia as soon as possible. Thank God the boy is not in Talia.'

The Mulhollands were staying in a little hotel on the Calle Specchieri. The lift was so tiny that only three people could fit in it together. So the family went up in it while a red-jacketed bellboy ran up the stairs with their bags. Their rooms were next to one another on the third floor. Dad gave the bellboy a huge tip.

The boy was back a few minutes later bearing a tray with three slim glasses and a bottle in an ice-bucket. Lucien was in his parents' room, opening their shutters to see what they had a view of.

'I didn't order anything,' said Dad. 'There must be some mistake.'

'*Offerto dalla casa*,' said the bellboy, grinning.

‘It’s prosecco,’ said Lucien. ‘It’s a bit like champagne. And I think he said it is on the house.’

‘The ’ouse, *sì*,’ said the bellboy. ‘*Salute*!’

And he was gone. Dad shrugged and opened the bottle with a pop. He poured three glasses of the cold wine and handed the smallest to Lucien.

‘I can see you’re going to be very useful here. Your very good health!’

‘Cheers!’ said Lucien.

In Talia the door slammed in one of the Duchessa’s dungeons. Arianna waited until the guards’ footsteps had faded away before she flung herself on a heap of straw and burst into tears.

Chapter 14

The Bridge of Sighs

The Mulhollands were up early for their first morning in Venice, determined to beat the crowds in the Piazza San Marco. They were almost first in the queue for the Basilica and spent some time in its shadowy interior. Lucien was not as bowled over by the mosaics as his parents were. They seemed garish to him in gold, used as he was to the cool silver finish of the mosaics in Bellezza's Basilica of the Maddalena.

He soon retreated up the steep precarious stairs to the museum, with its gilded bronze horses, and stepped out on to the loggia with the copies, and looked out over the square from what had been Arianna's hiding-place in Bellezza. It was breathtaking. The sky was an incredible postcard blue, swirled with sudden flights of pigeons over the square and wheeling white gulls out over the lagoon. Elegant black gondolas bobbed on the water along the Piazzetta and the Saint and the winged lion stood on their tall columns guarding the city.

And yet. Lucien could no longer think of this as the real city and Bellezza as the alternative. It was stunningly beautiful and a great deal cleaner than the Talian city, but to Lucien it was like a painting in a gallery compared with its subject. It was hard to believe that the water was really moving, the birds flying and the tourists milling around the square.

He rejoined his parents in the doorway of the cathedral. His mother had her guidebook in her hand. 'That was lovely. Now let's go and see the Doge's Palace.'

They set off towards the water, threading their way between other tourists and the pigeons underfoot, avoiding the stalls with their gaudy jesters' hats and gold-sprayed plastic gondolas. The rose-coloured palace along the side of the Piazzetta was attracting its own share of visitors and a queue was forming.

The high spot of the tour was walking through the covered Bridge of Sighs to the Doge's dungeons, following the route of the despairing condemned prisoners. People were queuing to get through. But ever since they had entered the palace, Lucien had been feeling uneasy. The State rooms were all so dark and gloomy with their panelled wood and huge paintings grimed with age. Even the Doge's private apartments were nothing like the Duchessa's. There was no Glass Room, and nowhere a room like the one with the peacock sconce and the secret passage. In fact, Lucien had been able to see from outside that there was no palazzo corresponding to Rodolfo's. The differences between the two cities were giving him a headache.

But his parents were already lining up for the Bridge of Sighs, so he tagged along. Half-way across the bridge the pressure inside Lucien's skull became unbearable but strangers had interposed between him and his parents. He was borne along by the crowd. On the other side of the bridge were the tiny cells. They were now filled with T-shirted and shorted visitors ghoulishly imagining the previous inhabitants.

Lucien didn't know what was happening to him. It wasn't like being ill before. He had difficulty breathing and his head pounded. He was propelled into one of the cells and immediately thought he was going to be sick. A feeling of dread and terror had hold of him. And he had a strong sense of someone else's fear, someone who had been incarcerated here before a horrible death.

'Whoa there!' said an American. 'What's with the kid? Looks like he's going to pass out.'

That brought Mum and Dad to Lucien's side in a flash and soon there was a flurry of people saying, 'Stand back' and 'Give him air' like extras in a film. His parents got Lucien back across to the other side of the bridge. The further away they were from the dungeons, the better he felt.

'I'm OK, really,' he said to his parents, who were muttering about doctors.

'It's the atmosphere in that place,' said the American, who had caught Lucien just as he was about to lose consciousness and come with them across the bridge. 'Hundreds of men went from there to their deaths. Something like that's pretty well bound to leave its mark. Your boy's just more sensitive than most, I'd say.'

The young woman took a boat to Burlesca, with a heart as full as her purse. There were some in her family who had doubted that Enrico would ever name the day; they had been engaged rather a long time. But now, with her money from the Duchessa and the extra silver that her fiancé had given her, she was in a position to order her wedding-dress. And where in the lagoon would you go for white lace if not Burlesca?

There was one old woman whose work was so light and delicate that her fame had spread beyond her island. Paola Bellini might charge more than the other lacemakers of Burlesca, but then she was the best. Giuliana's friends had told her how to find the lacemaker. 'Look for the white house,' they said. 'It's the only one.'

*

Rodolfo sculled Dethridge swiftly, by the backwaters, to a convent in the north of the city where the Duchessa was presenting a gift of silver for the orphan girls in their care. As she came out, her eyes widened when she saw him at the stern of his own vessel. In a moment, she had dismissed her own mandolier and stepped instead into the Senator's craft. She looked curiously at the white-haired man already seated in the cabin. He doffed his hat and introduced himself as Gugliemo Crinamorte, though his tongue stumbled over the name.

Rodolfo took the mandola into a side canal and tied it to a pole. He jumped down into the cabin.

'Why all the mystery?' asked the Duchessa. 'And who is your companion?' But the smile died on her lips when she saw Rodolfo's expression.

'It's not often that I tell you something is a matter of life and death,' said Rodolfo. 'But today that is exactly the case. Did you know that a warrant has gone out for a foreigner seen in the city on the Giornata Vietata?'

The Duchessa nodded. 'Yes, I signed it this morning. Unusual, isn't it? I suppose it will turn out to be a misunderstanding.'

'I hope so,' said Rodolfo. 'Do you know who it was for?'

'No,' said the Duchessa. 'You know how many papers I have to sign every day. I didn't look at the name – just noted the offence.'

'It was for Luciano,' said Rodolfo, and was astonished by her reaction. All colour drained from her face and she clutched her throat as if unable to catch her breath.

'It is al righte,' said Dethridge, patting her other hand. 'The yonge mann was not at home. Hee is goon backe to his own worlde and will not bee backe hir for a while.'

'But, I've remembered something,' said the Duchessa, still in distress. 'I signed *two* warrants. I'm sure the Commander of the Watch said that one was for a girl. I didn't look at the name on that one either, but wasn't it the day after the Marriage with the Sea that Luciano first came to Bellezza? And wasn't that when he met that girl Arianna?'

Rodolfo was surprised. He had never told the Duchessa who it was that was teaching Lucien about the city. And he didn't know about Giuseppe and her own investigations.

'We must get back and I will go to see the girl's aunt, Leonora,' he said. 'It is a terrible fate to hang over so young a girl.'

'No, Rodolfo, you don't understand,' said the Duchessa bitterly. 'This is not just any girl. There is something I have to tell you.'

Lucien's parents took him to the coffee bar in the Doge's Palace. It was a place worthy of Bellezza, where you could watch gondolas skimming past the window while drinking your cappuccino. The American tourist had shown them where it was before going back up to finish his tour.

'Now, what was all that about?' asked Dad, when they were sitting down with their frothy coffees and hard little almond biscuits.

'I think it was just the heat and all those people,' said Lucien. 'I suddenly felt claustrophobic.' But he knew it had been more than that. For now, though, he had to convince his parents that he was completely well and didn't need to be taken straight back to the hotel.

Lucien wondered how long it would take, if he recovered from his cancer, for his parents to stop treating him like a piece of Merlino glass. Would they always have that anxious, haunted look every time he sneezed or yawned? And what about if he didn't get better? Lucien didn't usually mind being an only child but now he longed for a sibling to take from him the pressure of being the sole vessel for all that parental love. 'I know how Arianna feels,' he thought.

In a white house on the island of Burlesca an old woman was showing piles of lace to a young one. The bride-to-be was cheerful and chatty, choosing the material for her dress, her veil and various undergarments for her honeymoon, as well as lace edging for the linen already stacked in a cedar chest in her parents' house. The old lacemaker was curious as to how this admittedly pleasant and attractive but clearly uneducated girl could afford such a luxurious Corredo dalla Sposa.

But choosing and commissioning such a quantity of material took time and over the course of the day, Giuliana became communicative. Being so close to the achievement of her ambition made her careless and she dropped so many hints that it wasn't difficult for Paola to fill in the gaps. And she did not like the sound of that Enrico or his wealthy Chimici employer.

If Giuliana was surprised at the number of fittings the old woman thought would be necessary, she didn't show it. She was quite content to spend more days such as this, sitting among the foaming lace and chatting to a sympathetic person about her wedding.

*

Arianna wanted her mother. So far she had been

treated quite kindly, but not allowed any visitors. She was in an agony of uncertainty. Had Lucien been arrested too? Or had he stravagated back home before the guards came? At least he would have been with Rodolfo, who had more influence than Aunt Leonora.

The night in the cell was the worst. It was dark, much darker than her bedroom on Torrone or the one in Leonora's house, because there were no candles in the cell and no torches in the passageway. The straw of her bedding was clean at least, but all night she was kept awake by its rustling, terrified that it might be caused by rats.

And she had no hope of rescue. She had committed the crime of which she was accused. If there were witnesses, she was done for. Of course she had known what the penalty for discovery was. When she had laid her plans, they were all based on not getting caught. She had calculated that if she were taken on as a mandolier, by the time she was discovered to be a girl it would be that which would attract all the attention, not the day on which she had enrolled. And there was no penalty for pretending to be of different sex.

Now she had to face up to the truth. The invariable sentence for the crime she had committed was death by burning. No one in living memory had been convicted of defying the law on the Giornata Vietata, but there was no doubt in anyone's mind about what would happen to them if they had.

And there had been other burnings, for other crimes, such as treason, in Arianna's own short lifetime. She knew that the fires were built between the two pillars, the one with the Maddalena and the one with the winged ram, which stood guarding the entrance to the city from the water. The burnings were public events, Bellezzans believing that anyone who would betray the city deserved no mercy and no pity.

Arianna had never seen one; her parents would not have taken her to such a gruesome spectacle. But she had seen the remains of one such bonfire and she had a vivid imagination. Here in the Duchessa's cell, it was all too easy to picture the flames, the smell of her own flesh singeing, the agonizing pain. Arianna could not bear it – she screamed out loud. But there was no one to hear her.

And then an extraordinary thing happened. A vision of Lucien appeared in the cell, surrounded by strangely dressed people. He was looking straight at her, with such a stricken expression that Arianna forgot her own suffering. The image lasted only a moment before fading, but after that, she felt much calmer. Though she was in terrible danger, so was Lucien and he was completely innocent.

He had no knowledge of the law and had not known he was breaking it. But the truth would not save him, for who would believe it? Arianna felt responsible too. If she had not taken him away from where she found him, perhaps he would have returned to his own time and place sooner?

Thinking of how she might help him and planning to get a message to Rodolfo, Arianna fell into a troubled sleep.

Lucien was feeling much better. He had one further moment of queasiness, passing between the two pillars on the way to the vaporetto stop, but it soon passed. Looking back, he noticed that only tourists walked through that gap; all the locals skirted round the pillars, even if it involved a detour. Lucien made a mental note to look it up in Mum's guidebook.

'It says here,' she said, 'that you can buy a season-ticket on the vaporetti. Let's do that, David. Let's get three weekly seasons and go everywhere by water like true Venetians.'

Lucien smiled at her enthusiasm and she smiled back, her worries over his health temporarily suppressed. It was really good of them to bring him on this amazing holiday and he was determined to enjoy it to the full. He might be a bit old for holidays with his parents but, as an only child, he had always got on well with them and enjoyed their company

Now he stood on the San Marco landing stage, looking across at the huge domed church of the Salute, standing roughly where the Chiesa delle Grazie was in Talia. It was from here that the bridge of boats had taken the fake Duchessa over to the church, while the real one had been threatened by the assassin and Lucien had gone diving for treasure in the filthy canal.

The vaporetto came and they went the five stops to the Rialto, crossing back and forth over the canal. Venice was so much noisier than Bellezza that it was sometimes possible to forget about the Talian city for whole hours together. This was especially true on the Rialto, where cheap trinkets for tourists mingled with unaffordable gold jewellery.

The only thing here that reminded Lucien of Bellezza was the masks, shop after shop and stall after stall of them. Many of the Venetian masks were the kind that covered the whole face, to be held up before it on a gilded stick. But there were others that were more like the Duchessa's or those of other Bellezzan women Lucien had seen. These just surrounded the eyes and the bridge of the nose and in Venice were held in place at the back by elastic, though the ones in Bellezza were tied with velvet or satin ribbons.

'Would you like one?' asked Dad, seeing Lucien stare at the masks.

'Oh, no thanks, Dad. I mean I do want a mask, but I haven't seen one I really like yet.'

'There are enough of them, aren't there?' said Mum. 'I bet there are hundreds more Venetian masks used as ornaments in people's homes around the world than have ever been worn here at Carnival.'

'What's that one with the beaky nose that they have in all the shops?' asked Dad.

Mum consulted her book. 'It's the Plague Doctor mask. Apparently they had the plague very badly here in the sixteenth century and doctors wore the beaky mask to protect them from the germs.'

'But they didn't know about germs in the sixteenth century, did they?' said Dad and they started one of their meandering discussions that Lucien knew from long experience he could just tune out of. As they walked back towards San Marco through the back streets, he thought about the plague that had wiped out a third of all Bellezzans just before Arianna was born. Surely if the doctors had known how it was spread, it would not have claimed so many lives?

'I can't believe it!' Mum suddenly said loudly, as if she had found a germ herself. 'That's disgusting!'

Lucien looked where she was pointing. There in the

corner of a square was a McDonald's. His mother was practically foaming at the mouth. She was famously anti what she called the pollution of American chains in the most beautiful cities of Europe.

'Fancy a burger and chips, Lucien?' said Dad winking.

'Don't wind her up, Dad,' laughed Lucien. 'Perhaps we could grab a slice of pizza?'

When they had found a bar that sold pizza slices and focaccia sandwiches and cans of cold drink, they sat on the stone wall of the fountain in the middle of the square, eating their lunch and watching the passers-by, Lucien's mother wincing at the ones munching on burgers. Then they continued their walk, following the bright yellow signs with their confusing bent black arrows pointing the way back to the Piazza San Marco.

'Look, Lucien,' said Dad, stopping suddenly. 'Here's a shop that sells books like that one I gave you. You know, the one that got you interested in Venice in the first place.'

They went in. It was an Aladdin's cave of marbled paper and beautiful notebooks from pocket-size to the kind you'd need an executive desk for. The prices were astronomical. Dad was disappointed until Lucien found a pencil decorated with exactly the same purple and red swirls as his precious notebook. He took the somewhat battered book out of his pocket to compare.

'Are you sure that's all you want?' asked Dad. 'I agree it's a perfect match. Shows the old book up a bit though, doesn't it? What have you been doing with it, writing in the bath?'

Next to the paper specialist was a very superior

mask shop. There Lucien found a silver mask shaped like a cat's face, which reminded him of Bellezza. It was much better made than the ones in the Rialto stalls and Mum and Dad were happy to buy it for him. Then they found a stall selling figured velvet and bought a green scarf for Mum and a pair of red slippers for Dad. They made their way back to the hotel in a very good mood.

The Duchessa swept over the Bridge of Sorrow, her dress swishing on the flagstones. As soon as the guard had unlocked the cell, she dismissed him. As the man hesitated, she waved him away impatiently. 'I hardly think a girl is much of a threat. I presume you searched her for weapons? But if she attempts to suffocate me with her straw mattress, I promise to call out for help.'

The man lit a torch in the corner of the cell, then turned and walked back over the bridge.

The girl was asleep. She looked exhausted, her hair tousled and full of straw-stalks. The Duchessa closed the cell door quietly behind her. But even that sound woke the girl, who sprang up and stared at her visitor. Then she sank down again, disappointed.

'Oh,' she said. 'I thought you were my mother.'

The Duchessa winced but said with her usual asperity, 'Is that any way to speak to your sovereign? No wonder you are in here for an act of treason.'

Arianna leapt up again. 'Your Grace,' she stammered. 'I'm sorry. You surprised me. I didn't mean to be rude.'

Chapter 15

The Language of Lace

Rinaldo di Chimici was fuming. Only half his plan had worked and it was the weaker half. The girl was safely in prison and he was pretty sure the evidence he had bought would see her convicted and sentenced to death. But would Senator Rodolfo care enough about the girl if the boy were not caught? And it was as if the boy had simply vanished into thin air. He wasn't at the Senator's house and no one had seen him leave.

Di Chimici had two other spies employed full-time to watch outside the Palazzo and pounce on the boy as soon as he returned, Enrico having been promoted to more important duties. But the Ambassador was now worried that Rodolfo knew where the boy was and had tipped him off so that he was lying low. And if the boy was what he suspected him to be, he had places to hide that were not open to Chimici spies.

The trial was not far off; it was not the Bellezzan way to delay on something so momentous. Council would meet in a few days and the outcome would be swift. With the girl dispatched, the Ambassador doubted if the boy would ever return.

'We must find the boy!' fretted di Chimici to Enrico. 'Or I shall have no bargaining power with the Duchessa! And she must sign that treaty!'

*

He might have been happier if he could have seen Rodolfo pacing the night away on his roof garden. The Senator had been racking his brains about how to get a message to Lucien, to prevent him from returning unwarily to Bellezza and walking straight into a trap. It was true that Lucien usually stravagated direct to the laboratory, but Rodolfo didn't know what the effect would be of a week having passed in Lucien's own world, with his being out of his accustomed place. If he stravagated in the middle of his night, he might go straight to Arianna's.

Ever since the day Rodolfo had had him transported to his laboratory from the Scuola Mandoliera, Lucien had not missed a morning's lessons until his parents took him away from England. As far as Rodolfo could understand it, Lucien's nights in his world were the daytimes in Bellezza, just as they had been for William Dethridge. If Lucien stravagated in either direction more than once in the hours of daylight or of night in either universe, he would arrive back in the other world only moments after he had left it. But if he left it till the next night to stravagate, a day had passed in Bellezza.

But the break of a week in Lucien's regular departures from his world brought an unprecedented absence in Talia and Rodolfo did not know how long it would last. He and Lucien and William Dethridge had spent hours discussing the time differences between Lucien's England and their Talia.

Dethridge told them that the date of his first, unplanned, stravagation, on the day he was trying to make gold, was 1552, twenty-five years ago according to Bellezzan history. But it was four hundred and twenty-five years behind Lucien's time. If the gateway between worlds behaved consistently, one year in Talia equalled nearly seventeen in Lucien's world. But that was the trouble: the gateway didn't behave consistently. During the period of Lucien's visits, the dates had matched one to one in the two worlds, but at other times the difference between one and the other had obviously been accelerated and it was impossible to tell when that would happen again.

'Even if I go away for a week and don't visit Bellezza,' Lucien had reasoned, 'I should still be back here in a week at the most.'

But none of them really knew whether this would happen. When Dethridge had told the Duchessa that Lucien would be away a while, he really thought they might not see him for a week. Now, on their way back to the laboratory, Rodolfo was worrying that time in Lucien's world might have speeded up again and that he could be back within hours. He was calculating whether he or Dethridge could get a message to Lucien by stravagating to his time.

'I am willinge to goe,' said Dethridge, 'yf it wolde holpe the boye.'

'Thank you,' said Rodolfo. 'It is good of you. But I think it would not help. You would find the twenty-first century very confusing and difficult. I certainly found the twentieth century so. And I am sure the time you would arrive in would be after Lucien's next stravagation so you would be too late to warn him.'

'Thenne we moste fynde anothir waye,' said Dethridge simply.

Unaware of how many thoughts were focused on him in Bellezza, Lucien continued to explore Venice. His parents were overwhelmed by his knowledge of the city, even though he would occasionally lead them by a Bellezzan route to something that did not exist in Venice or was in a completely different place. Still, he became more and more skilful at covering up these discrepancies and most of the time showed an impressive familiarity with the city and its customs. 'Your reading's certainly paid off,' said Dad.

Today they were going on a boat trip to the islands and Lucien had to keep the names right. Merlino was Murano, Burlesca was Burano and Torrone was Torcello. The boat took them to Murano first and the endless glass shops with their touts outside pouncing on tourists to drag them in for demonstrations of glass-blowing in their 'factories'.

'*Ingresso libero*,' Dad read on the doors. 'But doesn't that mean "entrance free"? Why wouldn't it be? They're shops for goodness sake!'

None of them liked the brightly coloured and hideously expensive glass very much, though Lucien did buy a plain glass ram, without wings. He longed to tell his parents what real lagoon glass could be like. The museum was nothing like the one on Merlino. There was no Glass Master, no fateful mask. Even though his parents were interested in the old and broken bowls and jugs, Lucien soon got bored and went to sit in the cool, cloistered garden, where semi-wild cats played in the long grass.

The best bit of Murano was having lunch in a restaurant by the canal, sitting on a little terrace overlooking the water. On the other side of the canal was an ancient church which, according to Mum's guidebook, housed the bones of a dragon killed by the spit of a saint.

Burano was more like its Talian equivalent, except that there was no single white house, though Lucien searched hard for it.

'Oh, just look at that lace!' cried Mum, and Lucien saw with a jolt that there was a white-haired old woman making lace outside her front door. It was a blue house and the work was not as fine as Paola's, but it was beautiful nonetheless and Lucien was thrilled that his mother had seen it. He insisted on buying her a tablecloth, even though it took virtually all the money he had brought with him to Venice.

'No, Lucien, you can't possibly,' she protested, but nothing would have stopped him.

'Remember my dream,' he said, 'about the lace – when you couldn't wake me up? I really want you to have it.'

Arianna was astonished. The Duchessa regained her composure with some difficulty and began a story so improbable that Arianna found it difficult to take in.

'You believe yourself to be the child of Valeria and Gianfranco Gasparini, do you not?' the Duchessa asked.

'Believe? No, I know I am,' said Arianna.

'Yes, I know your story,' said the Duchessa. 'The *Figlia dell'Isola*, the only child born on Torrone for years. Only you weren't.'

'Weren't what?'

'Born on Torrone. You were born here, in Bellezza, in this very palace, and smuggled to the island when you were only a few hours old.'

'I don't believe you,' said Arianna. 'How do you know?'

'Because I was present at your birth,' said the Duchessa, with a touch of her old humour. 'In fact I was very closely involved in it. Can't you guess how?'

Arianna tried to imagine the Duchessa as a midwife but couldn't.

'I gave birth to you myself,' said the Duchessa, gently. 'You are my daughter, Arianna, and I had you brought up by my older sister Valeria and her husband.'

Arianna's head was whirling. Valeria and Gianfranco not her parents? That was like saying that Bellezza wasn't a city. It just didn't make sense. And the Duchessa her mother? Everything Arianna had known about herself until today seemed to be untrue. But among all the many emotions swirling through her, one fact burned in her brain: if she had been born on Bellezza, then she was guilty of no crime on the Giornata Vietata! She would not be burnt. She seized that thought and held on to it.

'What are you thinking?' asked the Duchessa.

'Many things,' said Arianna. 'But if what you say is true, then I don't need to stay in this cell a moment longer.'

The Duchessa sighed. 'That is true, but I would prefer it if you remain here voluntarily until your trial in a few days' time. I shall produce evidence enough to convince the Council that you are a true-born Bellezzan, but I should prefer to keep your parentage a secret a little longer. It puts us both in danger.'

Then Arianna grasped another thought from the whirl of ideas in her head. 'If Gianfranco is not my real father, then who is?'

Torcello was just as Lucien remembered Torrone, apart from the mosaic in the tiny cathedral, which was gold instead of silver. The whitewashed houses beside the canal where Arianna lived, the stalls selling lace and glass, though they had no merlino-blades, the grassy area outside the cathedral, all made Lucien feel more at home than he had so far on this trip, even though he had been to Torrone only once.

He was tired on the walk back along the canal to catch the ferry back to the city, but happy. But as they passed what he thought of as Arianna's house, he had another strange experience. It wasn't as bad as the one in the Doge's prison. There was not the same terror. But there was a strong sense of danger and this time it seemed to involve him.

As soon as he had escorted the Duchessa back to her Palazzo, Rodolfo dropped Dethridge off at the laboratory, where the two guards who had presented the warrant were still waiting at the foot of the stairs.

'If Lucien returns,' whispered Rodolfo, 'get him through the secret passage and safe with the Duchessa and I'll come to him there. Now I must go at once to Leonora.'

Arianna's aunt was in a terrible state. That this should have happened while her niece was in her care was unthinkable. She had not yet been able to bring herself to tell Arianna's parents what had happened to her and Rodolfo immediately offered to make the journey to Torrone.

'You stay here in case any message comes from the Palazzo,' he said. 'Don't worry, Leonora. I can promise you that no harm will come to Arianna. And I shall send my friend, Dottore Crinamorte, to sit with you as soon as I can spare him.'

The boat ride to Torrone went quickly, Rodolfo brooding the whole way about what the Duchessa had told him. He had not asked about the girl's father but it hurt him deeply to realize that the child had been conceived while he and Silvia had been, as he thought, at their closest. It was while he was still spending much of his time in Padavia and was often away from Bellezza. But he had always thought that Silvia had been faithful to him.

Now he cursed the naïve young man he had been and questioned whether he had been deluding himself in the years since that time. Who could Arianna's father be? Surely not Egidio or Fiorentino? That had all ended, Silvia had assured him, when he first presented himself at the Scuola. But perhaps he had been a fool to believe her? Perhaps Silvia did not love him at all? And yet... what about this year's Marriage with the Sea? Silvia had given him good reason then to believe that her love was as strong as ever.

He thrust such thoughts aside and concentrated on the girl. Now that he thought about it, he could see that she was very like a young version of Silvia. The eyes were the same, and the smile.

He strode down the canalside towards the Gasparini house, thinking only of the girl and how Silvia could reveal enough of the truth to save her life, without putting her in new danger. And suddenly he halted in mid-stride. An image of Lucien appeared before him on the towpath. Rodolfo didn't stop to wonder how it had happened. He just concentrated his mind on letting Lucien know that he must be careful, that his life was in danger. And then the vision dissolved and Rodolfo had to go and tell Arianna's foster-parents what had happened to her.

*

Enrico was rapidly becoming Rinaldo di Chimici's right-hand man. And under his influence the Ambassador was becoming impatient to force Bellezza to join the Republic.

'Forget about the boy,' said Enrico. 'Or at least have another plan up your sleeve. I don't see what's wrong with assassination, as long as you've got another Duchessa lined up – one who will sign the treaty.'

'I do have a candidate as it happens,' said di Chimici. 'She is a member of my family – a cousin. She is Francesca di Chimici, from Bellona.'

'But she has to be a citizen of Bellezza to qualify to be Duchessa,' objected Enrico.

'That can be arranged,' said the Ambassador. 'She merely has to marry a Bellezzan citizen. My family can easily ensure that, with the size of her dowry.'

'And I suppose your family's money would buy the election result too?' said Enrico.

Di Chimici didn't like Enrico's familiar tone. 'I am sure the citizenry of Bellezza would find my cousin a worthy candidate,' he said stiffly.

'Then let's not wait for the boy. I know the trial was my idea but I think we should just go ahead and bump the lady off.'

'My last venture did not go well,' said di Chimici coldly.

Enrico tapped the side of his nose. 'That's because you didn't have me working with you. That nancy-boy you hired was a Bellezzan – you shouldn't trust anyone from the city to do the job for you. They all get sentimental about the lady in the end.'

'Are you offering your services?'

'Well,' said Enrico, 'for a price, of course.'

'Of course,' said di Chimici. 'But I still want the boy. He has something I need.'

'Oh, you'll have him,' said Enrico confidently. 'And Bellezza too. Just trust me.'

*

Giuliana enjoyed her fitting sessions on Burlesca. The old woman was kind and a good listener. She had got a younger woman to help her with the actual dressmaking and the three of them spent so many days on the trousseau that Giuliana moved in with the young dressmaker for a while, so that she should not have to undertake the double water-journey so often.

The sessions passed with Giuliana in a dream about her impending wedding. It was 'Enrico this' and 'my fiancé that' all day long and the other women didn't seem to mind how much she talked about him.

'He has such an important job at the moment,' she said. 'But I can't tell you what it is because it's top secret. Only I can tell you that if he pulls it off, we'll have enough silver to buy our own house! Imagine – I'd like one of these pretty coloured ones here on Burlesca but he says we might have to leave the lagoon after— after this job I can't tell you about.'

'It sounds rather dangerous, my dear.' said Paola mildly. 'I do hope it's nothing illegal.'

Giuliana simpered. 'Well, let's just say we might be better off in Remora when it's over. They might be very grateful to us there.' Paola's bright dark eyes belied her gentle manner as she spent the rest of that session probing her customer for more information. And by the end of the day she knew what she needed to know.

That evening, Paola took out her lacemaking cushion and worked over a candle until late at night, long after her husband Gentile had gone to bed.

*

Arianna was moved from her poky little cell the same night that the Duchessa visited her. The new one was bigger, with rugs on the stone flags, and was not so cold. Arianna had a soft mattress to sleep on instead of a bed of straw. But she could not close her eyes again for thinking about what she had been told. Her first thought was that the Duchessa had gone mad. But what she had said all made a weird kind of sense. Arianna's brothers were much older than her and she had never felt truly at home on the island. And she had always been drawn to Bellezza; it was the place of her heart's desire. Then another part of her mind would cling fiercely to all she had ever known and refuse to give up her familiar parents for a new and dangerous mother and an unknown father.

Early the next morning the door opened and the Duchessa was there again, this time with servants bringing furniture. When it had all been arranged to her satisfaction, she dismissed them and signalled to Arianna to sit beside her on the sofa. Arianna sat, pulling the last stalks of straw out of her hair. She was determined not to speak first.

'You are angry with me,' said the Duchessa quietly.

'What did you expect?' said Arianna bitterly. 'You gave me away and forgot about me for more than fifteen years. I don't know why you decided to tell me now, unless it was to save my life.'

'Of course that's a part of it,' said the Duchessa. 'But everything is changing now. I have known for some months that a crisis was coming in my affairs and those of the city.'

'How? What crisis? I don't understand,' said Arianna.

'Let me try to explain,' said the Duchessa. 'Perhaps it would help if you could see more of my face.'

And she lifted her hands to the silver ribbon and undid the blue silk mask she was wearing. She looked steadily into Arianna's eyes and the girl felt her heart lurch. If all she had been told was true, she was seeing her mother's face for the first time. And in the back of her brain a little voice told her that she was also looking on the unmasked face of her city's absolute ruler, the most powerful person she was ever likely to meet. It was all too much. Arianna had to look away. But not before she had realized that she and the Duchessa were very much alike.

'When I knew that I was going to have a child,' the Duchessa continued, speaking to the back of Arianna's head, 'I was afraid for myself and for you. Knowing that I had someone so dear to me would have been an awful weapon in the hands of my enemies. I had long since decided to remain unmarried and without children. My city was family enough for me. So I decided – and perhaps I was wrong, but you will be my judge – to have the child looked after by someone I could trust, someone who would never betray me. My own sister. Valeria agreed, when I sent for her, and she was rewarded with a daughter, something she had longed for after her two sons.'

'But how did you manage it?' asked Arianna, her natural curiosity getting the better of her. 'I mean, didn't anyone notice that you were, well, getting bigger? And what about my mother, I mean, your sister?'

The Duchessa smiled. 'It wasn't easy. I have one serving woman whom I trust above all others. Her name is Susanna and she knew everything. I could not have carried off the deceit without her. For a long time there was nothing to see, but as the child grew, I took to wearing looser fashions and it was given out that I was unwell with a stomach disorder that lasted some months. At the same time, Valeria took to padding her undergarments and she let her women friends know that she was expecting again. They were very surprised.'

'Yes,' said Arianna. 'I'm always being told what excitement there was on Torrone when they knew I was coming.'

'That was the hardest part,' said the Duchessa. 'The women of Torrone had put their childbearing years behind them and they were so interested in the coming baby. Of course they wanted it to be one of them that delivered it. But Gianfranco said he would have a midwife from the city, since there had been no call for one on the island for many years.'

'And when the midwife came, she brought me with her, I suppose?' said Arianna.

'That's right. I had taken to using substitutes on State occasions, once my body's changes were beyond concealment. A young woman was appearing in my place, wearing my gorgeous clothes at the Epiphany banquet, while I lay upstairs in my chamber, with only Susanna and the midwife to attend me, getting on with the business of giving birth to you.'

There was silence in the cell. 'Didn't you care about giving me away?' asked Arianna.

The Duchessa took her hand. 'I had made up my mind to do it. I could not let myself care. I made no sound when I bore you and I said no word when I gave you away. I had already chosen your name and that was all I could do for you then. That and giving you to my sister was all I honestly believed I could do for you.'

'But couldn't you have pretended to be my aunt at least? I mean I never knew till last night that my...

that Valeria even had a sister, let alone that it was you.'

'That was also for the best. Of course people knew when I was first elected that I had come from the islands, though I too was born in Bellezza, as the Duchessa must be. Your grandmother, Paola, was on a shopping trip to the city when I was born. I, like you, was in a hurry to enter this world and came before my time. But people's memories here are short and even if they remembered that my parents lived on Burlesca, it would have taken a very persistent enemy to track down a sister on Torrone. And even if they had, then there would be no reason to doubt that you were her child.'

'But if it's worked for all these years, why change things now?' asked Arianna, moving her hand away.

The Duchessa sighed. 'A few months ago Rodolfo came to me with a strange story. He had been making his divinations as he does every full moon, and had come up with a repeated pattern that he could not quite understand. Whether he asked the cards, or cast the stones or threw the dice, an urgent message was being revealed to him but he lacked the one piece of information he needed to interpret it. He didn't know about you.'

'What was the message?' asked Arianna.

'About a young girl and danger, about a mage and a young man, about a talisman and a new Stravagante from the other side, about the dukedom and the number sixteen. Once he told me about it, I knew that some of it referred to you and your coming birthday and that I must take steps to ensure your future safety. So I sent messages to my sister and mother and waited to see what plan of my enemies would bring danger to you – or to me through you.'

Arianna was silent for a while. 'Is Rodolfo my father?' she asked in a low voice. The Duchessa got up with a gesture of impatience and walked to the other side of the cell.

'Don't you think you owe me the truth about that too?' Arianna persisted.

'I told you last night, I have never spoken to your father about your existence,' said the Duchessa. 'That was essential for your concealment. When I consider it necessary to tell him, then you will know too. Until then the less you know, the safer we shall all be.'

Her voice was quite hard and Arianna could see that she was going to get no further with this line of questioning today. So she tried another.

'And have you been content to know nothing of me for all these years?'

'What makes you think I have known nothing of you?' said the Duchessa, turning back with her eyes flashing. 'I knew when you cut your first tooth, when you said your first word – it was 'no' if I remember rightly – when you took your first step. I knew when you went to school and how you were pert with your teachers, I knew that your brothers and Gianfranco spoiled you and that you were the darling of the island. I knew everything about you except what you looked like. As soon as I saw you with Luciano I had you followed and my hunch was confirmed. But I never guessed that you had come to Bellezza on the forbidden day. Of all the fates I have considered, I never dreamed that the danger would be brought here by you yourself!'

Arianna couldn't bear to leave the Duchessa the advantage of standing tall over her. She sprang to her feet, expecting to meet her ruler's angry gaze, words of self-justification springing to her lips. But then she saw that the Duchessa's eyes, so like hers, were bright with tears.

The week in Venice was over. Lucien had done everything he had meant to. He thought he would never forget the view of the city from the water when they had taken the boat back from Torcello, which called at the Lido and then crossed the lagoon to the piazzetta. The whole city seemed to float on the water, its gold spires and domes and gilded towers glowing in the setting sun.

It reminded Lucien of his last boat journey back from Torrone, when he had been with Arianna and had suddenly stravagated home. Then the city had been silver but both were magical.

On their last evening, Dad had hired a gondola with lanterns and they had been serenaded in the manner of an ice-cream commercial.

'You have to pay extra for the singing,' whispered Dad. 'I wonder how much extra you'd have to pay to get him to stop?'

Lucien had chosen the gondola, picking the best-looking gondolier, in honour of the Duchessa, though he was clearly over twenty-five.

'You're so funny, Lucien,' said his mum. 'Why does it matter what the man looks like?'

'I just think everything in Venice should be perfect,'

said Lucien, 'and it would be distracting if the gondolier was ugly.'

They floated lazily up the Grand Canal in the balmy evening air and forty-five minutes later they were back in the Piazza San Marco. Lucien noticed again how only tourists walked between the two columns with the statues on top. He had a very strong feeling that he didn't want to go near them himself.

'What does it say in your guidebook about those columns, Mum?' he asked.

She looked it up. 'The columns of San Marco and San Teodoro,' she read, 'were the site of a gruesome spectacle. Executions of criminals took place here up to the eighteenth century. Even today, superstitious Venetians will not walk between them.'

In spite of the warm summer evening, Lucien shivered.

'Ugh,' said Dad. 'Let's go for a last drink.'

They went to one of the expensive cafés with tables outside in the Piazza. Since it was their last night, Dad ordered Bellinis – cocktails made from prosecco and white peach juice.

'Can I have an ice-cream too?' asked Lucien.

'Let's all have them,' said Dad. 'It will be a long time before we taste proper Italian ice-cream again.'

The Duchessa sat in her glass audience room, waiting for the Ambassador. She had commissioned the glass for the room soon after her election and after nearly twenty-five years it still gave her satisfaction. Each wall was decorated with patterned and mirrored glass from Merlino. But each section had been separately commissioned and only the Duchessa and one craftsman knew the secret of how they fitted together to form deceptive reflections.

It gave her the edge on negotiations in all formal audiences, unnerving and disconcerting her visitors, who were never sure which Duchessa they saw was the real one. This suited Silvia very well, particularly in the long wearying sessions she had had in this room with the Reman Ambassador. She sighed at the thought of having to go through another one of them again today.

There was a knock at the door and a manservant came in bearing a small package.

'Excuse me, milady,' he said. 'I know you are expecting the Ambassador. But the messenger was most insistent that you should have this straightaway. He said it was the lace you ordered from Burlesca and that you were in a hurry for it.'

'Quite so,' said the Duchessa, who nevertheless had ordered no lace. 'Thank you, you did quite right.'

She dismissed the manservant and opened the package. The lace panel was intricate and delicately worked. The Duchessa held it in front of her, as if it were a book to be read. As indeed for her it was. Her mother, the old lacemaker, had taught both her daughters what she called the language of lace.

Ever since Silvia had visited her on the island, her mother had known that a crisis was coming. The existence of the child would not be a secret for much longer. And now, by a stroke of luck, she had learned information that might save her own daughter's life. Paola had put all she knew about the di Chimici plot into that piece of lace and, before the Ambassador arrived, the Duchessa knew exactly what he was plotting.

'Good,' she said under her breath. 'I shall have it made into a bodice and wear it in front of the stupid man. It will take more than Rinaldo di Chimici and his grubby little henchman to take Bellezza from me.'

Chapter 16

The Glass Room

Lucien had benefited from his week in Venice in more ways than one. For a start, he had slept like a log every night, catching up on months of sleep loss. And it was a city that, in spite of its reliance on waterways, required a lot of walking. The exercise had done him good. And the change of scene had been wonderful. Just to get out of the house and see new places would have been good after his months of confinement. But for that new place to be Venice...

And yet, ever since that moment on the towpath in Torcello, he had been feeling a sort of low-level anxiety. All the time he had been so ill and having treatment, he had known that his life was in danger but this was quite different. He was sure that this new threat had its roots in Bellezza and he couldn't wait to get back and find out what it was.

The Duchessa's gaoler had known nothing like it. First an obvious miscreant had been well treated and then released without charge and now the girl-prisoner, charged with one of the most heinous crimes in Bellezza, was being treated like an honoured guest. The Duchessa had ordered her moved to a larger, airier cell with its own garderobe. And then furniture had been moved in! A red velvet sofa, an armchair, a little escritoire and a stack of books.

The prisoner had her own oil-lamp and candles and a rug to cover the flagstones. The cell was snugger and more cosy than the gaoler's own apartment. He might have been envious, except that the girl really was a fetching little thing and he had come to the conclusion that she must be innocent of the charge. He certainly hoped so or she would face a horrible fate. But then, if she was innocent, why did he have to keep her locked up?

Arianna was actually relieved to be in prison. She had so much to think about that she didn't want anyone or anything to distract her. After her second interview with the Duchessa, Rodolfo had brought her parents to her and, as soon as she saw them, she had clung to them sobbing, begging them to tell her it wasn't true. Though they were surprised to find she knew the secret of her birth, they did not deny it. They just looked at her gravely, relieved that that same secret would now save her life.

And then they had held her tight and cried their own tears, promising that they would always love her as their own child. And Arianna had sobbed all the harder, feeling that now there would always be a barrier between them.

The Duchessa had come a few times since, bringing small presents of food or clothing. Once she had sent her own woman to wash and dress Arianna's hair. Arianna submitted to all these attentions like someone in a dream. When the Duchessa had first made her revelations, she had been angry. She had always loathed the idea of the arbitrary ruler and as soon as she had met the Duchessa in person, she had a new reason to hate her. But she couldn't, not after she had seen how moved the Duchessa had been. Arianna felt torn in two.

She must learn to think of her parents as her aunt and uncle, her brothers as her cousins. The only thing that was still the same was that her grandparents really were her grandparents. That was a rock to cling to in a sea of swirling uncertainties. But even that rock had its sharp and uncomfortable edge: Paola and Gentile had lied to her just as much as Valeria and Gianfranco had.

Bigger than all of this was the idea that her own real mother was a person so powerful and charismatic as the Duchessa. It gave Arianna a completely different view of herself. She wasn't the child of gentle, elderly parents, a housewife and a museum curator. She was the daughter of the most powerful person in Bellezza, the only head of State able to hold out against the di Chimici, the centre of political intrigues and assassination attempts. And the worst of it was that, despite everything, Arianna found herself excited by the idea.

All her life she had wanted adventure and incident and now she would have more of it than she could handle. She would no longer have to fear being married off to someone dull. She needn't marry at all if she didn't want to; the Duchessa hadn't. And that would set her off on the other round of thoughts. Who was her father?

It was all very well for the Duchessa to say that the less she knew, the safer she would be. Arianna still hoped it might be Senator Rodolfo, even though she was a little afraid of him. She knew, as everyone did in Bellezza, the rumours about his relationship with the Duchessa. But he had looked so grim and distant when he brought her parents to her – her aunt and uncle, she corrected herself – that she did not think he could possibly be her father. And though she still wanted to ask the Duchessa more about it, now whenever she came she had a waiting-woman with her and Arianna had to remain silent.

The trial before Council was set for the next day and Arianna was no longer afraid that she would be convicted. But she was worried about Lucien. Rodolfo had said, in answer to her question, that there was still no sign of him and he didn't know when he would return.

As soon as they were back home in London and had unpacked, Lucien pleaded tiredness and the need for an early night. He took down the mirror above his bed and hung the silver mask on its hook; it would do for now. He propped the mirror against the wall at the foot of his bed. He put the pencil on his bedside table and the book in the pocket of his pyjamas. As soon as he was ready for bed, he lay in the dark for a long time, touching the book and waiting for sleep to take him to Bellezza.

William Dethridge had not been idle. He had spent some time comforting Leonora, who was still distracted with worry, in spite of Rodolfo's assurances, and now he was trying to find a way to communicate with Lucien that would be less uncertain than stravagating forward to an uncertain time. Rodolfo had shown him the way in which his mirrors worked and he was now trying to open up a link with the world he had come from and where Lucien still lived. The combination of his occult knowledge from one world and Rodolfo's science from another was formidable and he was beginning to make some progress.

In one of the mirrors, an image was forming which he didn't understand. At first he thought it was somewhere in Bellezza, because he could see a silver mask. But underneath it was a boy's head on a pillow. He had just realized that it was Lucien, when the face in the bed closed its eyes and Lucien himself appeared in the laboratory.

'Master Lucian!' said the old man. 'I am righte glad to see ye! But ye moste not stay here. Youre lyfe is in daungere. Ye moste goe in the peacocke passage and wait for Maister Rudolphe. He wol explaine it all.'

Dethridge did not allow any questions; he was already propelling Lucien towards the wall and grasping the sconce. Within seconds, Lucien found himself inside the secret passage without any source of light. But it was all right. Lucien had used the passage several times and now knew it well enough to make his way along it in the dark to the Duchessa's side. Still, he was glad to realize that he still had his merlino-dagger in his belt, since he didn't know what to expect when he got there.

He could hear voices on the other side of her door and hesitated for a while until he was sure that one of them was Rodolfo's. Cautiously, he pushed against the door and found himself the centre of attention.

Rodolfo was obviously pleased to see him. Although he was smiling now, Lucien thought his master looked a lot older, as if a lot had happened to worry him in the short time that Lucien had been away. The Duchessa was also warm in her welcome. But they had such a lot to tell him that Lucien was overwhelmed.

'Arianna arrested?' he said. 'Can I see her?'

'Why not?' said the Duchessa, laughing. 'The last place my city guards will be looking for you is in one of my cells. And she will have more to tell you.'

'I'll take you,' said Rodolfo. 'We can go through the Council chamber and across the Bridge of Sorrow. But you mustn't stay long and we must find a way of keeping you safe from trial.'

*

'Maister Rudolphe,' said Dethridge, when the

Stravagante returned to his laboratory. 'I thinke I may have foond my olde worlde.'

He showed Rodolfo what he had done with his mirror and the two Stravaganti found themselves looking into Lucien's bedroom. It took a while to work out what it was because it looked nothing like a room in either Rodolfo's Talia or Dethridge's England, but they recognized the sleeping boy. They watched in silence as the figure breathed lightly almost without moving.

'That is how I moste have semed whenne I was a-stravaging here,' said Dethridge. 'Noe wondir is it that I was ofttimes taken to be dede. It toke mee some tyme to fathome that I moste travel onlie at nighte.'

'Fascinating!' said Rodolfo. He clapped the old man on the shoulder. 'Well done, Dottore, you have done something quite remarkable – and it may turn out to be very useful to the Brotherhood.'

*

The Bellezza Council soon dispatched the smaller transgressions on the day's list. Everyone was eager to get on with the main business of the day. Council proceedings were not open to the public so Rodolfo was not there. Nor was Rinaldo di Chimici, but he had a Councillor in his pay, to spy for him.

The prisoner was led in, looking remarkably fresh and pretty for someone who had been shut up in a cell for a few days. The evidence against her was produced in the shape of the landlord of the little bar.

'Yes, I saw her on the forbidden day,' he said, grudgingly. 'She came and drank hot chocolate in my bar with the other one, the boy.'

'Your Grace, the boy has not been found,' said the prosecutor.

'Very well, let us hear no more about the boy,' said the Duchessa. She had not enjoyed a Council session so much for a long time.

'I shall now prove that the girl is not a citizen of Bellezza,' said the prosecutor. 'Call Gianfranco Gasparini.'

Gasparini was called and took the oath.

'Signor Gasparini,' began the prosecutor. 'Tell the Council where you live.'

'On Torrone,' said Gianfranco. 'I am curator of the cathedral museum there.'

'And do you recognize the accused?' asked the prosecutor.

'Yes,' said Gianfranco. 'She is my foster-daughter.'

Arianna blinked back her tears. It was still upsetting to hear him say it. There was a murmur throughout the Council chamber.

'Foster-daughter?' said the prosecutor, riffling through his notes. 'You mean you are not the girl's natural father?'

'Quite so,' said Gianfranco. 'She was raised by my wife and myself, but she is not our own child.'

'But my information,' said the prosecutor, 'says that she was well known on Torrone as the *Figlia dell'Isola*, the only child to be born there for many years.'

Gianfranco nodded. 'Except that she was not born there.'

There was a sensation in the Council.

'And where was she born?' asked the prosecutor,

though he had a horrible idea he knew what the answer would be.

'Here in Bellezza,' said Gianfranco.

'Your Grace,' said the prosecutor, unnerved by the way his examination was going. 'This is new information. The witness must offer proof. Otherwise anyone accused of this crime could claim to have been born on Bellezza.'

'Indeed,' said the Duchessa. 'Do you have proof, Signor Gasparini?'

'If Your Grace would allow another witness to be called, one Signora Landini, your prosecutor could ask her for proof.'

The Duchessa nodded and the witness was called. Arianna had no idea who she was and nor, it was obvious, did the prosecutor.

'Please give your name, Signora,' he said.

'Maria Maddalena Landini,' said the woman, who was plump and about sixty years of age.

'And what is your connection with the prisoner?'

'I was midwife at her birth,' said the old woman.

'And where did that birth take place?'

'Here, sir, in Bellezza.'

'And who was the mother?'

The Duchessa was impassive behind her mask. The old woman looked straight ahead.

'I don't believe I have to answer that,' she said.

'Your Grace?' appealed the prosecutor.

'The child's parentage is not the issue,' said the Duchessa. 'Only her place of birth. If that is Bellezza the case will be dismissed.'

'What happened after the child was born?' asked the prosecutor.

'I showed her to the mother, who was a gentlewoman,' said Signora Landini, 'and she asked me if I would take her to a couple on Torrone, who had agreed to raise her.'

'And that is what you did?' asked the prosecutor, feeling the case slip through his fingers.

'I did,' said the Signora, 'I took the baby by boat that same night to a family on Torrone by name of Gasparini. The mother paid me handsomely and that was the end of the matter.'

The Duchessa intervened. 'It seems clear to me there has been a mistake. There is clearly no case to answer. Release the prisoner to her foster-father.'

*

The Duchessa returned from the hearing in high spirits. Lucien was waiting in her apartments with Rodolfo until the Council session was over.

'How's Arianna?' asked Lucien. It had been traumatic visiting her in the palace dungeons, although she had seemed quite comfortable.

'Free and happy, I hope,' said the Duchessa. 'Gianfranco will have taken her back to her aunt's I think.'

'Can I see her?' he asked.

'It would not be safe for you to go out in the street with the warrant still out,' said Rodolfo.

'I shall recall that warrant,' said the Duchessa. 'I can say that the dismissal of one case has cast doubt on the validity of the other. Go back through the passage with Rodolfo and I will send a message to Arianna when the danger has lifted. Then she can go to you or you to her without fear.'

'But please remember to come back here before you go home,' said Rodolfo.

Lucien felt a weight lift from him. And now he looked at the Duchessa in a new light. Knowing that she was Arianna's mother made him look for resemblances. And the Duchessa in a good mood was like her daughter, full of a good humour that was infectious.

'Now go, both of you,' she said. 'I have other important matters to arrange.'

*

Enrico whistled as he walked along the canalside. He had a very useful new piece of information. His friend, Giuseppe, the Duchessa's spy, had another friend, on Merlino, who knew the craftsman who had put together the Glass Room. And along this fragile chain of links had passed silver in one direction, getting less as it passed through each set of hands, and information in the other, growing slightly as it progressed from mouth to mouth.

And now Enrico had a sketch of how the room had been put together. He was ready to make his fortune.

*

Giuliana had been asked to impersonate the Duchessa again. She was not going to say no, of course. Her love of silver had begun to eclipse even her love for Enrico. This time she planned to keep it all for herself and so she didn't tell her fiancé about the new commission. This time she didn't have to appear in public, only to receive petitioners in the Duchessa's audience-chamber. She would not have to speak; a waiting-woman would explain that the Duchessa was suffering from a sore throat. All she had to do was to dress up in the Duchessa's clothes and appear to listen to some requests and then report them to the Duchessa afterwards. The ruler's judgements would be communicated to the petitioners later.

Giuliana was surprised to learn that the Duchessa used doubles for minor indispositions; she had thought it happened only on State occasions, but she was willing to go along with the deception. She gazed at the growing pile of beautiful clothes in her cedar chest. She could hardly close the lid on them now. Giuliana was beginning to have far stronger feelings about the idea of her finery and the house she would one day have than her feelings for Enrico. At times he just seemed a necessary evil, a signpost on a route to a better life.

*

Arianna was practically dancing round the fountain when Lucien found her. It was too late to go out anywhere together. It was nearly time for him to stravagate home. But just to walk through the streets without that dull dread which had been hanging over him for days had felt very good.

'Will you go on with your lessons?' asked Arianna. 'And shall we still have our afternoons?'

'I don't see why not,' said Lucien. 'I still have a lot to learn about stravagation and about Bellezza.'

He didn't tell Arianna about a new worry of his. What would happen to his life in Bellezza when he had to go back to school in September? It was going to be hard enough to catch up on all the work he had missed and get back into doing a full school day, without losing night after night of sleep.

For the time being, he would enjoy what was left of the holidays, in both his worlds, but he could feel a change coming and he didn't like it.

*

'Have some more wine, Dottore,' said Leonora.

'Thanke ye,' said Dethridge. 'Ye are moste kinde. And where are the yonglinges now?'

'Out somewhere in the city, making the most of their time together,' said Leonora. 'It's nearly dark. He will have to get back to Senator Rodolfo's and go home soon.'

'So ye knowe whatte hee is?' the doctor asked.

'Oh yes,' said Leonora calmly. 'I've always known. But he's a good boy and that matters more than what world he comes from, doesn't it?'

Dethridge was thoughtful. 'Ye knowe thatte I was the same as hee?'

Leonora looked at him. 'No, but you say "was". What happened?'

Dethridge sighed gustily. 'There was daungere and an accident. It is too longe a tale for now. Some daie I may tell ye. But it sufficeth thatte I am noe longire like unto maister Lucian. I am here now – for gode.'

Leonora reached out and patted his hand.

'I'm glad,' she said.

*

Rinaldo di Chimici was furious about the result of the Council trial and even more so when he heard that Lucien's warrant had been countermanded.

Enrico just shrugged. 'You win some, you lose some,' he said. 'What will it matter tomorrow, when the Duchessa is dead?'

Di Chimici couldn't repress a shudder. The man's bloodthirstiness appalled him. Having to use him to achieve his aim was like eating an exquisitely prepared dish with a dirty knife. But he was too far gone with the plot now to back out. His cousin Francesca was already in Bellezza, awaiting her role in the plot. He had one or two Bellezzan nobles lined up to marry her quickly if the assassination succeeded.

'But we can still get the boy if you want,' said Enrico. 'When we have a new Duchessa and are part of the Republic, you can get him under your new witchcraft laws. There's definitely something unnatural about him.'

Di Chimici was relieved. He still needed the boy. In fact he might not wait till Francesca's election. Why not just get this dirty tool of his to rob the boy? But he would wait till after tomorrow.

*

Once a month anyone in Bellezza could come to the Duchessa with a petition. It did not have to go before Council if it was a small complaint; she could settle for herself disputes between neighbours, inheritance claims among family members, landlord and tenant quarrels.

Silvia normally enjoyed it, sitting in the Glass Room which was reserved for more weighty embassies the rest of the month. She was quite aware that Bellezzans, who were notoriously litigious, often came before her on little pretexts, just to see the great lady face to face and have some discussion with her. It was one of the customs that made the citizens most devoted to their ruler.

They came away even more in awe of her powers and confused about what they had seen. The Glass Room led straight off the Duchessa's private chamber. A sliding door between them admitted her into the audience-room. But today it was her substitute who stepped through to sit on the Duchessa's glass throne.

The room gave Giuliana a vertiginous sensation. She wouldn't have dared get up off the throne to take two steps across the room. All was illusion and deception; she couldn't tell which was the reality and which the reflection. Giuliana shuddered; there was something spooky about this room. Only a mind like the Duchessa's could have dreamed it up.

With the first three petitioners, Giuliana scarcely listened to the details of their pleas. Her gaze, behind her red feathered mask, flitted around the extraordinary room which reflected her image back to her over and over again, fractured into splinters by the intricacy of the mirrored panels. It was giving her a headache.

But the fourth petitioner jolted her out of her reverie. It was Enrico! She couldn't speak to him, of course, but she blushed behind her mask until she felt her face must match her dress. What was he going to ask? She felt sure that it was going to be something to do with the wedding.

But he said nothing. Perhaps he was confused by the room like the other people? But no. He was looking straight at her, not misled by the mirrored glass at all. Suddenly, he nodded, bent down and seemed to bowl something like a ball under her chair. Then he turned and left the room in a hurry.

*

Rodolfo heard the explosion from his laboratory. Lucien had just arrived for his morning lessons. There was a deafening boom followed by the sounds of crashing and splintering glass.

Rodolfo knew where the Duchessa should be at this time and on this day, just as he always knew. In fact, one of his mirrors was trained on the audience room. Rodolfo looked in horror at the mess of glass and blood. She couldn't possibly have survived. But he was prepared to tear through the glass shards bare-handed to find her.

The quickest way to the Duchessa was the secret passage. Leaving Dethridge and Lucien behind, he wrenched the sconce round and ran in the dark, not waiting to use the firestone. He could hear his own breath rasping loudly in the stone corridor. A voice was moaning, 'Please, goddess, no!' and he was quite unaware that it was his own.

Chapter 17

Death of a Duchess

Enrico walked as slowly and calmly as he could coming down the stairs of the Duchessa's palace and across the square. But as soon as he was among the usual crowd of tourists, he heard the explosion and ran as fast as he could all the way back to his lodgings. He had agreed not to contact di Chimici. He had given a false name at the Palazzo and he was going to lie low for a few days. As soon as he had the money from the Ambassador, he would collect Giuliana and leave for Remora. It was foolproof.

Rinaldo di Chimici heard the explosion too, in his rooms on the Great Canal. The sound was followed by a silence, in which all Bellezza seemed to hold its breath. And then a roar, as people went running to the Palazzo, guards trying to keep them out of the building while others were picking their way through the wreckage to the Glass Room.

Di Chimici was fighting to behave normally. What would be normal for a Reman Ambassador suspecting carnage at the Palazzo, he wondered. He must make an appearance in public, must seem surprised, distressed even, or he would be suspected of involvement. He rang his bell to call his servant for news and, when none was forthcoming, except that there had been an explosion in the direction of the Piazza Maddalena, he descended to his mandola at the landing stage.

As the vessel cut through the water, he could see lots of traffic heading in the same direction. The square was thronged with people as if a feast was in progress. But the black smoke pouring from the roof of the Palazzo belied the carnival atmosphere. The Bellezzan fire-fighting team were pumping water from the lagoon to the Palazzo as fast as they could.

As the Ambassador leapt from his mandola on to the Piazzetta landing-stage, he heard the first cry of '*Bellezza è morta!*' It stopped him in his tracks. After what had happened at the Feast of the Maddalena, he could not believe the plot had succeeded. But the shouts meant only one thing; the Duchessa was dead.

*

Rodolfo ran into something soft in the dark – a person coming from the opposite direction. At first he grabbed it by the shoulders to cast it out of his way, but something stopped him. A scent, a caught breath like a sob, and he had the figure in his arms. He did not know how she had survived, but this was Silvia, beyond any doubt.

'Thank the goddess!' he whispered.

The woman sighed and took a long, shuddering breath.

'The goddess might have helped,' said Silvia, in a shaky voice, 'but I gave her a hand.'

The two seemed to stand in the dark tunnel for a long time, until their heartbeats returned to normal and they walked slowly back to Rodolfo's side of the passage.

'Hevene bee praysed!' said Dethridge when he saw them emerge. 'Wee thoghte the worste had happened.'

'It very nearly did, Dottore,' said the Duchessa. 'But it takes more than a di Chimici to kill *me*.'

'Luciano,' said Rodolfo. 'Give her some wine. She has had a shock.'

'What happened?' asked Lucien as he went to a cupboard and poured wine into Rodolfo's best silver cups.

The Duchessa drank deep before she answered. She was wearing the crimson dress and feathered mask that they had seen in Rodolfo's mirror only seconds before the explosion. Apart from a little dust and a few cobwebs picked up in the secret passage, her ensemble was undamaged. Rubies glowed at her throat and ears and the fan she still clutched was of blood-red lace.

'I used a double for my public audience today,' she said, with only the slightest tremor in her low voice. 'It was a good idea as it turned out.'

Lucien was appalled. An innocent woman had gone to her death. He knew that a ruler lived with danger. He had helped her survive one assassination attempt already. But suddenly he had the horrible thought that the Duchessa had known very well what she was doing when she sent a substitute into the Glass Room.

Rodolfo obviously had the same thought. 'You knew that something was going to happen?'

The Duchessa nodded. 'I had a warning.'

'Do you know who it was?' asked Rodolfo through clenched jaws.

'The instrument was a common rogue, who thought he was murdering Bellezza when in fact he was killing his own fiancée,' said the Duchessa. 'But of course the real assassin was the same as last time – Rinaldo di Chimici.'

'How did you know all this?' asked Lucien, still shocked that the Duchessa would send another woman to a certain death, even if that woman was somehow connected with the plot.

'My mother, Arianna's grandmother, makes lace on Burlesca,' said the Duchessa, as if she were answering his question.

Lucien wondered if the shock had been too much for her.

'I know,' he said 'I have met her.'

'Ah yes, I forgot,' said the Duchessa. 'Well, if you have seen her work, you must know it's very good. People come to her from all over the lagoon when they want something special made. And a young woman recently went to see her about a splendid set of wedding-clothes. That woman was boastful about the money her intended husband would be getting for a secret job for Rinaldo di Chimici.'

'What a coincidence!' said Lucien.

The Duchessa rubbed her eyes behind the mask. 'I

don't believe in coincidence,' she said. 'It was Fate. My mother managed to get a message to me in a way that only I would have understood. When I had unravelled it, I decided to use that young woman as a substitute today – I had used her before.'

'But why did she agree if she knew the danger?' asked Lucien.

'I don't suppose she knew when it was going to happen. Probably she didn't understand herself half the clues she had passed on to my mother. She was greedy and she liked the offer of more money. And she had broken the agreement we made on the occasion of her first impersonation.'

The Duchessa looked at them a shade defiantly, as if challenging any of them to protest against this reasoning. Lucien thought again that she was the most ruthless person he had ever met. He thanked his good fortune that he was on her side in the dangerous and violent world of Talian politics.

'What happens now?' asked Rodolfo. 'Shall I send your guards to arrest di Chimici?'

The Duchessa got up and looked in the mirror which showed the wreckage of the Glass Room.

'No. When I left my chamber, I was alone. I just wanted to get away from the noise and the confusion. But in that dark corridor, I realized that I could make today work to my advantage in another way.'

She turned back and looked at them, then slowly, deliberately, untied her crimson mask. 'I have decided that the Duchessa is dead.'

*

The funeral was the most magnificent Bellezza had

ever seen. A public day of mourning had been declared. Six of the Duchessa's guards carried the silver-inlaid ebony coffin into the cathedral, where the Senators and Councillors awaited it. Two of the guards had been among the first to reach the Glass Room and knew how little remained of the great lady to bury. The scraps and fragments of red silk and feathers, all stained a darker red, were the only way of identifying the pathetic human remains after the explosion. No one doubted that the elaborate coffin held the Duchessa. It was Giuliana's last impersonation.

The Bishop of Bellezza performed the rite in the silver Basilica. Senator Rodolfo, in his public role as senior statesman and his private one as the widely acknowledged favourite of the late Duchessa, was Chief Mourner. He followed the coffin into the cathedral, his face set and grim. Behind him walked Rinaldo di Chimici, representing Remora and the Pope.

Those Bellezzans who could not get into the cathedral stood with bowed heads in the Piazza, listening to the music and the solemn sounds of the Requiem Mass coming from the great silver doors, which remained open throughout the service.

After the service, two hours later, six of the Duchessa's best mandoliers carried the coffin to the black 'mandola di morte' waiting in the lagoon, as the single bell tolled from the campanile. The funeral mandola was draped with black lace, but the curtains were tied back to allow citizens their last glimpse of their beloved ruler's coffin.

The mandoliers took it in turns to scull the vessel

the length of the Great Canal and out at the northern end, towards the Isola dei Morti.

The whole city was in mourning. There wasn't a single Bellezzan old or young who had not managed to be part of the thousands lining the canal. The two bridges across the great waterway were so thronged with people that they looked in some danger of collapsing. Bellezzans had camped out on the Rialto all night to be sure of a place near the parapet from which to bid the Duchessa farewell. Whoever owned a room overlooking the canal, or had a friend in one, was out on their balcony watching the water cortège.

A little beyond the Rialto stood a family group showing less emotion than other Bellezzans. Two middle-aged women and two men of the same years, with a young girl, not yet old enough to wear a mask. Behind them was a tall young red-headed man. The women were soberly yet well dressed, in black, like the rest of Bellezza. Even the girl had her brown curls hidden under a black lace veil. Leonora and Arianna had not attended the funeral, for the simple reason that its subject stood beside them. The handsome woman with the violet eyes was wearing one of Leonora's dresses; luckily Leonora had a good wardrobe of mourning clothes.

As soon as the Duchessa had decided to maintain the charade of her own death, she had sent Lucien to Leonora's to tell Arianna what had really happened and to borrow some plain clothes. The Duchessa's senior waiting-woman, Susanna, the one who had hired Giuliana on the last day of her life, had eventually guessed what had happened and made her way through the secret passage. She was the only one who knew of its existence. Her emotion on finding her mistress alive had so moved the Duchessa that the two had pledged themselves to stay together in hiding.

The men of the little party by the canal were also not as inconsolable as most Bellezzans around them. Egidio and Fiorentino were two more of the small number of people who knew that their Duchessa was not in the coffin. Guido Parola was also in on the secret. He had suffered such agonies when he heard that the second assassination attempt had succeeded that the brothers, who had been told the truth by Rodolfo, had begged Silvia to let them take the young man into their confidence.

Now they watched the funeral mandola slowly making its way up the canal, followed by the State vessel with Rodolfo and the Reman Ambassador, another with the Bishop and his priests and then the Barcone, with many Councillors and Senators on deck, beside a band of musicians playing a dirge, their plangent harmonies clashing with the single note of the campanile bell.

The canal was filling up with flowers as Bellezzans hurled blooms at the passing coffin. Some landed in the mandola, so that its severe black lines were now blurred into a mass of colour. But most fell unheeded into the water, where they floated along in the wake of the cortège, alongside cheap golden ornaments representing the goddess.

And all the time the great bell of the campanile kept tolling.

As the mandola bearing the coffin passed by the little family party, Silvia observed closely the citizens around her. All were weeping, many fell to their knees and crossed themselves as the mandola went by, or made the 'hand of fortune'. Many cried out 'Goddess bless her!' or 'Bellezza is dead!' or other laments. An old woman near Silvia said, 'There will never be another Duchessa like her – not in my lifetime!' Silvia had to pull her veil low over her face to hide the smile of pleasure she felt forming there, but she was genuinely moved.

Then the State mandola passed by them. 'Hypocrite!' she whispered. Rinaldo di Chimici was holding his handkerchief to his face as if afflicted by grief.

'He does that because he just can't stand the smell of the canal,' she muttered.

Rodolfo sat upright beside the Ambassador, as if frozen in grief. But in fact the little party knew that he was rigid with nervousness at the part he had been called upon to play. His face looked more deeply lined, as if the events of the past few days had aged him. The crowds were all sympathetic to him, seeing in him the romantic figure of a man who has lost the love of his life as well as his ruler like the rest of the city.

'Poor fellow!' said a bystander. 'I've heard she led him a hell of a dance.'

Silvia darted him a vicious look, but he had already been suppressed by the people around him, who would take no criticism of their Duchessa today.

Round a bend in the Great Canal, Lucien and William Dethridge were among the watchers. Lucien felt the unreality of the spectacle and stood dry-eyed as the funeral mandola passed by. But William Dethridge wept openly for the Duchessa, even though he knew her to be alive.

'She was a grete ladye,' he said to Lucien, who knew he was not play-acting. 'What will the Citie doe without hir?'

And then Lucien found himself caught up in the great wave of emotion. He knew that Silvia still lived, but in a way it was true that the Duchessa had died. Never again would he see her in one of her fantastic masks, wearing her beautiful jewels and gorgeous dresses. She was just plain Silvia Bellini, a citizen of Bellezza, and he couldn't imagine what she was going to do with the rest of her life.

The crowds remained, still and silent at their posts, while the funeral mandola, the mourners and the Barcone went out to the Isola dei Morti. The interment there was short and solemn and then the funeral mandola returned the way it had come. There was not a sound as it retraced its way down the Great Canal, now empty of its burden, except for the occasional soon-stifled sob from the banks. No more flowers were thrown and the musicians had ceased playing.

When the mandola reached the jetty, the bell stopped tolling and all Bellezza seemed to let out a collective sigh. The Duchessa was gone indeed.

*

In the north of the city, the little party held their own wake. They were soon joined by Lucien and Dethridge. Bellezza was now like a ghost town. There was no one on the streets. It would change later, when everyone had consumed enough wine at home. Then the streets would be full again and eventually the citizens would start to sing and some sort of impromptu parties would break out, but for now each home needed time to recover from the emotions of the morning.

Gathered in Fiorentino's house were under a dozen people who knew that the Duchessa had survived. Silvia herself, Arianna, Valeria and Gianfranco, Lucien, Leonora and Dethridge, who were now firm friends, Egidio, Fiorentino, Guido Parola and Susanna the waiting-woman. They were soon joined by Rodolfo, who had absented himself from the funeral banquet. No one had questioned his decision, assuming he was too overcome by grief to remain longer in public.

With his arrival, the group was complete and there was a sense of expectation. Everyone looked to Silvia to make some sort of speech, but in the end it was Rodolfo who asked, 'What happens now?'

'First,' said Silvia, 'we drink to the memory of the Duchessa, like all the other loyal citizens of Bellezza.'

'To the Duchessa!' The voices overlapped and the group drank their red wine.

'And now—' Silvia tried to go on but Rodolfo stopped her.

'Before you say any more, we should drink to the unfortunate woman whose remains are in that coffin, and pray for her soul.'

Silvia looked for a moment as if she was going to argue, but raised her glass anyway. 'To Giuliana, family name unknown, may she rest in peace.'

They all drank again.

'May I continue?' asked Silvia, looking around the room. There was silence.

'As most of you know,' she resumed, 'when the explosion happened, I was in my chamber alone. I ran to Rodolfo's by a hidden passage, terrified by the noise and the smell of burning. I had no plan about what to do next. But I am tired. I have been Duchessa of this great city for twenty-five years, serving it as well as I could. I decided that I would take this opportunity to lead the life of a private citizen again.'

Lucien still had not got used to seeing her without her mask, but it was a perfect disguise. Hardly anyone outside this room had seen her without it for quarter of a century. With the action of a moment, she had rendered herself invisible.

'But I shall not give up my opposition to Remora and the di Chimici,' she continued. 'It will just take a new form, working behind the scenes.'

'Where will you live?' asked Fiorentino. 'You know you can always have a home here.'

'Or with me,' added Egidio hastily.

'Or me,' said Leonora. Rodolfo said nothing, though Lucien could see that William Dethridge was very obviously nudging him in the ribs.

'Thank you all,' said Silvia. 'But I shall not continue to live in Bellezza. It will be too dangerous, even on the islands. I was thinking of going to Padavia. It is less than a day's journey away, so that I can return here easily if I am ever needed. Susanna has brought me enough of my private fortune through the secret passage for me to set myself up under a new identity, as a wealthy widow from Bellezza. Susanna will come with me and, I hope, young Guido.'

Parola blushed and leapt to his feet. He bent over Silvia and kissed her hand. Lucien felt fiercely jealous.

The last time he had seen Parola he had been trying to kill the Duchessa and it was hard for him to believe that he would now be her protector, even though he had been told the assassin was a reformed character. Lucien wanted to offer his own services but what could he do? He wasn't even sure that he would be able to come to Talia for much longer.

'What about di Chimici?' asked Fiorentino. 'Are you going to let him get away with it, like last time?'

'No,' said Silvia smiling, 'but there are better ways of punishing him than taking him to law. Besides I could hardly give evidence in Council of my own death, could I?'

Lucien could stand it no longer. 'But I don't understand what is going to happen. Who is going to be the next Duchessa? What will happen to Bellezza? How can you just walk away from it? Surely the di Chimici will make it part of the Republic now?'

'I don't doubt that Rinaldo di Chimici has a candidate of his own lined up, Silvia,' said Rodolfo.

'You are probably right,' said Silvia, turning her violet gaze on him. 'But then so do I.'

'Who do you mean?' asked Lucien.

'You don't know much about our political system, do you, Luciano?' asked Silvia. 'But perhaps you have heard that Duchesse can be succeeded by their daughters. They have to be elected, of course, but no other candidate has ever won against a Duchessa's heir. And I think that Arianna will make an excellent Duchessa!'

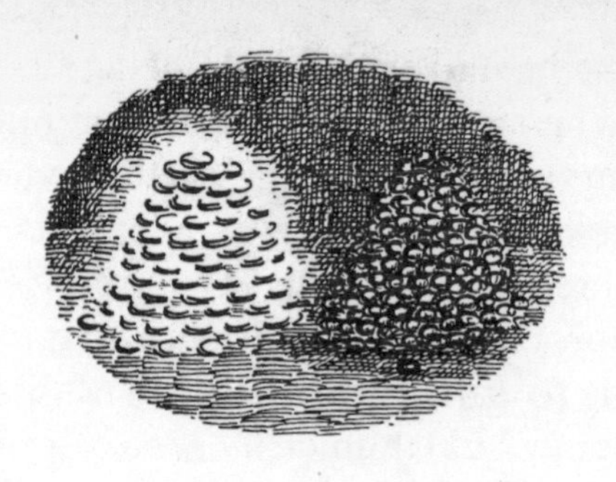

Chapter 18

Viva Bellezza!

Lucien woke with a start. His alarm clock was ringing violently in his ear and for a moment he couldn't remember why he had set it. Then it came back to him; today was the big day – his check-up. It seemed almost impossible after what he had been through earlier in the year, but he had been so caught up in the events in Bellezza that he hadn't been giving today any thought, even though he'd had another scan two days before.

Not so Mum and Dad. But they tried not to show their nervousness throughout breakfast and the journey to the hospital. Somehow that made Lucien more apprehensive.

He knew that he felt a lot better than when he was having treatment. He had lost that awful tiredness, which had been replaced by a much more healthy feeling of never having quite enough sleep, because of his night-time activity in Bellezza. And the returns from Bellezza were no longer as agonizing as that first one, when it felt as if he were re-clothing himself in a suit of lead.

But as he entered the swinging rubber doors to Outpatients, all his old fears returned. It was something to do with the smell, he decided. It was a mixture of disinfectant used on the floors, the pink Hibiscrub liquid that the doctors washed their hands in and the distant smell of overcooked cabbage coming from the kitchens. It was irrational but it made Lucien's stomach bunch into a knot.

As they sat in the Oncology waiting-room, he tried to take his mind off the appointment by thinking about what had happened in Bellezza last night. At first, Arianna had been furious with the Duchessa. 'You can't just boss me around the way you do everyone else!' she had fumed. 'You're no longer the Duchessa so I don't have to obey you. And don't think it makes any difference that you are my blood mother. You abandoned me. My real mother is the one who brought me up. And she wouldn't dream of announcing decisions for me without even asking me my opinion first!'

Everyone but Silvia had been embarrassed by this outburst. The Duchessa had just let it run its course, until Arianna collapsed sobbing and exhausted in Valeria's lap. The two women's eyes met over the tousled brown curls.

'What would you have then, Arianna?' the Duchessa had said, very mildly for her, Lucien thought. 'Bellezza must have its ruler. And it must stay independent of Remora. You agree, don't you?'

The curly head nodded in Valeria's lap.

'Then who is it to be? I have not been grooming anyone to follow me. It is only recently that I have thought of stepping down. And then these assassination attempts convinced me that I could do more good behind the scenes. You will have to have a Regent – you are too young to rule on your own. But Rodolfo could do that. And I shall be only a few miles away in Padavia, willing to help you whenever you need me. I have only ever wanted what was best for you, Arianna, that was why I had you raised in secret. You would have made the perfect hostage to get me to sign the Chimici treaty, or anything else they wanted. There will be several people in Bellezza who know the real situation. The people in this room and your grandparents. You will not have to do this alone.'

Lucien remembered these last words as his name was called. He flashed a glance of gratitude at his parents. 'I'm glad you're both here,' he whispered, as they went into the consulting room together.

Enrico was completely unprepared for the visit from Giuliana's father. Vittorio Massi was a big, broad-shouldered man and he was in a bad mood. He forced his way into Enrico's lodgings, demanding, 'Where is she?' He followed this up with various incomprehensible threats, involving horsewhipping and calling his daughter 'trollop' and other even less complimentary names.

Enrico was astonished. 'Do you mean Giuliana?' he said. 'I haven't seen her for days. Not since before the Duchessa died, goddess rest her.'

Vittorio automatically crossed himself and made the hand of fortune to be on the safe side, but he was not placated. 'Nor have we,' he said. 'She told us that morning she was off to Burlesca for another of her wedding fittings, but the dressmaker has sent to say that she missed her appointment and to ask if she was unwell. So I guessed she had come here to you. Although shame on my family name that she should do such a brazen thing and the wedding only ten days away!'

He raged around the room, but it was clear as day that there was no young woman in it and nowhere to hide one. Enrico felt a gnawing fear. Suppose she had run off with the silver?

'Has she taken any of her things?' he asked.

'Come and see for yourself,' said Vittorio. 'As far as I can tell, everything is where it should be.'

Vittorio, who had never liked his future son-in-law, was beginning to understand that he really did not know where Giuliana was. He felt mollified. And then began to be even more worried. If his daughter was not with her fiancé, then where in the lagoon was she?

*

The clearing up at the Palazzo lasted long after the funeral. The Glass Room was totally wrecked, of course, but all the pieces had to be sifted through, first for the grisly business of identifying the Duchessa's remains, then to look for clues to the assassination, finally to see if there were any pieces of the costly glass that could be saved, repaired or preserved. Only after that could the unwanted débris be carted away.

And there was extensive damage to the rooms around the audience chamber too. The Duchessa's own private chamber, the Council room, the map room with the two great globes, one of the earth and one of the heavens – all would need repair and redecoration. But no decisions could be taken until a new Duchessa was appointed.

Meanwhile, no one took any notice of Susanna, as she quietly packed and removed her mistress's personal possessions. People just assumed she was following orders to take bequests to the Duchessa's heirs, whoever they might be. Caskets of jewellery and silver, fine undergarments and nightwear, books and papers and a precious portrait by Michele Gamberi, but none of the fine dresses and masks that would have given Silvia away in her new life.

Mr Laski, the consultant, had Lucien's bulging file on the desk in front of him. He spent a few moments refreshing his memory about its contents, once he had greeted them. Lucien could tell that those moments seemed an age to his parents, but he felt quite detached about it. Mr Laski didn't have his fate in his hands; that was already decided. He was only the messenger.

'It's bad news, I'm afraid,' said the consultant. 'The MRI scan shows the tumour is growing back.'

Lucien felt his blood go cold and noticed with detachment that that was what really did happen; it wasn't a figure of speech. He heard his mother gasp.

'What does that mean exactly?' asked Dad. 'Can you get rid of it again?'

'The sixty-four-thousand-dollar question,' said Mr Laski. 'Patients always want to know the answer to that and I simply can't give it. We shall resume treatment, of course, and we hope to gain further remission from the disease, but I have to warn you that this recurrence is a bad sign.'

There was silence in the room while everyone tried to take this in. Lucien thought wearily about more chemotherapy, more exhaustion, losing his fine fuzz of hair again. He wished he could use a body double like the Duchessa. But this was London, not Bellezza, and he knew he had to face up to the treatment himself.

'Is there anything else you'd like to ask?' said Mr Laski, gently. Sometimes he hated his job.

'There have been a couple of times lately when I haven't been able to wake Lucien up when I've called him in the morning,' said Mum, talking fast to conceal her anxiety about the diagnosis. 'I don't just mean he was sleeping deeply. The first time it was only a few minutes. But the second it was nearly half an hour and I had to call our GP. Then he just woke up as usual.'

'Oh, Mum!' said Lucien. 'What does that matter now?' But Mr Laski was very interested and asked lots more questions and looked into Lucien's eyes with a little torch.

'I can't explain it,' he said at last, 'but I'd like you to keep an eye on it and bring him in if it happens again. You can call my secretary for a quick appointment. I'd like to examine him on the day that something like that happens. Meanwhile, I'll make the arrangements for Lucien to start chemo again as soon as possible.'

There seemed nothing else to say, so they shook hands and left.

Arianna's head was in a whirl. In a few days she had gone from being a simple island girl, in danger of execution, to the potential next Duchessa. When the Duchessa had first told her about her birth, her emotions had been a mixture of disbelief, resentment and excitement. Now she was contemplating ruling the city she loved and she just couldn't imagine what it would be like.

About the Duchessa, she still felt the same. She simply could not think of her as her mother. That role would always be Valeria's, the lovely, squashy warm presence, smelling of baking bread and herbs, who had been with her all her life. The Duchessa was a ruthless, selfish, stubborn, bossy woman, who couldn't be bothered to raise her own child.

But as the days went by, Arianna began to feel that perhaps she did have something in common with her blood mother after all. Although the thought of becoming Duchessa a bit short of her sixteenth birthday terrified her and the prospect of Rodolfo advising her was scarcely more comforting, she was beginning to be attracted by the sheer glamour of it.

Something similar had happened when she first discovered the secret of her birth: an initial revulsion followed by a fascination with the idea of a life so different from the one she had thought mapped out for her. It seemed a very long time since her highest ambition had been to train as a mandolier.

In the end, before making her decision, she asked to go back to Torrone and spend some time with what she still thought of as her proper family. She would listen to their advice and be guided by it.

'Let her go,' said the Duchessa, when Leonora told her of Arianna's wishes. 'She's my daughter – she'll be back.'

*

Bellezza had ten days of mourning before the election of a new Duchessa. Posters had begun appearing in the streets with the name Francesca di Chimici hastily painted on them. Citizens began to talk listlessly of the future. The whole city was gripped by an apathy most uncharacteristic of the people of the lagoon. It was not their way to give in to depression and gloom. But nothing in the city had ever happened that was as bad as the murder of their ruler. Not since the night of the glass mask a hundred years ago had something affected them so severely.

No one felt any enthusiasm for a di Chimici ruler, who would spell an end to Bellezzan independence, but there seemed to be no alternative candidates. It was part of the seeming immortality of the Duchessa that she had made no arrangements for the succession. Not many people could remember her election, as a young woman of twenty. No one remembered her family name or history.

She had just been a brilliant politician and orator, gaining a seat on the Council when still in her teens. The previous Duchessa, a childless middle-aged woman called Beatrice, had taken a fancy to the young Bellezzan, who had been born in the city but grown up on Burlesca, and had groomed her to be her successor. It had happened sooner than expected, because of the plague. It was no respecter of persons and had carried off the old Duchessa as one of its very first victims.

Bellezza had been disorientated then too, and the young Silvia had put her name forward while the city was still at a loss and looking for a strong leader. At that time the di Chimici were still building their power-base in the west of the country, so there was no real competition for the role.

If there had been any opposition to such an inexperienced politician taking on the rulership, it had been overcome by her beauty and intelligence and her steely devotion to the city, and it had been in any case forgotten a long time ago. For many years now the Duchessa had been regarded as irreplaceable.

*

For Lucien, the time after the Duchessa's funeral was very strange. Arianna was away on Torrone and he had no one to roam the city with in the afternoon. He missed her, but found a melancholy pleasure in wandering through the streets of a Bellezza now quiet with loss. It fitted in well with his mood. He spent a lot of time thinking about his prospects in his own world.

So far he hadn't started to feel ill again there but he knew all that would change when he resumed treatment. And somehow he didn't think he was going to make it this time. He could tell that Mr Laski didn't think so either. What should he tell his friends in Bellezza? For the moment he was numb and could do nothing but be glad that, at least when he was in the beautiful city, he was without the disease that might kill him.

He enjoyed the city even more now that he had seen the real Venice. It wasn't as clean, of course, but it was somehow fresher, the buildings more recent and the whole city more alive and full of hope. Until the catastrophe with the Duchessa of course.

Lucien thought again how convenient it would be to have a body double for all the difficult things you didn't want to face. And death was the ultimate of those. It had worked for the Duchessa. He leaned his arms on the stone parapet of one of the little bridges and looked down into the murky water, remembering the conversation with his parents after the diagnosis.

Dad had been trying to tough it out, saying reassuring things that Lucien was sure he didn't believe. But Mum, small and feisty, was fuelled by a new anger that Lucien hadn't seen before.

'We must help him, David,' she had said, running her hands through her black curls that were so like Lucien's own had been. 'Lucien, we need to talk about the possibility that you might not be lucky a second time.'

'I know, Mum,' he had said as calmly as he could. But they couldn't do it. Not then. They postponed that talk till another day and Lucien had fled to Bellezza as soon as he could, pleading the need for an early night.

His morning with Rodolfo had taken on a different flavour. The three Stravaganti spent their time discussing whether Arianna would agree to stand for Duchessa. Silvia was still staying with Leonora, completely safe, concealed in the heart of the city that believed her to be dead.

Rodolfo was completely distracted. 'Silvia wants me to announce that Arianna is her child. Then I must offer to act as Regent. It seems that Arianna's age would be the only obstacle to her election if the people believe the story of her birth.'

'And you don't want to do it?' asked Lucien.

They were all in the roof garden, in the late summer sunshine. Dethridge swung in the hammock, while Lucien and Rodolfo sat on one of the marble benches. Rodolfo now looked seriously at his apprentice.

'It is not something I can talk about easily,' he said. 'Particularly to someone as young as yourself. I do not mean to insult you, but there are matters of the heart involved which I hope you will not have to suffer for many years. Silvia did not ask if I would be willing or not to take on this burden; she just assumed I would fall in with her wishes. That has been the pattern of our life together for twenty years, this last year most of all. And she knows that any true Bellezzan would do whatever was called for to serve his city. If it were any other young woman! But to look after another man's child...'

He broke off and jumped to his feet, pacing up and down the tiled terrace in the way that Lucien remembered from their first meeting.

'Aye, it is a bitere thinge to have an untrowe wyf,' said Dethridge. Rodolfo stopped in his tracks.

'Not that the ladye is that,' added the Elizabethan hastily. 'But the herte of your sorowe is the same. Ye sholde ask hir what ye wolde knowe.'

Lucien was surprised. He felt out of his depth with these two men, who were so much older and wiser than him. And he simply did not know how to ask Dethridge if he spoke from his own experience. The Elizabethan had never before referred to the wife he would never see again and he never talked about his children.

Now he saw that Rodolfo was looking at him. 'Luciano!' said his master, coming over and taking his hand in both his. 'I am greatly at fault. In the midst of my worries, I had forgotten that you had a very important event in your own world. Tell me what happened when you went to the hospital.'

Lucien had been dreading the question, but there was no point in beating about the bush. 'It's bad news,' he said. 'I seem to be getting worse.'

Dethridge got quickly out of the hammock and both men enfolded him in a silent embrace. They had tears in their eyes and Lucien felt a warm rush of affection for them both. It was bad enough fearing that he might have to leave the parents he loved, but now he had to think that he might soon have to say goodbye to Bellezza and all the people in it who had come to matter so much to him.

*

Rinaldo di Chimici was living on a knife's edge. There was no hint that anyone knew of his involvement with the assassination. His young cousin Francesca was in the city and a friar had already performed a marriage ceremony between her and an elderly Bellezzan Councillor, who had gambled and drunk most of his family fortune away. Francesca was now a Bellezzan and eligible to stand as Duchessa.

The next few days would see the fruition of all his hopes for advancement in the family. To secure Bellezza for the di Chimici would be a fine jewel in the crown of his ambition. But he was playing for even higher stakes. He must possess what the boy had. And to this end he sent for Enrico again.

But the spy would not come to the Ambassador's rooms. They met in the little bar by the old theatre. Di Chimici was shocked to see how much the man had changed. His old swagger had gone and he had a three-day growth of beard.

'What is going on?' he hissed, as soon as his patron had bought him a large glass of Strega. 'My fiancée has disappeared – no one knows where she is. And no one knows where her silver is.'

Di Chimici thought privately that she might have changed her mind about tying herself to such an unprepossessing husband, but he could offer no explanation. He said such soothing things as he could think of, but he had not come to talk about his spy's love-life.

'I need you to do something else for me,' he said at last.

'It'll cost you,' said Enrico automatically.

'Of course,' said the Ambassador.

'What is it?'

'I want you to, er, capture the boy.'

'Do you want me to kill him?'

Di Chimici shuddered. 'Not necessarily. Only if he puts up a fight. I want you to take all his possessions and bring them to me. Everything, mind, no matter how unimportant it may seem.'

Enrico straightened up. The prospect of more silver had shaken him out of his lethargy. And this was an easy job. He was used to following the boy.

*

When Arianna returned to Bellezza, she went straight to her aunt's house and was closeted for some hours with Silvia. Then they sent to Rodolfo's house and the three Stravaganti joined them in the garden with the fountain.

Arianna flashed Lucien one of her sunny smiles but soon looked serious again. Lucien thought she looked as if she had grown up a lot in the few days she had been away. He wondered if he looked older too.

'I've decided,' she said simply.

*

The day of the Ducal election had arrived. A wooden platform had been built in the Piazza Maddalena and a city official sat at a table with a list of the citizens. He had two crates of black and white pebbles which any citizen entitled to vote, that is anyone over sixteen, had to choose from. White for Francesca di Chimici, black for the other candidate, whose name had not yet been announced.

The chosen pebbles would be placed in bowls and counted in the Council chamber later and the result would be announced later in the evening. Rumours had been circulating that there was a real second candidate, not just a cipher, but no one knew who it was. Citizens were already gathering in the Piazza and the first ripple of excitement ran through the crowd since the assassination. The Palazzo was still shored up with great wooden poles. There were fewer tourists than usual, but those who were there were in for an unexpected treat.

As the campanile bell struck eleven, a small group of people mounted the platform. Rodolfo, Arianna and Signora Landini. Francesca di Chimici, now renamed Albani through her marriage, came from the other side with her supporters, her new husband, and the Ambassador. There was a murmuring in the crowd. The Senator was a familiar enough figure and some people recognized the girl who had been arraigned for treason, but no one knew who the midwife was. And it did the di Chimici's candidate no good to be seen with the ambassador, whose mission to Bellezza was unofficially well known.

The election official conferred with Rodolfo and then stood up.

'People of Bellezza,' he called out. 'We have two candidates. One, Francesca Albani, is a Bellezzan by marriage to the Councillor here. The other, Arianna Gasparini, is Bellezzan by birth. Both candidates will be introduced by their sponsors.'

Rinaldo di Chimici stood up and addressed the crowd. It was an uninspiring speech. He had not spent much time preparing it because he had paid enough Bellezzans enough silver, as he thought, to ensure the election result he wanted. He was also distracted by curiosity about the other candidate. What on earth did the Senator think he was playing at? The Duchessa's death must have unhinged him.

There was sporadic applause when di Chimici sat down and more enthusiastic clapping when Rodolfo stood up. People wanted to hear what he had to say.

'Fellow citizens,' he said. 'We have suffered together.' There was a groan of approval from the crowd. 'We have all lost someone we loved, someone we thought not to replace for a long time. Some might say that this loss of ours is not capable of restoration. And in some ways I would agree. But out of despair has come forth hope. In the darkness there is a gleam of a new dawn. The Duchessa did not die childless.'

There was a sensation in the crowd. Di Chimici broke out in a sweat, as his cousin cast him a vicious look. As Rodolfo prepared to continue, the crowd hushed, eager for his every word.

'This young woman, not yet sixteen, has already had to prove she was born in Bellezza, in order to rebut a treason charge maliciously brought against her. Signora Landini here swore in Council that she delivered Arianna of a Bellezzan noblewoman before taking her to the Gasparini family on Torrone to be fostered. She will now tell you the rest of the story.'

The elderly midwife looked apprehensively at the crowd which had grown with every minute and was now filling the square.

'The child's mother was the Duchessa of Bellezza. I delivered the baby in that Palazzo,' she said, pointing, 'and then took her to the Duchessa's sister, Valeria Gasparini, on the island of Torrone. This young girl, born nearly sixteen years ago, is the true daughter of the late Duchessa!'

The crowd erupted. No matter that their Duchessa had not been exactly as they thought her, no matter that the child had been kept a secret, now that Arianna stood on the platform, her head held high, her slim figure echoing that of her mother, her violet eyes gazing steadfastly out over the city, she was the beloved first choice of every red-blooded Bellezzan.

They scarcely listened while Rodolfo explained he would act as Regent, if Arianna were elected. They were descending on the table, shouting out their names and grabbing black pebbles from the box. Several citizens thrust back silver coins at di Chimici, much to his embarrassment.

By midday, the election official had had to send for more black pebbles, while the crate of white ones remained full. In front of Rinaldo di Chimici the pile of silver grew, which he pretended not to see. As the two candidates for Duchessa walked into the Council chamber for the formality of the count, his cousin Francesca hissed at him, 'Get me a divorce!'

Back in the square, the coins lay untouched on the table. No one in Bellezza wanted any reminder that they might have voted for anyone other than the Duchessa's own daughter.

As Enrico quietly pocketed the silver, the cry went up from outside the Palazzo. 'Viva Bellezza!' 'Viva la Duchessa!' Bellezza had a ruler again.

Chapter 19

Between Worlds

When Lucien heard the result of the pebble count, he hurled his hat in the air and cheered with all the rest of the crowd. He was standing with William Dethridge outside the Ducal palace and the old Stravagante linked arms with him and the two of them shouted 'Viva la Duchessa!' till they were hoarse. Luciano had completely forgotten about his cancer.

There was no way they could get to their friends through the mass of people jammed into the courtyard. Rodolfo and Arianna entered the palace by the big oak doors at the top of the white marble stairs and were lost to sight. Di Chimici and his furious cousin struggled through the mob pushing in the opposite direction. Lucien saw them coming and retreated with Dethridge into the Piazza, where an impromptu party was already starting up.

Wooden trestles were being set up, barrels of ale rolled into the square and handcarts trundled along, laden with cheeses and whole hams and flat Bellezzan loaves the size of cartwheels. The city had been preparing, in a half-hearted way, for the election of a new Duchessa, but the result had been better than the people had dreamed possible and now they were going to celebrate it in style.

'Let us drinke gode helthe to the new Duchess!' said Dethridge, flushed with excitement, and led Lucien over to one of the trestles, where ale was being sold in wooden cups. Lucien took a sip of the thin, sour beer and grimaced. It wasn't nearly so nice as prosecco but Dethridge was obviously used to drinking something like it and knocked it back quickly and went for a refill. He called so many toasts that Lucien's cup was soon empty too and then he found that the square was not quite stable underneath him.

'Whoa! Stedye there, yonge man,' said the Elizabethan, laughing. 'Ye seme not to knowe how monye fete ye have. Let me get ye sum vittels to settil ye.'

Lucien watched happily while Dethridge wove his way across to a food stall. He felt completely content; Arianna had been elected Duchessa and that had to mean the beginning of a lot more adventures. He still didn't know what the future held for him in either of his worlds, but for the moment, he was happy just to enjoy the present. He was among friends and was going to celebrate like a proper Bellezzan.

He hardly noticed when a man in the crowd took

his arm; all Bellezza was linking arms and embracing. But this man seemed to be leading him somewhere out of the square. When Dethridge returned, Lucien was nowhere to be seen.

*

Silvia was having her own private celebration in Leonora's garden. The two women sat drinking wine by the fountain.

'Won't you miss all the ceremony and grandeur?' asked Leonora, as they listened to the sounds of revelry coming from the square.

Her companion didn't answer straightaway. 'There will be times when I shall,' she said eventually, 'but it is a price I'm willing to pay. I want my freedom. I'm tired of sitting in Council every week, listening to the lists of crimes my people commit. I'm tired of hearing the petty grievances of the people every month. I want to walk the streets without wearing a mask. I want not to have to endure Rinaldo di Chimici's dreadful conversation and smelly handkerchiefs. And I want most of all for people to stop trying to kill me.'

'Would you rather they tried to kill your daughter instead?' asked Leonora quietly.

'They won't,' said Silvia quickly. 'They'll have to start negotiations all over again with a new Duchessa. It took years of politicking before the Chimici accepted I would never give in and sign their wretched treaty and resorted to murder instead. And they're bound to think they have a better chance with someone young and inexperienced.'

Leonora smiled. 'Even without you in the background, I somehow don't think they will find

Arianna an easy subject to persuade.'

*

In the Ducal Palace, Arianna was sitting on an elaborately carved wooden chair, wondering if she would ever be comfortable again. Susanna had suggested to her that she should keep on all the remaining waiting-women, who had been very anxious about their future since the supposed assassination. They had all been sent for and were now lined up to hear her will.

Arianna spotted a masked woman much younger than the rest, who looked not much older than herself. She seemed especially nervous and the new Duchessa felt an immediate bond with her.

'What is your name?' she asked, pointing to the girl.

'Barbara, milady,' said the girl, curtseying.

'I shall need a personal maid to dress me,' said Arianna. 'Would you like to do that?'

Rodolfo looked over at her and slightly shook his head.

'I mean,' said Arianna more firmly. 'That will be your new rôle.'

'Thank you, milady,' said the girl, gratefully.

'The rest of you will continue in your accustomed tasks until further notice,' said Arianna. 'That will be all for now.'

It was the first moment she had had alone with Rodolfo since being led out into the Piazza that morning and they were both exhausted. Arianna wondered whether she dared broach the subject of her father with him, but it seemed as if Rodolfo might be nodding off to sleep. But he suddenly sat up and exclaimed, 'Luciano!'

They both realized at the same moment that it was very late.

'I hope he hasn't got so caught up in the celebrations that he's lost track of time,' said Rodolfo. He moved towards the door. 'I must leave you for a time, my dear, and get back to my Palazzo. Why don't you rest for a while? The people will expect to see you on the loggia later.'

With that, Arianna was alone at last, the new Duchessa of her beloved Bellezza. She took a candlestick and explored the Palazzo. It was strangely still and empty. Most servants were in the kitchens, preparing for a night of feasting. This was the first time she'd had the chance to roam the palace on her own. The blackened door of the Glass Room was sealed up and she passed it with a shudder.

Up and down marble staircases she went, the candle casting huge wobbly shadows before her. How she wished Luciano were here to share this strange night with her! On the ground floor, she lost her bearings and pushed open a heavy door to see what room lay behind it. And almost dropped the candlestick. The room seemed to be full of Duchesse, arrayed in magnificent clothes and all staring straight at her.

Shaking, she tried to hold the light steady. Then she realized it was the gallery of the last Duchessa's dresses worn on important occasions. Case after case of mannequins moulded to look like Silvia, wearing gorgeous silks and satins and brocades, their faces hidden behind jewel-studded masks. Arianna shuddered. 'I can't do this,' she thought. 'I'm too young.'

A sound behind her made her spin round, spilling hot wax on her hand.

'I'm sorry, milady,' said Barbara. 'I have been looking for you to ask what you would like to wear tonight.' Her gaze followed Arianna's to the magnificent dresses of the last Duchessa. 'They are lovely, aren't they, milady? But there are lots more in the Duchessa's chamber and if you would choose one, I could pin it to fit you.' She dropped a curtsey, wondering if she had been too forward.

'I'll come,' said Arianna, her lips almost too numb to speak, but she was now resolved. If she had to take her mother's place, she would do it properly.

*

'What do you mean, disappeared?' said Rodolfo, running his hands through his silver hair in frustration. It was clear that Dethridge was more than a little drunk.

'No grete matere,' said the Stravagante. 'Hee was with sum othere revellers. Withoute doubte hee has gone home by nowe.'

'No,' said Rodolfo. 'He can't have done.'

He left Dethridge with strict instructions to keep Lucien in the laboratory if he should turn up, then, shrugging off his weariness, ran down the stairs and all the way to Leonora's house.

'How is she?' asked Silvia, alarmed to see him so distracted.

'She is managing well,' said Rodolfo. 'I should get back to her soon, to present her to the people. But I'm worried about Luciano. Has he been here?'

Both women shook their heads, but neither could

understand why Rodolfo was so worried. 'Would you give us a few minutes together, Leonora?' asked Silvia and the widow retreated into the house, leaving them on their own, sitting side by side on the wall of the little stone fountain. But before he could tell her about Lucien, Silvia had launched into her own speech.

'There's something I need to talk to you about,' she began, looking at his brooding face. 'There will be objections raised about Arianna's legitimacy as soon as the Chimici have regrouped, maybe as soon as tomorrow and certainly before the coronation. They would grab at any straw to overturn the election and instate their puppet.'

Rodolfo waited. 'It is time to reveal the truth,' Silvia went on. 'You must tell them that she is my legitimate heir. You will have to reveal our marriage.' It took Rodofo a few seconds to realize what Silvia was telling him.

'Our marriage has no effect on her legitimacy,' said Rodolfo thoughtfully. 'Not unless ... are you telling me that Arianna is our child?'

When Silvia said nothing, Rodolfo took her chin in his long fingers and turned her face towards him.

'I must know,' he said as gently as he could. 'It has been driving me mad.'

*

The effects of the ale had worn off and Lucien was wretched, with a throbbing headache, shut in a room somewhere near the Great Canal, he guessed. His companion had been a man in a blue cloak, who looked vaguely familiar. But once out of the Piazza, he hadn't seemed friendly at all, gripping Lucien's wrist and threatening him with a merlino-blade, if he should try to break loose. Once in a side alley, he had gagged the boy and tied his hands, then blindfolded him.

Lucien stumbled along, protesting through the gag, but the few passers-by took no notice. He was taken up some stairs and flung in a stone-flagged room and the door slammed and locked. Later, someone came back, the same man by the smell of him and searched Lucien carefully. He took all his belongings; in spite of his struggles and cries, he had to give the notebook up along with everything else. Much later, a woman brought a cup of ale, the last thing Lucien wanted, and a hunk of fresh bread. But she did not untie his wrists. Through the blindfold, Lucien could see how dark it was getting. He lay down on the cold floor and gave way to despair.

Mr Laski was in his Harley Street consulting-rooms when Casualty bleeped him. Within minutes, he had rearranged the rest of his morning appointments and was in a taxi on his way to the hospital.

David and Vicky Mulholland looked white and strained in the curtained-off cubicle. Their son lay on the examination table, relaxed and apparently fast asleep. It took all Laski's training and experience to relate to them sympathetically, instead of plunging straight into an examination. He couldn't wait to get his hands on the patient, but he forced himself to listen to the mother's account and to ask questions.

'It's much worse this time than the other two,' said Vicky Mulholland, her voice unsteady. 'I had to call the ambulance – he just wouldn't wake up. I tried everything – shaking, shouting, wet flannels. And then I just panicked. I phoned my husband and he said to ring 999 and he'd meet me here.'

She was screwing a paper tissue in her hands as she talked. 'What is it? Is it the tumour affecting his brain?'

'I can't say until I've examined him,' said Mr Laski soothingly.

'It's not normal, though, is it?' said David Mulholland, tensely. 'You didn't say at his check-up that we should expect anything like this.'

'Just let me examine him,' said the consultant. 'We'll need to run some tests.'

In Bellezza, Lucien was wide awake, though it was the middle of the night. He kept rerunning in his head the scene that would be playing out in his home world. It was such an agony to imagine what his parents would be going through that it was a relief when the door of his room opened, even though he feared for his life.

With his eyes still blindfolded, Lucien's other senses were heightened. There was the rank smell of his captor and then a sharp, strong scent, like aftershave. Two people then, and they were whispering. Through the coarse cloth, he could see a bright light, as if someone were holding a lantern close to his face. Then it moved away a bit and there was a sharp intake of breath.

Lucien couldn't stand it. 'Why have you brought me here?' he said, in a voice that sounded pathetic in his own ears. 'I want to go home.'

'Ah,' said a cultured voice. 'But where exactly is home? And can you go there? Or do you need something we have taken from you?'

Lucien's heart sank. They knew he was a Stravagante! They must be Chimici. But perhaps they didn't know which of the items they had robbed him of was the talisman? After all, the book was Bellezzan. Perhaps they were now going to torture him to find out?

'You have no right to take my things,' he said. 'I want to go back to Signor Rodolfo.'

Smelly and Stinky was how Lucien thought of the two men. Smelly said something he couldn't hear and Stinky said, 'Of course you can go back to the Senator. Eventually. My friend here will take you.'

'And I want my things back,' said Lucien.

'You can have them,' said Stinky, adding, 'all except the book, of course.'

Lucien couldn't help wincing and he heard the little grunt of satisfaction from Smelly. 'Brilliant,' he thought. 'Now I've told them what they need to know. At least they won't torture me. But perhaps there's no reason to keep me alive now?' He imagined Smelly taking him through the back streets to Rodolfo's and silently sliding the merlino-blade between his ribs. In a way, he almost hoped for it, because perhaps that would return him to his real body in the other world. But alive or dead? Maybe he would just live long enough to tell his parents he was sorry.

*

Dethridge was sober now. Before Rodolfo returned from presenting Arianna to the people as their new

Duchessa on the Loggia degli Arieti, he had ordered Alfredo to take the old man into the roof garden and hold his head under the pump. The wet and chastened alchemist was holding his aching temples and trying to think of something he could do to help.

'Wee coulde looke in the glasse,' he said eventually. 'Methinks I can telle whethir hee is in his bodie or nay.'

Rodolfo sprang to the mirror. He had forgotten about the window which Dethridge had opened on to Lucien's world. It always showed Lucien's room, with him in his bed, although Luciano was in Bellezza. A few movements with the levers and the mirror showed the accustomed room. Sunlight streamed through the window but the bed was empty.

'That meneth noughte,' said Dethridge, looking at Rodolfo's anguished expression. 'Hee will be aboute his lyf, like as not.'

'No,' said Rodolfo bitterly. 'He has not gone back. I know it and it is my fault. His parents have taken his body somewhere, perhaps to their physician. Goddess save us if they think he is dead.'

'Ay,' said Dethridge, now troubled too. 'Pepyle oftimes thoghte that I was dede when I was merely stravayging.' He was moved to reveal one of his worst fears. 'Mayhap I was enterred in my coffin and coulde not brethe? That may have bene how I came to be stronded hire.'

Rodolfo clapped the old man on the shoulder. 'We must make sure nothing like that happens to Luciano. We have to find him and get him back.'

*

The sun poured into the new Duchessa's bedchamber as Barbara flung back the wooden shutters. Arianna woke from a deep, sound sleep, at first unsure where she was. Then she remembered: she was Duchessa now.

The events of yesterday came crowding back – the madness of the election, the roomful of dresses, dressing up in a blue satin gown full of pins to make it fit and standing on the Loggia degli Arieti with Senator Rodolfo. He had been even more remote than usual, though she had longed to talk to someone about the last time she had been on that balcony, the night of the Marriage with the Sea.

'I wish Luciano could be here,' was all she had said, waving graciously to the crowd beneath. She assumed he had stravagated back home but she was sorry he had not said goodbye.

But Rodolfo had turned his big black eyes on her and said quietly something that sounded like, 'I wish he were not.'

She hadn't been able to ask him what he meant. She was learning what the life of a Bellezzan Duchessa was like and it involved never being on one's own. There were always servants and guards in the way and a hundred little decisions to be made every hour. Arianna wondered how her mother had borne it for a quarter of a century.

It was starting again now, as she sat up in bed sipping her hot chocolate. Barbara was prattling away about clothes, when the dressmaker would be summoned to make all the garments she would need, including a coronation gown.

But Arianna was only mildly diverted by the

thought of a whole new wardrobe. Unlike Silvia, she was not vain. What was worrying her now was all her State duties, sitting in Council and the Senate, appearing in public, dealing with the Reman Ambassador. She gave Barbara her cup and burrowed back under the bedclothes. It would have been much easier to be a mandolier.

Lucien was in intensive care. He had had another MRI scan, X-rays and an electro-encephalogram. It was eight o'clock in the evening and he had not woken up. Now he lay in his pyjamas in the hospital bed, his face pale but peaceful, while his mother sat beside him holding his hand.

Mr Laski studied the chart and was looking serious. 'The tumour is a little bigger than at the last scan,' he said. 'But there is nothing to explain why he should be unconscious.'

'So why is he?' asked his father, trying to hold down the panic he felt.

Mr Laski shook his head. 'I simply don't know. But it's early days yet. I'd like to monitor his breathing and his brain activity for twenty-four hours and see if there's any change. And he'll be examined by a neurologist. Try not to worry too much. This unit has seen a lot of patients come out of comas.'

'Coma?' said Mrs Mulholland. 'Is that what it is?'

Rodolfo had not been to bed. He stayed up all night

training his mirrors on likely places in Bellezza and even other cities in Talia where Luciano might be. When day broke, after a hasty breakfast, he left for the Duchessa's palace by the open route, not the secret passage. He walked slowly through the Piazza, where people were clearing up after last night's celebrations. How was he to tell Arianna that Luciano was missing? He hadn't even told her that the boy was ill again. And there was something even more momentous that he had to tell her. But he could not face everything at once.

He stopped and rubbed his tired eyes. Although the Chimici had not succeeded in killing Silvia and in spite of the fact that the new Duchessa was a replacement of her own choosing, this morning Rodolfo felt for the first time for many months that the enemy were winning.

He found Arianna in a temporary audience chamber.

'Good morning, Your Grace,' he said, bowing formally.

'Good morning, Senator,' said Arianna, 'but I'm not yet, am I? Your Grace, I mean, not till my coronation.'

'That is so,' said Rodolfo, 'and one of the things we must discuss is arrangements for that ceremony. We have to consider how long it will take to make the necessary robes and so on.'

If Arianna hadn't been sitting down, she would have stamped her foot. 'Clothes again! Is that what being a Duchessa is all about? I want to know how much money I've got, how many hours a day I have to work and when I can start making laws. Otherwise, I'm not sure I want to go through with the coronation, election or no election.'

Rodolfo looked at Arianna for a long time before answering, then sighed and brushed his hand over his face.

'You are quite right,' he said at last. 'No one asked you if you would like to be Duchessa. You are scarcely more than a child and, though I am sure you will one day be an excellent ruler of the city, it will be years before you can make decisions unaided. There will be many tedious duties and the work will rarely be glamorous or enjoyable. But if you believe, as Silvia and I do, that the Chimici are not to be trusted and that their dominance of our country must be stopped, there is nothing to do but carry on with the resistance in Bellezza. And that we can do only if you go ahead with the coronation.'

He paused and searched her face with his penetrating eyes. 'And you did think about all this on Torrone? You did talk to your parents?'

'Foster-parents,' corrected Arianna. 'Yes. We talked about it all for ages. But I didn't know it would be so hard.'

For all her spirit, Rodolfo saw her for the first time as a little girl. He pushed aside his fears for Lucien for the moment and smiled wearily. 'Let me try to answer your questions. Firstly, money. Silvia, as you know, has taken her personal jewellery and some other precious objects. She has left almost all her grand clothes, some of which could perhaps be altered to fit you. And there are a great number of State jewels, which you will wear on important occasions.

'Silvia has taken enough silver to start her new life in Padavia as a wealthy private citizen. But every new Duchessa has considerable wealth from the taxes paid by citizens. It is carefully allocated to the city coffers to pay for things which all citizens enjoy, but there is a substantial sum which will be yours to spend in whatever way you choose. I shall be here to help you with any advice you need and you also have a State treasurer.

'As to laws, they have to come before the Senate, your twenty-four senior advisers. But anything proposed by the ruling Duchessa would be favourably looked upon, I'm sure. Did you have something in mind?'

'I want to make a law that says girls can train as mandoliers,' said Arianna, sniffing slightly. It seemed such a little thing now that she had the burden of ruling Bellezza on her shoulders, but she wanted to make that small difference as soon as possible, even though she would never now benefit from it herself.

'Once you have been crowned, I shall make sure it is on the agenda for the first Senate meeting,' said Rodolfo.

'And I want to get rid of the horrible custom of young women having to wear masks,' said Arianna.

'It would be a lot harder to convince the Senate of that,' said Rodolfo. 'May I suggest that you do not rush in and try to change too much at once? The city needs continuity.'

'What about the Palazzo?' asked Arianna. 'Can I change things in here?'

'Again, once you are crowned, you can make whatever changes we agree together. Do you have ideas already?'

'I want to get rid of the Glass Room,' said Arianna, shuddering. 'It gives me gooseflesh.'

'I should be happy to agree to that,' said Rodolfo. He got up and walked to the window. 'Now, if I have calmed your immediate fears about being Duchessa, I have to tell you something about Luciano. And it may be serious.'

Chapter 20

Out of the Shadows

Lucien was suffering his first full day of captivity in Bellezza. His hands had been untied so that he could remove his blindfold and he could see that he was in a small stone-floored room with very little furniture. There was a chair, a straw mattress which had been put in for his use, and a locked wooden chest, with a bowl and jug of water for washing on top. In a corner was a bucket for him to relieve himself in.

There was one high window and, once the feeling had come back into his wrists, he took down the bowl and jug and dragged the chest underneath it so that he could climb up and see out.

The view was not very revealing; it confirmed that he was several storeys up and, from his knowledge of the church spires and bell-towers of Bellezza, he could work out roughly where this building must be.

But that wasn't much help. He was pretty sure that he must be in the Reman Ambassador's apartments. But what mattered was not where he was but how he could get the book back. If he had that, he could stravagate back home in an instant. Without it, he was almost as stranded in this world as William Dethridge was.

As the weary hours stretched on, he would have settled even for escaping back to Rodolfo's. At noon, if the light through the high window was anything to go by, a woman brought him more ale and bread and some hard cheese and olives. But she wouldn't talk to him and backed out of the room hastily as soon as she had put the food inside the door. She turned the key in the lock just as soon as she was outside again.

Lucien cursed himself for being such a wuss. He could easily have overpowered the woman but everything in him rebelled at the idea of attacking someone unarmed and harmless who was bringing him food. Nevertheless he determined to do it the next time she came in.

For now he ate the food and even drank the ale, then lay on the straw mattress and slept for the first time since he had been captured.

*

'I have founde sum thinge!' cried Dethridge, who had been watching over the magic mirrors in the laboratory almost constantly since Lucien's disappearance.

Rodolfo was instantly at his side and peering into the mirror which Dethridge had trained on to Lucien's world. A woman lay on Lucien's bed, his pillow in her arms. There were no sounds in the mirror but it was obvious that she was crying. Rodolfo motioned to Dethridge to step back and he drew the silver curtain over the mirror.

'What dost thou thinke?' asked Dethridge. 'The mothire?'

'I'm afraid so,' said Rodolfo, his own face lined with grief. 'She is suffering and there is nothing I can do to help her. I wonder if I should stravagate to Luciano's world?'

Before Dethridge could answer, Alfredo came to the door, panting from climbing the stairs too quickly.

'Master,' he said. 'Di Chimici has organized a People's Senate for tomorrow. There are posters all over the city.'

The Ducal Senate met every month at the Duchessa's bidding to deal with all civil matters. But it was the right of any citizen, if he had the backing of eleven others, to call a 'People's Senate' in extraordinary circumstances. Then the twenty-four Senators would convene in the large Council Room instead of their usual Senate Chamber. The twelve citizens who had called the Senate would put their case and the hearing would be open to the public. Bellezzan citizens would pack into the room usually filled by the two hundred and forty Councillors.

It was a very rare event, but perfectly constitutional. Di Chimici hadn't called it himself, since he was a citizen of Remora, but he had bribed twelve Bellezzans to do it. They were not difficult to persuade because, now that the excitement of the election was over, they were open to doubts about the new Duchessa.

That evening, there was an emergency meeting in Rodolfo's laboratory. Alfredo escorted the two women from Leonora's house and Arianna, having received a message from Rodolfo, used the secret passage for the first time. She emerged into the candlelit room and found the others looking serious. She wished with all her heart that Luciano were safe and beside her there among these solemn grown-ups.

'What's happened?' she asked.

'Rinaldo di Chimici has organized a People's Senate for tomorrow,' said Rodolfo, 'and we'll have to let it go ahead.'

'But you won't have to preside,' said Silvia quickly, 'since you aren't confirmed as Duchessa till your coronation. Rodolfo will take charge of proceedings, as Principal Senator.'

'Will I have to be there?' asked Arianna, her heart sinking.

'I'm afraid so,' said Rodolfo. 'We suspect that the motion will concern you. Di Chimici will be exploring every loophole to get your election overturned.'

'What can he do?' asked Arianna.

'He can challenge your legitimacy,' said Silvia. 'It has never bothered Bellezzans much, but there is a clause in the constitution that bars illegitimate children from election. I should have had it changed while I had the power.'

Arianna was appalled. 'But then my election *will* be overturned!'

'Wait, child,' said Leonora.

'We can block this particular motion,' said Rodolfo, glancing over at Arianna, 'but we don't know what else they are planning. I'm worried that they may be behind Luciano's disappearance. I've had people searching the city and there's no sign of him. He must be a prisoner somewhere. But there is something else that is worrying me.'

He started pacing the room. 'Luciano told Doctor Dethridge and myself that his illness has come back. Whether he is imprisoned or not, I know he has not gone back to his world. We have no way of knowing how much time has passed there, nor what his parents will be thinking about his apparently lifeless body. According to the Doctor, he will be like one asleep – breathing but unconscious.'

'But that's terrible!' cried Arianna. 'Will they think it's the illness that's doing it to him?'

Rodolfo and Dethridge both looked grave and Arianna was really scared. She had been so absorbed in her own situation that the news about Lucien's illness had come as a shock. Now she felt devastated by the thought that she might never see him again.

Mr Laski and the neurologist, Ms Beaumont, had run out of ideas. Lucien's coma had now lasted nearly three weeks. After a few hours, he had had to be fed by tubes. After a few days, he couldn't breathe on his own and more tubes were needed. He now looked very pale and thin.

'We're going to have to tell the parents today,' said Ms Beaumont. 'There's no sign of any brain activity. He can't recover. There's nothing for it but to pull the plug.'

The People's Senate was due to start at three. From late morning, citizens started to drift across the Piazza, wanting to be sure of a seat. Once all the Councillors' places were filled, people took up position standing round the walls. It was soon very hot in the Council Room.

Lucien was blindfolded and bound again. He hadn't had to wrestle with his conscience the night before, since his food had been brought by the man with the dagger. He recognized him both as Smelly and as the spy with the blue cloak, who had been following him round the city for weeks.

This morning the man had come back and, after binding and blindfolding him, had led him out of the room and down the stairs. They left the house and Lucien felt the warm Bellezzan sun on his shoulders. The blindfold was removed and he could see he was near the Piazza. He took deep breaths of the mild air, not even minding the faint whiff of canal.

'Do as I say,' whispered the man. 'Remember I have the dagger. Now walk normally. We're going to the Duchessa's palace.'

'But it's too soon!' said David Mulholland angrily. 'You said the cancer wasn't the reason he's in this coma.'

'It is unusual,' agreed Mr Laski. 'But now that it has lasted for so long, the chances of his waking up are sadly minimal.'

'But three weeks is nothing,' said a white-faced Vicky Mulholland. 'You often hear of people coming round after months, even years, in a coma.'

'Not people with brain cancer and only when there has been some brain activity monitored during that time,' said Ms Beaumont, gently. 'I'm afraid, as we told you, there are signs that Lucien must have undergone some brain damage. I must repeat there is no sign of any brain activity at all. To all intents and purposes, he is dead already.'

'So you're saying there's no hope? No alternative to turning off the machines?' said David Mulholland.

Both consultants remained silent. The two parents clasped hands beside their son's body.

'All stand!' said the Clerk of the Senate and hundreds of Bellezzans struggled to their feet, while the Senators filed into their reserved places on a raised dais. The front row of Councillors' seats was also reserved. Soon Arianna and Leonora took their places; Silvia had wanted to come with them but everyone had convinced her that it would be too dangerous. The twelve Bellezzans who had called the Senate filed in beside them. There were still some places empty in the front row when Rodolfo declared the session open and everyone resumed their seats.

'Who calls this Senate?' asked Rodolfo formally and the clerk read out the names of the twelve citizens, who stood and doffed their hats one by one.

'What is the cause?'

The first citizen, one Giovanni Ricci, stood back up,

coughed, shuffled his feet, and gave a rehearsed speech. 'With all due respect to the memory of the late Duchessa, Goddess rest her, and to her daughter recently elected in her stead, we wish to raise the issue of the young woman's birth. We all heard the evidence of Signora Landini, the midwife, that she delivered the Duchessa of a daughter. But is it not the case that the Duchessa of Bellezza must be legitimate?'

Ricci sat down, relieved that his task was over. There was murmuring in the hall. Bellezzans did not want to be deprived of their new Duchessa so soon but they wanted the matter cleared up. Arianna noticed that Rinaldo di Chimici had slipped into a front row seat.

Rodolfo stood to address the Senate; he had a sheaf of papers in his hand.

'Senators and citizens of Bellezza,' he began. 'Signor Ricci is correct. I have consulted the constitution and there is a clause, number 67c, to be precise, that requires the Duchessa to be of legitimate birth, as well as of unblemished record and in good standing with her fellow-Bellezzans.'

There was much loud murmuring from the public.

'However,' Rodolfo continued. 'You will remember that it is also part of Talian law that any ensuing marriage legitimizes the offspring of the two parties. And I have here a document that records the marriage of the late Duchessa, Goddess rest her indeed, to the father of the new Duchessa, Arianna Gasparini.'

The murmurs rose to a roar and di Chimici could be seen passing a message to his spokesman. Ricci rose to his feet, turning his hat nervously in his hands.

'Senator,' he began. 'I am naturally pleased to hear it. But might we know who the father is?'

'Certainly,' said Rodolfo. 'You and the eleven other citizens who called this Senate may peruse the marriage lines, which I shall first pass round to my fellow-Senators. There you will read of the marriage between her Grace, the Duchessa Silvia Isabella Bellini, and myself, Senator Rodolfo Claudio Rossi, which took place on the day of this year's Marriage with the Sea.'

At this point the Council Hall erupted, but as far as Arianna was concerned there were only two people in it – herself and the man who had just calmly announced to the world that he was her father. Now he was looking straight at her and she felt her colour rising. Leonora took her hand.

'Why didn't he tell me he was my father?' Arianna hissed at her aunt.

'She didn't tell him until the night of your election,' Leonora said. 'Goodness knows how she persuaded him to marry her in secret when he did, though he would always have done anything for her. I'm sure your mother had her reasons for the timing. But she told him the truth about you only the day before yesterday. I don't think he's taken it in yet.'

The Senators had finished with the marriage certificate and Rodolfo now handed it to Signor Ricci. He and his companions made a great show of studying it carefully, but Arianna was sure they wouldn't know if it were genuine or not. Indeed she doubted if all twelve could read.

Rodolfo gave them a few minutes then said, 'I also call on Brother Lodovico, who officiated at the ceremony, in the Duchessa's private chapel, to corroborate the evidence of the document.'

A small brown-robed figure mounted the dais and Arianna remembered that she had seen him the night she had hidden in the Loggia degli Arieti. He was the monk she had seen on one of the wooden walkways high in the roof of the cathedral. He must have performed the marriage between her parents just before the feast, only a short time after Silvia's other marriage, the one with the sea. But Arianna suddenly remembered that her mother had probably not taken part in that first ceremony. She had probably used a double.

The room was unbearably hot now; the dramatic revelations of the last hour had made the volatile Bellezzans sweat profusely. Arianna felt herself growing dizzy in the heat and the smell. And then she found she could think nothing more.

'I can't bear it, David,' said Lucien's mother. 'I think I shall go mad.'

'I know, I know,' was all her husband said, holding her tightly and burying his face in her hair.

'I can't bear to think of him lying there getting thinner and thinner and wasting away. It was bad enough hearing the cancer had come back,' said Vicky, 'but I never thought it would be like this, without any time to say goodbye.' She thought she had cried all the tears she had in her but still more seemed to come when Lucien's father said, 'At least we had that holiday with him in Venice.'

‘In the light of today’s news,’ said Signor Ricci, carried away by being able to speak without notes in the great Council Hall, ‘I hope I may express, on behalf of my fellow-citizens, our sincere condolences to you, Senator, on the death of your wife, as we now know our beloved Duchessa to have been.’

‘Well said,’ echoed round the room, as Arianna came to with the acrid scent of Leonora’s smelling-salts under her nose. She thought she was still not quite conscious when she saw di Chimici spring to his feet and call out, ‘There is another cause!’

Rodolfo said calmly, ‘Ambassador, as an honoured guest of Bellezza, you are of course free to attend our public Senate and most welcome to do so. But I’m sure you realize that cause can only be given by one of our own citizens.’

‘Of course,’ said di Chimici, sitting down. ‘Forgive me. It is just that I heard these citizens discussing the case and I remembered that there were two causes.’ He glared at Ricci, who jumped back up.

‘Oh yes, Senator. I was forgetting in all the excitement over the marriage,’ said the foreman. ‘We are also disturbed by allegations of witchcraft among the new Duchessa’s intimate friends.’

‘Witchcraft?’ said Rodolfo. ‘Can you be more specific?’

‘Magic,’ said Ricci uncomfortably. ‘Consorting with spirits.’

Rodolfo merely raised one eyebrow.

‘She has a friend,’ Ricci ploughed on. ‘A special

friend with whom she has spent a lot of time, a young man.'

'You are referring to my apprentice, Luciano, perhaps?' said Rodolfo.

'Yes, indeed, Luciano is the name. We have evidence, incredible as it may seem, that he is not actually, er, how can I put this? Not exactly a mortal being of this world.'

'What is this evidence?' asked Rodolfo.

'Well, with your permission, Senator, we shall bring him forward and demonstrate it.'

There was a new sensation in the hall as Enrico walked up to the front dragging Lucien with him.

'Luciano!' cried Arianna at the same time as Ricci said, 'As you will see, the boy has no shadow.'

'Are you ready?' asked Mr Laski.

Lucien's parents nodded. They were on either side of him, each holding a hand. 'Goodbye, darling,' said his mother.

The sun had disappeared behind a cloud for a moment but was coming out again to shine with all its brightness through the tall glass windows of the Council Hall. The windows were behind Lucien and faced west and he knew he would stand revealed as the Stravagante he truly was. Everything had gone horribly wrong. He looked at Arianna and wondered what it would mean for him and her.

At that moment, Rodolfo called, 'Luciano, catch!' and threw something towards him; automatically he put out his hands to catch whatever it was but they were still tied together and to Enrico. He muffed the catch and the object fell on the floor.

At that moment the sun came out fully and shone through the window and Lucien saw what he had never seen in Talia before – his shadow stretched out on the floor in front of him. He felt a new kind of solidity and before he had time to realize what it meant, he saw that Leonora had just beaten di Chimici to picking up the thing that Rodolfo had thrown, which she pocketed, and then he heard that the whole Council Hall was filled with laughter.

'There seems to be no absence of shadow to observe,' said Rodolfo, though he was keeping his voice steady only by a great effort of will. 'If there are no further causes, I declare this People's Senate closed.'

The doctor closed Lucien's eyes.

Chapter 21

The Man in Black

Lucien was in a state of shock. Enrico had quickly untied him and then disappeared. Leonora took Lucien back to her house, with Arianna dancing anxiously round them. She took him into her elegant little sitting-room with its spindly chairs and rang the bell for wine. Before it was brought, Silvia had joined them and Rodolfo was shown in minutes afterwards.

He took Lucien's pulse as the boy lay on a little red velvet sofa.

'What happened?' he asked. 'Are you all right?'

Lucien nodded. He was numb and Leonora had to force some wine between his lips. The red liquid was like a blood transfusion, giving him the strength to speak.

'Di Chimici's man, the one in the blue cloak, took

me from the Piazza the night of the election,' he said. 'He tied me up and threatened me and locked me in a room. I was blindfolded at first, when he brought someone to see me, but I'm sure it was the Ambassador. They took all my things.' His voice broke. 'They took the book – I couldn't stop them.'

He drank some more wine, to steady himself.

'Perhaps they don't know what it does?' said Arianna.

Lucien shook his head. 'They know all right. It's only a matter of time till they work out how to use it.' He turned to Rodolfo. 'I've failed you, master.'

Everything was bleak; the Chimici would stravagate and the whole rotten business of plundering the twenty-first century would begin. There was nothing anyone could do to stop it. And beyond these grim thoughts lay a terror that Lucien could not even contemplate yet.

'No,' said Rodolfo, his face full of pain. 'It is I who have failed you. I could not find you in time to send you back home and now it is too late.'

The room was very quiet.

'Just what did happen at the People's Senate?' asked Silvia.

'Di Chimici had trumped up a second cause,' said Rodolfo. 'To investigate Arianna for witchcraft, on the grounds that she had a familiar demon – our friend Luciano. Di Chimici's mouthpiece claimed that the boy had no shadow.'

Silvia gasped. 'So he is revealed as a Stravagante from the other world?'

The shutters were closed in Leonora's sitting-room,

to stop the sun from fading the upholstery. Rodolfo strode over to the window and flung them open.

'That is no longer what he is,' he said. 'See, he is as solid as you or me.'

Lucien stood up and walked to the window; his black shadow streamed out on the tiled floor behind him. 'I can't go back, can I?' he said.

Rodolfo put an arm round the boy's shoulders. 'No,' he said. 'You are a Bellezzan now, by night and by day. Your life in the other world is over. It is a bitter ending and I shall never forgive myself for it.'

Lucien blinked hard to keep back the tears. This was it then; he was dead.

A part of him was horrified at the realization. But slowly another part was telling him that he was at least still alive in Bellezza. He knew that the cancer would have killed him if he'd stayed in his world, and that he had been given a second chance that most people would kill for. He had to lock his feelings about his old life and his parents away until it was safe to take them out and look at them.

But there was a more immediate problem to deal with now – the fact that the Chimici had an important key to the science of stravagation.

'But the book, master,' he said. 'Can we steal it back?'

'No need,' said Rodolfo, with a rueful smile. 'I think Leonora has it.'

Astonished, Lucien saw Leonora produce from her petticoat pocket what was indisputably his book, his talisman to the other world.

'But how? Di Chimici's spy took it out of my pocket the night they captured me,' he said.

'No,' said Rodolfo. 'They took the substitute book that I made for you shortly after the Feast of the Maddalena. It was then that I realized how much danger you were in. You remember that since then I have been asking you to come back to the laboratory before stravagating home. I would make the necessary substitution again before you left.'

'But why?' asked Lucien. 'And how?'

'I was sure they were going to try to capture you and take it from you,' said Rodolfo. 'It wasn't hard. I got another book from Egidio and marked it and soaked it to make it look like yours. I wrote in it in your hand the notes you had put in it, even though I didn't understand them all. It was an exact replica.'

'It certainly fooled me,' said Lucien bitterly.

'I was wrong,' said Rodolfo. 'I should have told you what I'd done. But I didn't want to frighten you. And Luciano,' he added softly, 'the outcome would have been the same. The Chimici kept you prisoner for too long. It was only if I could have found you that I could have helped you home.'

Everyone was looking at Lucien and the sympathy in their eyes was more than he could bear. 'You're right,' he said roughly. 'Even if I hadn't been kidnapped, I was going to die in my world anyway. But I can't bear it that I didn't say goodbye to my parents.'

'I know,' said Rodolfo, 'I'm going to try to put that right. But there is just one thing I have to do first. Leonora, may I have a few words with Arianna in private?'

Arianna followed Rodolfo into the little garden as if

she were sleepwalking. For some minutes now she had stopped understanding what was happening around her. Her mind was just too overloaded with momentous information to take in any more. She remembered that she was angry with Rodolfo, but even that seemed to be about something that had happened long ago and that she was looking at from far away. She wondered if she were going to faint again.

Rodolfo looked old and grey-faced, as if he were burdened with some terrible tragedy. She didn't know what to say to him. But he saved her the trouble.

'I know that you are hurt by what Silvia has done,' he began. 'And by what I did in the Senate just now. We both thought that your genuine surprise about your parentage would convince the people that we had been successful in concealing the facts from everyone, yourself included. Otherwise they might not have believed our story. I could not let them know that I had found out about your existence only a few days ago and about my part in it even later.'

He paused. Arianna struggled to understand.

'You really never knew that the Duchessa had a child?'

Rodolfo shook his head. 'If I had known, do you think I should have let her get away with this mad plan? That I should have let her rob me of my child? No, I should have taken you myself and hidden with you in some far-off land and never seen her again rather than agree to such an unnatural scheme.'

Arianna felt a rush of warmth towards him.

'I have upbraided her for the lies and for the uncertainty in which she left me for days,' he continued, shaking his head. 'I should not wish to live through such days as those again. But in the end I must accept that she was acting in accordance with what she thought was right. But never think that you were not wanted, my daughter.'

He took both of her hands in his and kissed her gently on the forehead. 'And now we must go back to my palazzo, without the time to talk about this as we should. As a result of my distraction and ill-judgement there are even greater wrongs that have to be addressed. But I trust there will be time enough in the future to talk together and for me to piece together the years of your life that I have lost.'

*

William Dethridge knew straightaway that something was different about Lucien.

'Ah, well met, yonge mann!' he cried as soon as they all got back to the laboratory, but then, with a piercing look, 'Thou art translated and bicome as I am.'

After that he said nothing, but held the boy in his arms for a long time and then went to sit in a dark corner.

'You know that Maestro Crinamorte opened a window on to your world?' Rodolfo asked Lucien, using Dethridge's new Talian name.

'Yes,' said Lucien, wondering whether he would now have a new name too. He felt as vulnerable as an unbaptized baby.

'We have seen something in it which would upset you,' said Rodolfo. 'But I shall need to look again. Are you willing to look with me?'

Lucien nodded. He couldn't trust himself to speak. Rodolfo drew back the silver curtain. It was weird for Lucien to see his own bedroom – it would have been weird at any time. But now that he knew he was never going back there, it was almost unbearable. As he watched, Lucien saw his mother appear in the glass. He was shocked; she looked so much older than he remembered her, yet surely not much time had passed in his world since he last saw her?

She was thin and haggard. Perhaps it was more noticeable because she was wearing a black dress Lucien had never seen before. In the mirror she knelt on his bed and reached up to the silver Venetian mask and unhooked it from the wall.

'Can you understand what you are seeing?' asked Rodolfo. 'What does it mean?'

Lucien nodded. 'She only wears black to funerals, though that's a new dress. I can only guess about the mask. They gave it to me in Venice.'

Rodolfo looked at him seriously. 'Then I must go straightaway.'

He had not stravagated in all the time Lucien had been visiting Talia. 'It is early evening here,' he said. 'So it must be early morning in your world. Your mother is up earlier than usual, perhaps because she cannot sleep. Tell me your address so that I can find the house. You said it was near the school in Barnsbury. Maestro, come with us if you will.'

Lucien told him the address and the three Stravaganti went into an inner chamber, where Rodolfo slept. He took from a chain round his neck a silver ring, which he slipped on his finger. 'This is my talisman, Lucien,' he said, 'Doctor Dethridge gave it to me. Will you both watch by me while I'm away?'

And, waiting for nothing more, he slipped into unconsciousness.

The duty priest at the cemetery blenched when he first saw the dates of the person he must officiate over that Thursday. He hated burying young people. It was not just the tragic unnaturalness of it and the distraught parents; any priest might have to cope with that from time to time in his ministry. It was all the other young people who came to the funerals. Some in black from head to foot, even if they'd not been close friends, others trying to wear something cheerful under the impression that it was what the deceased would have wanted.

The girls were always in floods of tears and the boys not much better. And he would have to preach a sermon that would leave them all with some hope to cling on to, even the atheists and agnostics who would be the majority.

The parents, for example, who had been to see him. They had said they were not churchgoers. 'Even if I had been, I wouldn't go now,' the father had said rudely. 'I know there's no God after what's happened to Lucien.'

'Hush, David,' the wife had said, but she too had asked if the ceremony could be 'non-religious'.

'Well, you don't have to have prayers or hymns,' the priest had said as gently as he could, making allowances for their grief. 'You can have poems or other readings of your choice and the music you think appropriate for your son. But can I just suggest you read through the funeral service in the Book of Common Prayer? It does contain some very fine passages and some people find them comforting, even if they are not believers.'

In the end they had opted for the whole 1662 service, with two hymns, 'Come Down Thou Love Divine' and 'Jerusalem'. The mother had chosen all the other music and asked for one of her son's friends to read a poem and then, hesitantly, said that they would appreciate it if his sermon recognized they were not believers.

The priest did not take umbrage. If the Church failed people at their time of greatest need, it couldn't expect to make any headway with their doubts. All he said was, 'I shall take no belief for granted but my own.'

And now he mounted the small wooden pulpit to try to bring some sort of comfort to all those frightened teenagers. The door at the back of the church opened and a very queer figure came in. At first the priest wondered if it were a homeless person sheltering from the cold, but he quickly saw it was rather a distinguished-looking silver-haired gentleman. He was dressed as if for a part in a Shakespeare production, in black velvet knee-breeches, flowing white shirt and velvet waistcoat and cloak. He wore long black suede boots and his hair was long. He held an elaborate black velvet hat in his hands and followed the sermon most intently.

*

'Thank you, Tom,' said Vicky Mulholland after the service. 'You read that very well. It was good of you to do it.'

Tom nodded and shook hands with both Lucien's parents. A pale pretty girl held tightly on to his other hand.

'Who's that?' asked Lucien's father, indicating the strange man in black velvet who was talking to some of the young people. 'I thought he might be one of the drama teachers from your school come straight from a rehearsal.'

'I've never seen him before,' said Tom. 'But he asked me about what happened to Lucien. He seemed like a good bloke, very upset, even though he's so funny-looking.'

They were standing looking at the sea of flowers round Lucien's name card. The ones from Lucien's parents were a sheaf of white roses and they had spent a fortune to get old-fashioned ones that would smell. They would have to come back later for the ashes, which they had decided to take back to Venice and scatter in the Grand Canal. Lucien's ashes and those of the silver mask they had asked the undertaker to put in the coffin. Now they were waiting to speak to all the guests then drive back to the house for a funeral tea.

'Should we ask him back?' whispered Vicky.

At that moment, the man came over to them. He had the most wonderful mesmeric black eyes, so that when he took Lucien's mother's hand, she forgot to ask who he was and where he had come from.

'I am so very, very sorry,' he said, with evident sincerity. 'I wish it could have been otherwise.'

'Thank you,' said Vicky. 'This is my husband, David.'

The man shook hands with Lucien's father – and then he said the strangest thing.

'Your son still lives, you know, only in another place. And he will never forget you. He will think of you all the time as you think of him. He will grow up strong and happy and one day you will see him again.'

Tears blinded Vicky's eyes and when she could see again, the man was gone.

'A nutter,' said her husband. 'Obviously a religious nutter that hangs about funerals and talks about the next world. Don't let him upset you.'

'He didn't upset me, David,' she said. 'And he didn't seem like a nutter. I actually found him quite consoling.'

Lucien and Dethridge kept an anxious vigil by Rodolfo's bed. Candles burned in the inner room and they could hear the voices of the three women, who were still in the laboratory.

At last, the seemingly sleeping figure gave a deep sigh and opened his eyes. He sat up and took off the ring.

'Did you see them?' asked Lucien. 'Did you tell them anything about me?'

Rodolfo nodded. He took from his shirt a white rose and silently handed it to Lucien.

Lucien gasped. 'You brought something back!'

'There is a reason,' said Rodolfo. 'Now, if you don't

mind, Maestro, I need to speak to Luciano on his own.'

*

It was much later when the two of them came out of the chamber. Dawn was breaking and the pale blue light of Bellezza that is like nothing in the world, except the light of Venice, was filling the laboratory. Lucien was very pale.

Arianna ran and took his hand. During that long night, she had talked with Silvia and Leonora and Dethridge and understood more of what had happened. She was no longer angry with her mother and father or frightened of her responsibilities; there was no room for any emotion in her heart except the overwhelming sorrow for her friend.

Lucien smiled at her. He was deathly tired. But he knew that in this world he was cured. The cancer had never come with him to Bellezza and now he knew he had escaped any possibility of its doing so. But he felt it would be a long time before he would be normal and happy again.

'There are some things we have to settle,' said Rodolfo. 'Because of his involvement in the affairs of our world, Luciano has lost his own. We in this room must offer him our friendship, understanding and protection. I doubt if his dangers are over yet. And, as he is a minor, I hereby offer myself as a foster-father to him.'

'Nay,' said Dethridge. 'The boy hath nede of two parentes and ye cannot, with al respecte, gracious lady,' to Silvia, 'live with yore legill husbonde if ye are to kepe the secrete of yore survival.'

Lucien felt perplexed. The Duchessa's legal husband? Rodolfo was looking embarrassed and he guessed a lot had happened while he had been imprisoned.

'And I think perhaps Arianna would not want him for a brother,' said Leonora unexpectedly. Arianna blushed. It always disconcerted her to know how much her aunt understood about her.

'Then what is to be done?' asked Silvia. 'No one should have care of Luciano who does not know his secret.'

'It is simpil,' said Dethridge. 'I offire myselfe, althow olde, to be the boy's fathire and since this kind ladye has agreed to be mye wyf, she will bee as a mothire to him. I canne see no harme in the marriage, since I am dede to my olde lyf and cannot return to my wyf in the othire worlde.'

'Aunt Leonora!' exclaimed Arianna.

Even Rodolfo was amazed. Lucien didn't know what to say.

'Luciano, don't misunderstand,' said Leonora. 'We shall not try to take your real parents' place. But you can live with us in my house, which is near to the Palazzo and to here. You will be able to see Rodolfo and Arianna as much as you want.'

'I'd really like that,' said Lucien.

'You make me feel quite sorry that I shall be living in Padavia,' said Silvia, with a touch of her old humour. 'I shall be missing all the fun.'

'I think it will not all be fun,' said Rodolfo. He took her hand and kissed it, the first time that anyone in the room had seen him do such a thing. 'But yesterday was a day of sadness and today is a new day. We shall have much to celebrate. And if Luciano cannot be Silvia's and my adopted son, at least we can stand as sponsors for him in his new life as a Bellezzan.'

He turned to Lucien. 'We shall have our work cut out to get enough suitable fireworks ready for my daughter's coronation. They must be the most special I have ever devised.' It was the first time Arianna had heard him say 'my daughter' in public. Rodolfo took her hand and she felt for the first time that he really was her father.

'And now I shall get Alfredo to bring us some breakfast,' said Rodolfo.

Lucien suddenly felt ravenous. He had eaten nothing since the hunk of bread brought to him in his prison at midday the day before. He looked round the room. He now had a foster-father and a sort of godfather who were both powerful magicians, scientists or natural philosophers. He had a godmother who was supposed to be a dead Duchessa but was one of the most fascinating, clever and ruthless women he had ever met. He had a foster mother who was kind and sensible and motherly, although quite unlike his own. And he had a friend, a girlfriend, he even dared think, from the way she was looking at him, who was going to be the most powerful person in the city.

But the thing that made him feel best was the words Rodolfo had said to him in private.

'You are still a Stravagante, Luciano. Never forget that. All you need is a new talisman. Keep the book to remind you of past travels, but it is the rose that will take you back now. Once you are strong enough to undertake the journey. Only you will be a visitor from this world to that. You must always return here.'

Lucien patted the rose, now wrapped in fine tissue

and kept in his shirt pocket. Bellezzan from now on he might be, but he would find a way back to his own world. He had unfinished business there.

Epilogue: *Carnival*

For three days, Bellezza resounded to the sound of laughter, music and merry-making. Masked revellers danced in the streets or swaggered down them with linked arms. Bellezzans saved their best clothes of the year for carnival and everyone was dressed in bright silks and satins and figured velvet. The men wore masks too, as did women whether married or not, and it gave many opportunities for flirtation and seduction.

The streets were full of stalls selling food – polenta and cheese and frittata. Young men with lanterns stood round in the evenings waiting to earn a few scudi lighting people to their homes or boats. All the mandoliers wore masks and all the mandolas were hung with lanterns and coloured ribbons. Astrologers set up their stalls at every well-head, offering to read fortunes for young women in search of husbands and lovesick young men wanting to win the affections of their ladies.

Tightrope walkers ran with balancing poles on ropes strung between the two columns in the Piazza Maddalena, and any other high places they could find. In all the squares Bellezzans strolled just for the purpose of showing off their elaborate costumes and ever more exotic masks. But nowhere was this more popular than in the square in front of the great silver Basilica.

Beautifully dressed women sat in their balconies around the square, flirting with their fans, while agile young men tried to climb up to them with flowers and eggshells filled with scented water.

One young mandolier had a boatload of laughing guests. He was slim with black curly hair and a silver butterfly mask. In his craft sat a young woman, also masked, and two middle-aged men who found the boy's efforts highly amusing.

'Luciano!' said one of them. 'Who did you say was teaching you?'

'Alfredo,' said the young mandolier. 'But I've only had the mandola a week.' He was smiling. He had bought the beautiful black craft with the Duchessa's silver and Rodolfo's servant had been giving him lessons.

'You'll have to come up to our canaletto for a few more lessons, I think,' said Egidio.

'Yes, you wouldn't be the first we'd taught up there,' said Fiorentino.

'Don't take any notice,' said the masked girl. 'I

think you're not doing badly – for a beginner!'

'Come up here and show me how to do it better,' said Luciano. 'If you think you can.'

And the laughing girl took him at his word, taking over the oar and sculling expertly along the canal, while the boy watched and the men smiled with pride.

'You're a real mandolier,' cried Egidio.

'Well, it's in her blood,' said Fiorentino.

And Arianna, made reckless by the anonymity and licence of Carnival, realized her ambition as she sculled the mandola up the Great Canal.

The first time that Vicky Mulholland saw Lucien, she didn't tell her husband about it. He would have thought she was going mad. Goodness knows, she had often thought so herself in the weeks after Lucien's death.

That first time it was just a glimpse anyway, outside the school, and she convinced herself that it had been a trick of the light. It was only later, when she had seen him again, that she believed in the first sighting. And then she had to tell David.

'What?' he had said, stupefied. 'You mean you saw someone who looked like him?'

'No,' said Vicky. 'It was really him. I know it was.'

Her husband took her in his arms. 'Do you mean like a ghost, love?' he said, very tenderly.

'No,' said Vicky, tears streaming down her cheeks. 'Not a ghost – a real boy.' And David didn't know what to say.

The next time, they both saw him. He was outside

their house. He didn't speak, but he smiled and waved before he disappeared.

Over the months and years they saw him many times and in time they were able to speak to him and hear his version of events. They kept it a secret; it was so strange and disturbing. But it comforted them.

Down by the quay, two burly fishermen were explaining something, with much waving of their arms and measuring out of an invisible catch. The crowd around them were urging them on and plying them with wine and the fishermen were getting more and more merry.

'It's a miracle,' said one. 'That the merlino-fish is still alive.'

'Prosperity for Merlino is assured,' said the other, though this was a hard sentence for his wine-fuddled tongue.

'And for us,' agreed his brother.

'It's the least we can expect,' said the second, 'specially now our little sister is Duchessa.'

'Now I know you're lying,' said an onlooker in the crowd. 'Merlino-fishes come to life and our new Duchessa the sister of a pair of drunken fishermen!'

But Angelo and Tommaso were not to be put out. They had caught the merlino in their own net and let it go back into the sea where it belonged. They were content to wait for it to die of natural causes and leave its bones on the beach for them to find sometime in the future. But it was an omen and like all lagooners they believed in omens.

The Piazza Maddalena was full of dancers. The big party was inside the Duchessa's Palazzo, where all the dignitaries were wearing the most gorgeous costumes and masks and eating the grandest food. But that didn't stop the ordinary Bellezzans from enjoying their own party in the square. It was what the last three days had been leading up to.

Now they were all dressed in their very best costumes and were ready to dance all night to the music of the many players filling the colonnades around the Piazza. Everyone was masked tonight – men and women, old and young, married and unattached. Among the brightly coloured silks, satins and brocades, the glittering sequins and vivid ribbons, stalked the occasional black-clad figure, with the beaky mask of the Plague Doctor.

One such could be seen hurrying towards the Ducal Palace, late for the Duchessa's ball. He stopped to admire the young man sliding down the campanile on a rope, to the cheers of the crowd. He quickened his pace as he passed the bonfire between the two columns. He knew now that the figure to be burned was made of straw, but he still didn't like to see it. He reached the Palazzo, now restored to its former beauty but without the Glass Room, and was admitted up the silver staircase. He entered the great hall, looking for his friends, and stood in the doorway, gazing out over the packed dance floor. The first person he recognized was a woman, who sought him out.

'Where have you been?' asked the stately figure in purple brocade, with her silver mask trimmed with black feathers, approaching the sinister doctor without fear.

'Forgive mee, my dere,' said the Plague Doctor. 'I hadde to complete my experimente. Bot I am here now and ready to enjoy myselfe.' He took a goblet of wine from a passing servant. 'Where are owre friendes?'

The purple lady led him to the other end of the room, where two big men in dark blue velvet and black masks were engaged in a mock wrestling match. A red-headed younger man, even taller, in a harlequin's costume and white make-up, was urging them on.

'Fiorentino wins!' called out Harlequin as the slightly lighter-built of the blue velvet ones kept the other pinned to the ground.

'I demand a rematch,' said the heavier man, laughing underneath his brother.

'You see, even when they are in disguise, they are themselves,' said a silver-haired man in black velvet, with the silver mask of a fox, clapping the Plague Doctor on the shoulder.

'Gretinges, old friend,' said the doctor, returning the embrace affectionately. 'Where are the yonglinges?'

'Over there,' nodded the man in black, indicating a handsome couple about to take to the dance floor. Just then a woman in green silk, with a green sequinned mask, came up to the man in black and, with the boldness of all Bellezzan women at carnival, demanded a dance. He yielded reluctantly.

'Aren't you enjoying yourself, Senator?' asked the woman in a low voice, her violet eyes glittering behind the mask.

'Silvia!' he whispered, holding her more tightly. 'Aren't you afraid of being recognized?'

'At Carnival?' she mocked. 'I think I am safer here than at any other time.' She was wearing his silver ring on the third finger of her right hand. And he hers. It was something they could do to make up for the concealments under which they still lived.

The new Duchessa was dressed in silver taffeta, her mask a fantasy of silver lace, made by her grandmother on Burlesca. Her partner, a slim young man with black curls, was like her shadow, in his grey velvet cloak and silver cat mask.

They whirled around the floor together, creating a circle of space round them as the crowd gave way to make room for the Duchessa's wide swirling skirts and the dancers' flickering feet.

'You've been taking lessons!' said Arianna, laughing and out of breath as they finally stopped.

'Yes,' gasped Luciano. 'I bet you never guessed that Doctor Dethridge was a demon dancer in his day. He was determined that I should do him credit tonight.'

'You dance better than you scull,' said Arianna.

'Give me time,' said Lucien. 'I have plenty of teachers.'

The Plague Doctor was leading the applause of the crowd as the Duchessa and her partner left the floor.

'Let's have an ice,' said Arianna. 'This dress is so hot.'

She was much more at ease in the Palazzo than she used to be. Everyone had done their best to help her since the coronation at the top of the silver staircase, when she had officially become Duchessa of the city of Bellezza. It had been hard to accept that there would be servants surrounding her at every hour of the day, anticipating her every need and supplying her with whatever she wanted. Now a footman brought two glass bowls of melon-flavoured ice, its crystals sparkling like something in the museum at Merlino, before they had even reached the refreshment table.

Arianna nodded graciously to him and swept out on to the gallery running round the Palazzo's courtyard. Luciano stood with her, letting the ice melt deliciously on his tongue, cooling his throat. He had had much more to adapt to than Arianna had. In the first days after what Dethridge called his 'translation', he had made lists both mental and real of all the things he would never experience again.

They were all so small but seemed suddenly so important. He would never go to a football match, or see a film or eat a pizza or take a hot shower again. Never watch TV or eat popcorn or travel by Tube or swim in a swimming-pool. Never sleep under a duvet or buy a lottery ticket or use a *GameBoy* or chew gum. Never fly in an aeroplane or ride on a rollercoaster or wear jeans. He wouldn't do his GCSEs or AS levels, wouldn't ever vote or drink legally in pubs. The lists went on and on.

He never wrote anything about not seeing his friends or his family because his mind still shut down whenever he started to think about them. But gradually, with the help of Rodolfo and his new foster-parents, Luciano had begun to see that there were pluses to spending the rest of his life as a citizen of Bellezza. One of the best things was that he already had friends here, good friends. He had a comfortable home with Dethridge and Aunt Leonora, who were now married.

And his work continued as Rodolfo's apprentice,

which he had to admit was better than any job he could have hoped for in his old life. There was talk of sending him to university in Padavia when he was a bit older too. He realized that he was one of the most privileged people in Bellezza, close friends with the young Duchessa and her Regent. Best of all, of course, was that he had a life of any kind at all.

And he was quite rich in his own right, with the silver he had dredged up from the canal and the reward the last Duchessa had given him for saving her from assassination. The Duchessa! He was sure he had glimpsed her at the ball, dancing with Rodolfo.

That was quite typical of her. Although she now lived in Padavia, with Susanna and Guido Parola, the reformed assassin, as her confidential servants, she sometimes slipped back quietly into Bellezza, revelling in her new freedom to roam the streets unattended, picking up gossip which might prove useful in the ongoing struggle with the Chimici. And to see Arianna.

It was a strange family, Luciano reflected, finishing his ice, where parent didn't live with child and husband lived apart from wife. But he had to admit that the three of them got on better than many families he had known in his old life. The longer she was Duchessa, the better Arianna seemed to understand her mother. And, although she was still somewhat afraid of her new father, she respected him and trusted in him completely.

And yet, when her State duties became too much for her, the young Duchessa escaped back to the islands. She wasn't allowed to go alone, so Luciano went with her and Barbara, her waiting-woman, and a boatload of guards followed them. They ate cakes with Arianna's grandparents on Burlesca, and huge fish dinners with Valeria and Gianfranco and the gentle fishermen she still thought of as her brothers on Torrone.

'I would pay to know what you were thinking,' said Arianna now.

'What? Oh, yes, "a penny for your thoughts" is what we say,' said Luciano.

'Who's we?' teased Arianna. 'You're a Bellezzan now.'

'I know,' said Luciano. 'That's what I was thinking about.'

He touched the talisman which hung on a thong round his neck. It was a pressed white rose, encased in resin, something which Rodolfo had done for him. He had used it three times now to get back to his world. But he had only glimpsed his parents because stravagating was much harder now he was Bellezzan and he had been able to stay only a few minutes. Rodolfo had promised him it would get easier. He sighed.

'Listen!' said Arianna.

She held his hand as the bell of the campanile tolled midnight in the silence. At the last stroke a great cry went up from the crowd in the square as the bonfire was lit: 'It's going, it's going, Carnival is going!'

'Luciano?' said Arianna inquiringly. 'Are you all right?'

'Luciano' was how he thought of himself now; Lucien belonged to the past, for all he was a twenty-first-century boy. Luciano lived in Talia. He had even had his sixteenth birthday here, a few weeks after

Arianna's. Remembering hers, he smiled.

The Duchessa snorted in a very unducal manner. 'You can be so maddening!' she said. 'What now?'

'I was thinking of your first mask,' said Luciano.

It was Arianna's turn to smile. As Duchessa, she had had a very formal birthday celebration, culminating in the ceremonial fastening on of a white silk mask by Rodolfo, as her father and Duke Regent. How she had hated it! Thereafter she had had to wear a variety of elaborate masks whenever she appeared in public.

She still hated them but gradually had come to see that they had their uses. It was hard to see what someone was thinking behind a mask, even though you could see their eyes. That didn't mean she had given up the idea of changing the law, but she accepted Rodolfo's advice to go cautiously with the Senate. It was enough that they had passed her new law about girls being mandoliers.

For now, girls of sixteen would continue to wear masks until they married.

'Are you getting used to it then?' asked Luciano. 'That silver lace one is really pretty, you know.'

'Mmm,' said Arianna. 'Not exactly. But perhaps it doesn't matter. I don't think I'll be wearing a mask for long.'

And she gave Luciano a smile that was pure Duchessa.

A Note on Stravagation

William Dethridge, the first Stravagante, made his first journey to another dimension by chance, as the result of an alchemical accident affecting the rules of time and space. This happened in 1552, when Dethridge was officially teaching mathematics at Oxford University, but spending a great deal of time on his private study of alchemy.

The copper dish which he was holding in his hand while trying to commute base matter into gold, became his talisman enabling him to travel between the two worlds and was a reliable key to that travel for nearly quarter of a century.

But although Dethridge always arrived back from his journeys to Talia in his own time, the gateway he had accidentally opened was very unstable. Since his first journey, other Stravaganti, from the Talian side, have found themselves arriving in much later periods than Dethridge's Elizabethan England. Rodolfo left the notebook talisman in the twentieth century, for example.

All talismans work in both directions but must come originally from the opposite dimension to the traveller's. That is why Lucien needs a new one after his death in our world. And for this reason, his Talian notebook would not actually be usable by the Chimici, but they don't know that. Dethridge's copper dish is the only exception to this rule. Of course, once Dethridge has been 'translated', which happened when he died in his own body in England after fleeing in terror to Talia, his journeys to our world, if undertaken, would be subject to the same temporal instability of the gateway.

When in Talia, Lucien speaks and understands the Talian language, although he doesn't know Italian in his own world. Dethridge's language sounds old-fashioned to him, and only him, because they are both English, born about 450 years apart. And this is still true even after they have both been translated to Talia. For consistency I have kept Dethridge's words in Elizabethan English throughout, even when Lucien is not present.

A Note on Talia

The country of Talia is both like and unlike the Italy of this world. It exists in a parallel dimension and diverged hundreds of years ago from the Italy we know. The significant moment came during the dispute between the brothers Romulus and Remus. In the history of our world, which at that stage is not fully distinguishable from its mythology, Romulus won the contest and founded the city of Rome. In Talia, Remus was the victor and founded the city of Remora, capital of the Reman Empire and situated roughly where Siena is in our world.

One change leads to others and there are marked points in Talia's history, particularly in relation to Anglia, which is what they call our England, which differ from Italy's. The most obvious one is that Anglia never split from the Reman Church. Henry the Eighth of Anglia had a son by his only wife Catherine, who became Edward the Sixth but died young and was succeeded by his two full sisters, Mary and Elizabeth, both of whom died childless. There is no equivalent of the Church of England.

Talia is in some ways more advanced than Italy, in that in the sixteenth century it enjoyed Strega and Prosecco, and had cultivated the potato and tomato, as well as importing coffee and chocolate. However, it did not have tobacco.